THE BUILDER'S PRIDE

THE LEGENDARY BUILDER BOOK 3

J A. CIPRIANO

Copyright © 2017 by J A. Cipriano

All rights reserved.

No part of this book may be reproduced in any form or by any electronic or mechanical means, including information storage and retrieval systems, without written permission from the author, except for the use of brief quotations in a book review.

WANT TO GET THIS FREE?

Sign up here. If you do, I'll send you my short story, *Alone in the Dark*, for free.

Visit me on Facebook or on the web at JACipriano.com for all the latest updates.

ALSO BY J A. CIPRIANO

∼

World of Ruul

Soulstone: Awakening

Soulstone: The Skeleton King

∼

Bug Wars

Doomed Infinity Marine

∼

The Legendary Builder

The Builder's Sword

The Builder's Greed

The Builder's Pride

∼

Elements of Wrath Online

Ring of Promise

The Vale of Three Wolves

Kingdom of Heaven

The Skull Throne

Escape From Hell

The Thrice Cursed Mage

Cursed

Marked

Burned

Seized

Claimed

Hellbound

The Half-Demon Warlock

Pound of Flesh

Flesh and Blood

Blood and Treasure

The Lillim Callina Chronicles

Wardbreaker

Kill it with Magic

The Hatter is Mad

Fairy Tale

Pursuit

Hardboiled

Mind Games

Fatal Ties

Clans of Shadow

Heart of Gold

Feet of Clay

Fists of Iron

The Spellslinger Chronicles

Throne to the Wolves

Prince of Blood and Thunder

Found Magic

May Contain Magic

The Magic Within

Magic for Hire

Witching on a Starship

Maverick

Planet Breaker

1

"No. Just fucking no," I said, taking a step backward, one hand going to the hilt of my sword.

"No?" Lucifer asked, arching one delicate eyebrow at me. "What do you mean no?" The archangel cocked her head to the side before taking a step closer until her bare breasts were practically pressed into my chest. "Why would you refuse my offer, Arthur? Do you not want to defeat the Darkness?"

"Because you're the goddamned Devil." My fingers twitched, anxious to draw my weapon. I knew it wouldn't do any good though. Lucifer had just destroyed Royal Centre with a wave of her hand and had very nearly smashed Mammon underfoot like a bug. Fighting her would do absolutely nothing, and, she seemed to know that. No, that wasn't quite true. It seemed to amuse her. Greatly.

"We've been through this," she said, reaching out and touching my arm. Heat and desire exploded inside me. My knees shook, and a moan escaped my mouth as a wave of pleasure unlike anything I had ever experienced crashed into me. "I do not like being called the Devil." Her blood red lips quirked into a smile. "Then again, the devil is in the details, is it not?" She playfully walked her fingers up my arm. "They call me Pride, but is it really Pride when you are simply better than all others?"

I swallowed, trying to get my bearings as she met my eyes. Her perfectly crystalline orbs flickered mischievously. In them, I could see a thousand possibilities, each more indulgent than the last. With her, I could be better than all others. I could crush Dred beneath my heel, push back the Darkness. With her at my side, I would be an unstoppable army unto myself.

"If you're so great, why were you sealed beneath a town?" I asked, trying to keep my breath from catching in my throat, I failed miserably.

"Because I'm too amazing," she said, pulling her

hand away, and the absence of her touch nearly sent me into withdrawals. I wanted her, needed her. My body began to shake, and my stomach clenched as I fought the urge to reach out and touch her myself. No, that wasn't even quite right. As my knees started to shake, and I started to sweat, the urge to get just one more touch was so overwhelming, I nearly screamed, nearly begged, nearly promised her everything.

The only thing that saved me was the cold throb of the mark on my neck. Mammon's power called to me, let me know this was but temporary, an effect of Lucifer's power. She would never provide what she promised, and what's more, she couldn't be trusted. The mark told me all that and more with such absolute certainty that I knew it to be true.

And the craziest part? I didn't fucking care.

"You're too amazing?" I said, taking a deep breath and shutting my eyes. However, even with them shut, I could still see her in my mind. Her perfect breasts, her dark nipples, her milky skin.

"Yes," she said, and in my mind's eye, her hand slipped into my pants, and the feeling was nearly indescribable. "I am *most high*. There is nothing the others can do, that I cannot do better. Do you wish for sex, money, or power? All those things are mine to command." She clucked her tongue. "I can offer you anything you wish, and it will be better than anything else anyone could ever give you."

My eyes snapped open to find her still standing there, a bemused smirk on her lips. Her eyes caught mine, and she reached out, taking my hand again. This time it was like coming home and having a cold one after a long day. No, that wasn't right. It was like getting a fucking fix. All my pain, all my problems vanished into the ether.

"You wish to defeat the Darkness? Well, I can help you do that, Arthur." She placed my hand on her bare breast as she spoke. Now, I wouldn't say I was an expert on the female body, but I'd been around quite a few girls who broke the ten-point scale when it came to beauty. And in that moment when my hand closed around her breast, and her nipple pressed into my palm, I'd have rather touched Lucifer like this than fuck any of them.

As I looked up at the Devil herself, I realized we could do more. Do so much more that I'd cease to even remember the others. Not only that, but I wouldn't care.

A spark of heat niggled in my chest, and the suddenness of it was enough to shock me to my senses. It was Gwen. Somehow, someway, when I'd broken my sword Clarent, she'd become bound to me, and now? Now the succubus's inner spark was protecting me from whatever this was.

I pulled my hand away, and as I did, I felt the warmth in my chest spread out. It wasn't a lot, but while that touch of heat, that reminder of how I was tied to Gwen, wasn't nearly enough to combat the bolt of need and want that hit me like a thunder crack, it was enough to keep me from promising Lucifer anything and everything.

Disappointment flickered across the Devil's face. It was so brief, I nearly missed it. Then her lips parted, and she leaned into me, letting me know she was going to kiss me, and it would be absolute fucking Heaven. I also knew that if I let it happen, I'd be done. No, more than that, I'd be her slave.

"If I help you, we're going to do things my way," I said, taking a step backward. It was so hard, I nearly tripped. As it was, my movement barely separated us by a couple inches, but it was enough to stop the Devil in her tracks.

Her face froze mid-motion, and her eyes opened enough to peer at me through long black lashes. "What are your terms?" The question was surprisingly serious, given her current position.

"You're not mad?" I asked, confusion filling me. I'd half-expected to be smote where I stood. After all, this was Lucifer.

"Everyone always denies me at first." She licked her lips and straightened before gesturing at herself. "But I am patient, and I have much to offer. You will see that given enough time." Her eyes crinkled. "But I think you've seen enough. No more freebies." She swept her hand downward. In an instant, she was covered from throat to foot in form-fitting shining red armor. The thing was, it didn't diminish her beauty even slightly. No, if anything, it was enhanced because it left just enough to the imagination that I was desperate to see underneath. And I'd just seen her naked. It was fucking crazy.

"Fine, whatever," I said, trying to regain myself. It was hard because nearly everything in me wanted to leap on her, to throw her down and tear the armor from her body. Even worse, I knew she'd let me, that she wanted me to do it. "Stop."

"Stop what?" she asked coyly. "I am just standing here."

"You are hardly standing there," I said, staring up at the sky, and that was when I realized it wasn't stormy above. Normally the horizon was nothing but an endless storm cloud of crackling lightning. Only, it wasn't now. No, now it was a flat black sky filled with twinkling stars, reminding me of when I'd gone camping on the outskirts and could really see all the stars. How was that possible?

"It is beautiful isn't it," Lucifer said, moving next to me and pointing upward. "I do so enjoy the stars. They were always my favorite creations." She stuck her tongue out. "Not like man, with his breath and sweat." She snorted. "How I hate sweat."

"You're throwing a lot of mixed signals at me," I said, glancing at her.

"Oh, I don't mean you," she said, turning to look at me and giving me a once over. "I fixed that breath problem a long time ago." She quirked a smile at me. "Gave your whole race a breath mint." She scrunched up her nose. "Doesn't solve the sweat thing though."

"Are you talking about what I think you're talking

about?" I asked, wondering if she was talking about the apple and Adam and Eve. I ran a hand through my hair, and as I did, I realized I no longer felt the crazy attraction to her I had before. No, whatever spell or magic or force of will she'd been using before was gone.

"Perhaps," she said, crossing her arms over her chest. "Now tell me, Arthur. What can I offer you?" She sidled toward me, all lithe movement and sinewy grace. "I *really* want to know."

"Just like that?" I asked, gesturing at her. "What the fuck is going on with you?"

"Nothing is going on with me." She shrugged. "I want to help you, and I think you owe it to yourself to find out just how much I can offer you." She smiled. "Tell me what you want, Arthur."

"Oh," I said. I had no idea what I wanted from her other than to go away. Dealing with Mammon, the Archangel of Greed, had been difficult enough, and Lucifer? Well, that was way out of my league because every word felt like a trap. What I needed was Mammon. She'd be able to help with this.

"You don't know what to ask for, do you?" Lucifer asked with a laugh that would have summoned small forest creatures if we were in a Disney movie. "How cute."

"Great, the Devil thinks I'm cute." I shook my head. "You really know how to kick a guy in his pride."

"Yes. You might say it's my specialty." Lucifer met my eyes. "I wish for you to retrieve my hammer. It was lost to me when I was bound beneath this city. I can feel it, can lead you to it, but I cannot retrieve it."

"Your hammer?" I said, confused. "What do you mean a hammer?"

"All archangels have a unique weapon specifically created for us." Her gaze intensified, and for a second, I got the impression she could not only read my mind and see all my memories, but she could see all of my soul. "Like Samael's scythe and Gabriella's mace, I too have a special weapon, but it was long ago lost to me. I would just like for you to find it so I may help you confront the Darkness." She gave me a conciliatory look. "I know it sounds silly, but all I want is to help you, Arthur, and I will gladly help you in exchange for the chance to fight at your side. All you have to do is tell me what you want. I will make it so."

"I won't finalize any deals without Mammon and Buffy," I paused, and when she gestured for me to go on, I continued, "But I'd definitely want your Armament, and help with getting the others."

"Well then, that sounds fair." She smiled at me, and I couldn't help but feel like I'd been suckered. "Let us find Mammon."

"Well, she's back in the town." I turned to look at the gateway but found it had closed. That was no good. It'd take a while for the residual energy to recharge enough for us to use it. An hour or two at the least.

"Then we shall go to your town." She held out her hand to me as her wings extended from her back. They were huge, spreading out a good ten feet on either side. They were jet black for the most part, but every so often a feather would glitter like it was made from spun gold. "Ready to ride with the Devil?" Her lips curled into a smile. "Or would you rather run?"

2

The trip back to the Graveyard was awkward because I could feel Lucifer's breasts pressing into my back the whole way. Every time I tried to move to create some space, her arms would wrap tighter around me like some kind of Chinese finger trap until the entire length of my back was practically molded to her chest.

"Why do you fidget so much?" she asked, breath hot on my neck as we neared the gates. "If you keep it up, I might drop you." She intertwined her legs around mine. "And we wouldn't want that."

"I'm just not used to sharing my personal space so much," I said, taking a deep breath, but all I could smell was her. It was like inhaling desire, desperation, and cheap mints.

"Oh, am I making you uncomfortable?" she cooed, tongue flicking my earlobe as she spoke. "Do we need to take a minute so we can blow off some steam?"

"No," I said as we stopped just before the city. It was strange because I'd expected her to just land in the middle of the town, but I quickly realized why she hadn't. During my absence, they'd erected an energy barrier similar to the one Lustnor had. Only the sigils were different on this one, and even from here, I could feel their energy focused on keeping her out.

"Mammon," Lucifer hissed, one hand jerking out to point at the magical barrier encompassing the Graveyard of Statues.

"Mammon?" I asked, feeling slightly uncomfortable as Lucifer held me in the air one-handed. "What did she do?"

"Maybe it wasn't her," Lucifer mused, her wings beating the air as she arced around so she could drop us to the ground just in front of the gates. "This would cost a lot of energy to do, and she wouldn't have it after healing Samael." Lucifer inhaled sharply as we touched down. Then her eyes narrowed. "What is this?" She turned to look at me, and fear exploded through me.

Before I knew what I was doing, I had my sword out. If it bothered her, it didn't show because she kept staring at me like I'd pissed in her oatmeal.

"You have an archangel here," Lucifer said, taking a step forward. "Which one?"

"Oh," I said, realizing the problem. Of course, Lucifer wouldn't get along with the angels. After all, they had tossed her ass out of Heaven.

"'Oh,' does not answer my question." She moved forward, knocking my sword out of the way with one hand. The movement was so quick, I didn't even see it. One moment I had my weapon pointed at her, and the next it was buried in the ground next to us. Her eyes were inches from mine, and literal purple flames seemed to dance in them. The ground around us buckled as cracks spread out from beneath her feet. Overhead the once clear sky turned to a cacophony of lightning and thunder.

"Sister!" Gabriella cried, and the next thing I knew

Lucifer was engulfed in a hug that lifted her off her feet.

"Gabriella!" Lucifer's eyes filled with warmth as her arms snaked out to wrap around the other angel. "I've missed you." The Devil's eyes flicked to me then. "Has he been nice to you?"

"Who, Arthur?" Gabriella relinquished her hold on Lucifer and turned to look at me, her eyes blazing with good cheer and her smile bright enough to melt even the frostiest heart. "Yeah, he's the best." Gabriella bounced like a kid with too much sugar. "He bought me ice cream and popcorn." She turned back to Lucifer. "Have you had ice cream? It's soooooooooooooooo good."

"I'm afraid I haven't had the pleasure," Lucifer said, and there was something of both fondness and approval in her voice. "But I am glad you have. It pleases me you are well cared for." Lucifer's face fell slightly. "How are your sisters?"

"Michelle, you mean?" Gabriella ran a hand through her golden locks. "She's fine. Boring as ever, all war and no play." Gabriella stuck out her tongue.

"But she's safe?" Lucifer asked, and there was a strange amount of fear in the words.

"Yes, she's okay." Gabriella nodded furiously. "Sister is so strong, she once fought Dred for three days straight."

"Dred?" Lucifer asked, confusion filling her voice. "Who is Dred?"

"Oh, you don't know?" Gabriella asked, her face twisted in confusion.

"No. I've been trapped for a long time." Lucifer looked at me then. "The Destroyer?"

"Yes," I replied, and Lucifer rubbed her chin with one hand.

"Things are worse than I thought. If the Destroyer could fight Michelle at all, let alone for three days, it is more imperative than ever I find my hammer." She nodded to Gabriella. "Would you take the wards down so I can come inside?"

"Oh… I can't do that. Mammon will be mad." Gabriella huffed, blowing out an exasperated breath. "She wouldn't help Samael unless I made them. I wasn't sure why, but now I think I get it." Gabriella narrowed her eyes at Lucifer right before she poked the Devil in the chest with one long finger. "You didn't apologize, did you?"

"Why would I apologize—"

"You didn't. No wonder Mammon is mad." Gabriella shook her head. "You should say you're sorry." Gabriella crossed her arms over her voluptuous chest. "I won't take the wards down unless you promise."

I stared at the two women and almost wanted to laugh. Gabriella definitely seemed dead set on making Lucifer, the Archangel of Pride, apologize, and even a cursory glance at the Devil made me think that was never going to happen. Still, if anyone could make Lucifer say she was sorry, I was willing to bet it was Gabriella.

"Gabby," Lucifer said, dropping her eyes to the ground. "You know I can't."

"Forgiveness is the first step toward redemption, Luci," Gabriella shrugged. "Or you can stay out here. I'll come visit you, but it'll be awkward since I have lots to do."

"I will not apologize," Lucifer said, dropping her

eyes to the ground. "Even if I did, it'd hardly matter."

"It will matter if you mean it," Gabriella said, giving her sister a hug. "Actions matter, and besides, apologies are always two-way streets. One to forgive and one to accept. You can only control your actions, not another's." She nodded once more before blowing a lock of hair out of her face. "You taught me that."

"When did you get so smart?" Lucifer said, looking her sister over.

"I don't know." Gabriella flushed before turning her eyes to me. "Michelle always told me to keep my ideas to myself." She shrugged. "Arthur didn't think so, though, so I've been speaking my mind more." She turned her gaze back to Lucifer. "You really think I'm smart?"

The Devil was silent for a long while, and I realized she was thinking something over. "Yes," she said after a while. "You're definitely the smartest person I know." As Lucifer said the words, I got the impression she actually believed them. It was weird because while Gabriella was innocent and a bit naive, the way she looked at the words had a sort of sense to it, I often didn't see myself.

"Does that mean you'll apologize to Mammon?" Gabriella inquired, raising one golden eyebrow at her sister.

"Yes," Lucifer said begrudgingly. Then she kicked at a nonexistent speck on the ground. "Lower the wards, and I will apologize."

"Yay!" Gabriella said, grabbing Lucifer's hands and shaking them. "Maybe we can be a family again!"

"Don't get your hopes up," Lucifer said, taking a deep breath. "Actually… you know what, I have a couple things to do." Lucifer shifted uncomfortably from foot to foot.

"Wait, you don't want to come inside?" Gabriella asked, eyes full of confusion.

"I do, I just… I need to go get the crown for Arthur." She nodded, turning her eyes to me, and even though I didn't know her very well, I could tell she wanted my help.

"Oh, that's right. I'd forgotten about the crown." I shook my head like the whole thing was my fault as I put a hand on Gabriella's shoulder. "Lucifer said she would get me the Armament. She wanted to hurry and retrieve it, but I made her give me a ride back first." I looked sheepishly at the Devil herself. "Sorry about that."

"It's not a problem," Lucifer said before mouthing "thank you." Then she nodded to Gabriella. "I really have to be going. Arthur will need the Armament if he is to defeat Dred."

"Oh, you guys are so smart. I forgot about that." Gabriella flushed so hard, her neck turned red. "Always on task. Guess I should do that too." She gave Lucifer a small wave. "Come back soon?"

"Yeah…" Lucifer replied, looking up at the sky. "I'll be back soon. I just need to work through some things."

"Great! Maybe we can have ice cream when you come back." Gabriella hugged her sister before turning to me. "Come on, Arthur. Sister is busy, and I have something to show you!" The archangel grabbed my hand and began pulling me toward the gate while Lucifer stood there, unable to do more than watch us leave.

3

"Well, that was strange," I said, glancing at Gabriella as the gates shut behind us. "I didn't realize you guys were such besties."

"Who?" Gabriella asked, button nose scrounging up. "You mean Luci and me?"

"Yeah." I rubbed the back of my neck. "I had sort of assumed you guys would be, I dunno, enemies."

Gabriella shrugged. "I find it's better to get along with people." She touched my arm. "I know you say I'm smart, but I know I'm not." She bit her lip. "But I appreciate that you try to let me be me and don't tell me to let the grownups talk." She nodded back toward the gate. "Lucifer always did that too.

Thought we should have an equal voice." Gabriella swallowed hard. "She always thought I was special in my own way. My other sisters don't really think that." She looked at the ground. "It made me sad when she fell."

"That's a lot to take in," I said, stopping and looking at her. "Do you want to talk about it?"

"Not really, no." Gabriella shook her head, sending her golden locks whipping around her face. "I've never found rehashing the past to be productive." She smiled at me then. "It's why I'm so glad she's back. I know sister is scared we're all going to hate her for what she did, but I think it's been long enough for them to be able to forgive her. Even if they don't, she can stop carrying that burden and move on." She nodded. "That would be good for her. Luci has always felt like she needs to carry the world on her shoulders." She took my hands. "Sort of reminds me of you at times, Arthur." She looked at me, crystal blue eyes practically boring into my soul. "Both of you could stand to realize something important."

"What's that?" I asked, wanting to break her gaze but not daring to do so. Instead, I focused on her with everything I could. I owed her that much.

"That you don't have to do it alone." She smiled brightly. "We'll all help you if you'll let us."

"You know, I don't understand why anyone ever says you're dumb." I hugged her, pulling her close. "You're the smartest person I know."

"Thanks!" She hugged me back. "When you say it, I totally believe you." She stepped back and nodded at me. "It's why I like you so much." She flushed slightly, leaving me to puzzle over the reaction. "I mean, well, you know." She looked away. "Anyway, we need to go check on Samael. She'll want to see you, and then Saramana wanted to speak with you." She pulled out a scrap of paper and showed it to me, only I couldn't read her scribbles. "See. Gwen made me a schedule. I'm supposed to help you keep it."

"A schedule?" I asked, raising an eyebrow at her. "Why would I need that?"

"Gwen said, and I quote, 'Arthur is terrible about doing things when he's supposed to, and he's forgetful. You seem to be able to get through to him, so you need to make sure he gets everything done since he doesn't seem to care what I think,' then she handed me this list." She showed me the paper again. "Saramana is first."

I rubbed my face, making a mental note to talk to Gwen about this. I wasn't sure how I felt about Gabriella being assigned to me, and I knew that while Gwen probably wanted someone to keep me on task since she was my second in command, I was worried she'd assigned Gabriella to secretary duty just to keep her out of everyone's hair. After what had just happened, I wasn't so sure I was okay with that. Actually, that wasn't true. I knew I wasn't okay with that.

"And when do I see Gwen?" I asked, gesturing at the list. "I can't read that."

"Oh. Sorry. I didn't know. Let me check." Gabriella pulled the paper back and scanned it. "You have her at four." She glanced at the sky. "That's two hours or so from now."

"Ah, okay," I said, marveling at how she could tell time. The sky had changed dramatically since Lucifer had awakened, and now I couldn't tell what time of day it was for the life of me. Before the sky had seemed to follow a cycle, even if the general atmosphere never changed, but now, it just did whatever the Hell it wanted to. It made me wonder if Lucifer was the direct cause of that, and when the sky would return to normal, assuming it did at all.

"Great! So, let's get going." Gabriella took my hand and pulled me to the left, toward a building I didn't recognize. Actually, as we moved through the town, I realized a lot of the buildings had changed. It wasn't in the overall appearance so much as it was in little things. In fact, I probably wouldn't have noticed if there wasn't a pair of half-finished buildings next to it. The one on the right looked familiar in construction, while the one directly to the left of it was just a tiny bit, well, better. I could tell in the way the jousts were supported as well as the way it was generally framed out.

"Who designed that one?" I asked, pointing at the left one as we approached Maribelle. "The other one looks pretty familiar, so I'm guessing Maribelle designed that one."

"I designed it," Saramana said before Maribelle could reply. The head of the carpenter's guild turned to look at me and wiped her calloused palms on her overalls while Maribelle dropped her eyes to the floor, her cheeks flushed with embarrassment. "I've been teaching Maribelle a few things."

"Oh?" I asked, watching Maribelle fidget, obviously uncomfortable with the scrutiny, although I was pretty sure that had less to do with me looking at her and more to do with her guild head working beside her.

"Yes," Saramana said, nodding to me before moving toward the building. "These are some more advanced techniques." She gestured to the bracing at the corner of the building. "The way I've aligned the joints here will offer increased support with a fraction of the material." She pushed on it with one hand. "Go on, try to knock it down."

"I believe you. I can tell just from looking." I moved a bit closer and examined it, wishing I had Clarent. If I did, I could have seen exactly what sort of technique she'd used. "Although part of me is curious why Maribelle doesn't know it." I waved a hand at Maribelle. "She's a fantastic carpenter, but I can tell the general construction of this is well, better. I just watched our sculptor in the yearly competition, and I got the impression from watching it that the difference in skill was degrees. This though." I pointed at the building. "This is a whole different level."

"Well, erm, I—"

"You're being unfair," Saramana said, cutting off Maribelle's reply with the wave of one hand. Then she put that same hand on Maribelle's shoulder. "I *am* the Head of the Carpenter's Guild. Maribelle is a rank 10 carpenter. Now, she's my best rank ten carpenter by a huge margin, but she hasn't moved up through the ranks, hasn't learned the more advanced skills." She met my eyes. "She knows some stuff she shouldn't, but I assume that's from you. The problem is, she doesn't even know what she doesn't know, and I doubt you do either."

"Okay," I said, rubbing my chin. "You're saying she would have learned these skills, but she hasn't yet?"

"That is exactly what I'm saying." Saramana gestured across the road toward where Annabeth was busy sculpting a new fountain out of a chunk of stone. I wasn't quite sure what it was supposed to be, nor where she'd gotten the red rock, I'd learned was nearly impossible to carve, but what she'd made so far was definitely skilled, if rough around the edges still. "Your sculptor is using advanced techniques on the red rock, the kind that you only learn by moving up in the guild and studying hard. She has natural skill, sure, but it's been honed by practice and learning. Maribelle doesn't have that. She's working with the basics, which she's very good at, and relying on her impressive level of skill."

"Master has been teaching me," Maribelle squeaked, and a glance in her direction let me know she wanted to find a hole and hide within it. "I didn't mean to be so disappointing."

"No one is disappointed in you," I said, taking a deep breath. Normally in this situation, I'd look at Saramana's skill trees, assuming I could, and ask her about what to have Maribelle work on, similar to what I'd done with Annabeth and sculpting. Only, I couldn't do that without Clarent. What's more, Saramana was right in that I didn't recall Maribelle having that many skill trees. Sure, the ones she'd had were nearly maxed, but she hadn't unlocked new ones, and if they weren't unlocked, it would be a coin toss whether or not I could see them at all.

"Yes, you're doing very well." Saramana nodded

once. "It's why I'm showing you these things, so you can learn."

"Yes, but once you leave, I'll be stuck." Maribelle frowned and looked at the building. "I may get good at what you've shown me in the last few hours, but those are the only skills I will be able to improve." She bit her lip. "I need years more of study."

"You do, but I'll try my best to pop back in. Once I figure out what's going on in Ridge Tree, I'll see if I can spare someone to come help you learn." She looked to me. "Assuming that's okay with you."

"It's okay with me, but you'd have to clear it with Gwen," I said before stopping myself. "Wait, you're leaving?"

"Yes, that's why I asked the angel to bring you to me." She shrugged. "I'd already cleared everything else with Gwen. The way I figure it, I'm alive because of you, so I should return the favor by helping." She took a deep breath. "I just happened to be on my way here with a message from the guilds about your Stairway when the town blew…"

"You mean the Stairway to Heaven?" I asked. In all the excitement, I'd totally forgotten about it. The

Stairway was an item we needed to craft so we could open a portal to Heaven, although with the way things were going, I wasn't sure having such a portal was a good idea. After all, portals worked both ways, and I didn't know if I wanted the armies of Darkness to have an easy way into Hell.

"Yes," Saramana nodded. "Most of the Guild had agreed to help you make it." She waved her hand. "That doesn't matter now though. All the Guild leaders who survived will be returning to their towns to get things in order in the wake of the Royal Centre explosion." She took a deep breath. "That is why I'm leaving."

"You're returning to your own town?" I asked, suddenly confused. "I thought you lived in Royal Centre."

"No, well, at least, I don't. I spend time there, sure. More recently because you interest me." She looked me over. "But all the trades have their own towns that are dedicated to the pursuit of the trade." She touched her chest. "Mine is Ridge Tree, and I need to return to it. Once I have things sorted, I'll send a master carpenter to help you and to teach Maribelle."

"What's the catch?" I asked, glancing at Maribelle who was shifting from foot to foot uncomfortably.

"There isn't a catch." Saramana huffed out a breath. "You know I've felt that we need you to beat the Darkness. I want you to succeed. I guess that's the catch. You need to beat the Darkness."

4

"Hey, Sam. How are you?" I asked, slowly entering her door. I hadn't been sure what I'd find, but when I saw her sitting there reading a book, I'll admit, I was a touch shocked.

"Some light reading. Mammon said I have to sit here and Sally has been mother-henning me for the last few hours." She closed her paperback. "Sally just stepped out, so I thought I'd be able to finish my book."

"Ah, I was about to ask about Sally," I said, moving into the room. "Is your book interesting?"

She looked haggard and worn, but better, and if her current situation was any indication, she at least seemed like she should be getting better.

"Not really. It's about this guy Mac Brennan who sold his soul to a demon and got a magic arm. Only he can't remember why he sold his soul because he has amnesia and uses it as an excuse to kill everyone." Sam shrugged. "I think the author might be a hack."

"I dunno, sounds kinda cool to me. Does it have lots of explosions?" I pulled out the Once and Future Builder, the denser than a textbook manual for all things Builder I'd gotten from Gabriella when she'd first arrived in Hell. You know, assuming it had decided it wanted to reveal the information to me. "Because if it does, we can totally trade."

"Pass." Sam put her book on her lap and looked at me. "I'm fine by the way. I appreciate you coming to see me, but I know you have things to do."

"Yeah, here's the thing though. I need to have my sword rebuilt. Are you going to be strong enough to do that?" I looked at my shoes sheepishly. Here Sam was hurt, and I was about to ask her to help me. It seemed like a dick move and probably was, but at the same time, we were at war. Besides, I doubted Sam wanted me to coddle her.

"Theoretically." She watched me for a moment.

"But we still need the Stygian Iron, and unless I've been asleep for longer than I expect," she made a dramatic show of checking her watchless wrist, "I doubt you've found any."

"I have a plan for that. Well, Buffy has a plan for that." I sighed, waving off the comment. "That's not actually why I came here."

She gave me a sad smile. "Look, I'm really not up for the whole sex thing right now." Her eyes twinkled slightly. "Wouldn't turn down a topless sponge bath though."

"What?" I asked, feeling my cheeks heat up. "No, that's not why I'm here."

"I figured." She took a deep breath. "I was trolling you. Trust me, the absolute last thing I want is for you to give me a sponge bath. Not when Gabriella can do it." Sam gave me a wry smile. "She has the touch of an angel, don't you know."

"Ha ha," I said, rolling my eyes as I moved to the chair next to her bed and sat down. "I actually have an important question for you."

"Lucifer?" she asked, and the way she said it made me think she knew I was going to ask about it. In retrospect it made sense. She'd seen Mammon. No doubt the two had chatted about it.

"Yes." I opened the book and showed her the page detailing the archangel. I'd noticed it'd filled itself in after I'd talked to Saramana. It also had details on the crown, but unlike Mammon's gauntlets, it had no recipe nor characteristics for what the thing actually did.

"You can't trust Lucifer." Sam stopped herself. "Actually, that isn't true. You can totally trust her to do what she thinks is best." Sam tapped her cheek with one finger, lost in thought. "You know those leaders who are absolutely sure they are one hundred percent correct? The ones surrounded by yes men because they fire everyone who disagrees with them? That's what Lucifer is like." She shrugged. "It's great when she's actually right, but when she's not…" she gestured around the room as if to say, "see Exhibit A."

"Great, so as long as we're doing the same thing, I *can* trust her." I took a deep breath. "She seemed sort of straightforward to me. Powerful as fuck, but straightforward."

"That she is." Sam met my eyes. "Lucifer is power.

Likely the most powerful of all the archangels. It took the combined forces of Heaven to throw her ass out." She took a deep breath and searched for the words. "And then once she and her fallen were down here, they eventually took her down too. Think about that. She was the de facto leader of Heaven and was violently forced out. Then the same thing happened in Hell. The likelihood we'll need to force her out again is really high."

"But until then…" I muttered, not liking where this was going. I knew it was crazy, but I'd sort of felt bad for the Devil. It was absolutely insane, but she was also powerful and had an armament. Having her at my side *should* make dealing with the Darkness easier.

"Until then you'd better play nice because even if Mammon, Gabriella, and I were at full strength, she could snap her fingers and make us explode." Sam's voice had gone deathly serious. "That isn't hyperbole, Arthur."

"Oh." I swallowed. I'd know she was powerful, but if she could kill another Archangel with the snap of her fingers, how were we to do anything but what she wanted? "How was she defeated?"

"We took her hammer." Sam sighed. "It helps her focus her power. Without it, she has to spend a tremendous amount of her focus just to keep her own strength from consuming her. That's the key to beating her. It always has been." She watched me for a second. "When we battled in Heaven, we took her hammer and flung it from Heaven. Only then were we able to stand against her. I got the impression she never recovered it after that. If she had, who knows what would have happened. Nothing good, that's for sure."

"Well, see, that's the thing," I looked everywhere to avoid her laser-like stare, "she sort of wants me to get her hammer in exchange for the Armament."

"I figured," Sam said, voice somewhat bored. "Mammon and I talked about it, and there's nothing else we can think of that she'd rather have." Sam sighed. "It's definitely one of those 'doomed if you do, doomed if you don't' situations. Still…" she let the word trail off until I turned back to look at her, and I found her smiling at me. "I think you should do it. Give her the hammer and toss her ass at the Darkness. That's what she really wants, anyway. A second shot at glory and redemption. She won't say it, but I know *that* is what she really wants."

"Wait, you want me to power up the Devil?" I asked, sort of confused. "I mean, I get what you're saying, but… why would she care about redemption?"

"Because she's prideful." Sam watched me carefully. "Right now, her pride has been hurt. She'll do anything she can to make everyone see she was right. To do that, she must conquer the Darkness once and for all, put that genie back in its bottle so to speak. After that, well, all bets are off, but until then? Well, until then, I think we can count on her to actually help." She shrugged. "What's the alternative? Give up on the Armament? Dred already has five. You'll need at least five to stand against him. Lucifer has one. Not getting it from her is silly."

"That makes a certain amount of sense." I nodded. "I think I can work with that… That just leaves me with my last question, and then I'll leave you to your book."

"You want to know what the Armament I gave

Dred does." Sam gestured at me. "You should have figured it out."

"I should have figured it out?" I asked, confused. "You know I'm kind of dumb, right?"

"Only when it comes to women," Sam said, rolling her eyes. "The armor you have based on the augmentations to Clarent? That's my Armament. That's what I gave Dred."

"Wait, you mean the armor I summon with Clarent? That's the power you gave Dred?" I stared at her in confusion. "But you gave me that."

"And when you wore it, did you not feel stronger and faster? Did you not gain magic powers?" Sam shrugged. "It's not as powerful because I couldn't put as much power into it as I did Dred's as he saps nearly everything inside me, but the concept is the same." She touched her chest where Dred had once marked her, only now the mark was broken. "I honestly have no idea how it will function now that the bond between us had been severed."

"Does that mean what I think it means?" I asked, raising an eyebrow at me. "Because if you're saying Dred is about to lose one of his Armaments…"

"His armament will still function, just likely at the level your armor does unless he's found a way to bridge the power thing. The armaments essentially allow the user to tap into the giver's power for fuel. Perhaps the Darkness is fueling his Armament now. Either way, I wouldn't count on him being weaker."

"Fair enough. That's a bad plan, anyway." I sighed. "I guess that's it until I can find the sword." I got to my feet and kissed her on the forehead. Her skin was both too warm and clammy, reminding me of how I'd felt after a fever had broken. "Get well soon."

"I'll do my best," she said, picking up her book. I smiled, watching her for a moment, and as I did, she glanced up at me. "Yes?"

"Nothing," I said, taking a deep breath. "I'm really glad you're okay."

"You probably say that to all the girls, but I'm glad to hear it." She made a shooing motion with her hand. "Now go, I'm at the part where he steals a race car and drives it through a mansion."

"Right..." I rolled my eyes as I made my way back outside.

5

"Hey, Gabriella, could you go and find Buffy for me?" I asked as I came out of Sam's room. She'd been waiting outside staring at her notes like she was afraid she was forgetting something.

"Buffy?" Gabriella asked, looking at me in confusion. "She's not on the schedule."

"Is there anything on the schedule?" I asked, moving over to take a peek before I realized I wouldn't be able to read it. Man, not having Clarent's ability to translate everything into digestible tooltips sucked. I needed to get on that whole Stygian Iron thing so I could repair the weapon.

"Not until you meet with Gwen in about an hour."

She looked at me concerned. "Did I miss something?"

"No, it's fine. Go find Buffy and tell her to meet me over there." I pointed to a spot between the buildings. It was littered with rocks, and our carpenters had opted to avoid the space for now. They'd marked it out with stakes and rope, but clearly, they were choosing to work on easier areas first.

"Okay…" Gabriella took a deep breath before looking back to her notes and scribbling something. "I've added it to your calendar. I'll be back before you can say moose knuckle."

"Moose knuckle?" I asked as she turned to walk away. "I'm not familiar with the term."

Gabriella stopped and blushed. Hard. "Um… well…" she gestured at my pants. "It's when a guy's you know…"

"I honestly don't know," I said, looking down at myself. "Do I have one?"

"No. I mean, I didn't look or anything." She flushed so hard her chest and neck turned pink. "Sorry, I just, I have to get Buffy." She gave me a determined look and tapped the notes with one hand. "It's on the schedule. Silly me, gotta run." She pointed her chin in the opposite direction of me and walked off, taking over-exaggerated steps.

"All right…" I mumbled, shrugging my shoulders. Then I made my way toward the spot that had been marked off. It was easy to see why they'd avoided it. Chunks of rock were not only strewn across the dirt, but they looked to be embedded into the earth itself. Not just small chunks either, the kind that made you think what was visible was just the tip of the iceberg.

Still, this was just what I needed. I pulled my gauntlets, The Unrelenting Grips of Greed, on. They were the Armament provided by Mammon, the Princess of Greed, and allowed me to pull whatever I wanted from wherever I wanted with a weird sort of telekinesis, assuming, of course, that I was strong enough to actually do it. I took a deep breath as a wave of cold hit me, then I reached my hand out toward the plot.

The gemstones embedded into the palms and the back of the hands began to glow with silver light, and my skin began to prickle as Mammon's power fell over me. This must have been what Sam was talking about. Every time I'd used the gauntlets so far, I'd felt Mammon's presence like an ice cube down the back of my neck, and what's more, I'd gotten the impression she felt when I used the power.

The thought made me sick. Had Sam felt Dred use her powers to slaughter her friends and family? What a fucking bastard.

Pushing the thought out of my mind before it could distract me, I exhaled a breath of mist and raised my hand, focusing on the Armament I'd gotten from Mammon, the Relentless Grips of Greed.

Like Clarent, it allowed me to see stats and tooltips, but only of the objects I could extract with its power.

Instantly the whole field came alive with stat boxes and menus. The most common material was a stone called Coti. It was definitely the most plentiful stone here, but there was also limestone, and a few others. None of it looked particularly difficult to extract, and for a second I wanted to try to pull one of them out just to see what it was like in comparison to the Coti. Only, as I looked back at the menu for the gray stone, I noticed there were two new categories. Proficiency and Overall Proficiency.

Coti

Material Type: stone

Grade: B (Average)

Depth: 3 meters

Difficulty: 2

Proficiency: 1/100

Overall Proficiency: 0/100

A type of stone typically used in construction.

"I wonder what those do," I mumbled, flipping open the menu for Proficiency.

Proficiency: The user has demonstrated the ability to pull this type of material from its designated location. Each time this is successfully performed, a bonus equal to the proficiency rating will be subtracted from the overall difficulty calculation. Each material has its own, separate proficiency rating that must be raised.

"Okay, I guess I can get really good at pulling out

Coti." I shrugged. It would be useful to reduce the difficulty of extracting the different materials, but I wasn't sure what being really good at removing Coti would do for me in the long run. Somewhat dissatisfied, I opened the tooltip for Overall Proficiency.

Overall Proficiency: An additive bonus applied to the difficulty of extracting any material from its designated location based on the Proficiency rating of each individual material the user has achieved.

My eyes opened wide in shock. If I was reading the tooltip correctly, it meant that by raising the proficiency of Coti, it would contribute to my Overall Proficiency, and that *would* help me pull limestone, or even Stygian Iron, from the ground. Sure, I had no idea what sort of contribution it would make, but I was suddenly much more optimistic about the prospect of actually obtaining the Stygian Iron.

"Time to get on with it then," I said, suddenly excited. I was going to pull all the Coti in the town from the ground. After that, I'd move on to everything else, sweeping the town in waves to make the most use of my Overall Proficiency. I smirked. It was time to power level the crap out of this.

Nodding to myself, I moved to the closest piece of

Coti and dropped to my knees in the dirt. Then I placed my hand on the rock. I felt the connection between it and the gauntlets instantly, like a thousand invisible tethers reaching out and latching onto the piece of stone. I could instantly see the size and shape of the rock within the dirt, and while it seemed like there should be more detail available, there wasn't. No, it was sort of like I'd hit it with a sonar blast and was reading the echo. It gave me a general shape of what was around it but not much else.

Still, it was a lot more than what I'd seen when I pulled the first piece of stone from the earth. Perhaps I'd get more detail as I did it? I wasn't sure, but either way, I had to level up my Overall Proficiency. Once I did that, I could try getting the Stygian Iron.

The gauntlets began to glow with silver light, causing little sparks of lightning to flash within the gemstones. The one made from the Heart of Earth flashed brightly, glowing with a violent green color as the rock beneath my fingers began to move. The surrounding earth cracked, splitting open like the flesh of a ripe peach to reveal the pit.

My brow began to sweat, and my chest heaved

with effort as the stone began to move upward. Shutting my eyes, I concentrated and allowed Mammon's power to fill me. The cold touch of her strength washed over me like a bucket of ice water in winter, causing my teeth to chatter and my hair to stand on end. Gooseflesh sprouted across my arms and legs, but I ignored it, focusing on the coti.

"Come on," I wheezed, and jerked my hands upward. The rock exploded from the earth, a massive chunk that had to have weighed about forty pounds. It hung in the air in front of me for a moment before crashing to the ground.

As I looked at it just sitting there, I glanced at my proficiency rating and found it had increased to two. Excellent. A smile crossed my lips as I wiped my brow with the back of one hand. Then I pushed myself to the next piece of Coti. It had a similar difficulty rating, and judging on how much effort the last one had taken, I was pretty sure I could pull about five or six more without needing to rest. Still, time would tell.

"What did you want, Arthur?" Buffy said, marching over to me as I settled down to extract the next one. "Because I am *way* too busy to watch you pull rocks from the ground." She kicked idly at the stone before squatting down, so we were eye to eye.

"I'm going to pull every piece of stone out of this town and the surrounding areas. I want you to tell me which ones to do." I gestured at the field. "I'm going to start with Coti, but being that there is a ton of it, I'm sure it's not worth much. You're the one who knows what will sell. Draw me up a list of what to focus on so we can make some money."

"Arthur," Buffy said, swallowing hard. "As much as I love you taking the initiative to make money, none of this stuff is worth much. I've studied the resource maps for the whole area, and there's scant little that is Sure, we could sell all this rock, but it'd be better for us to use it…"

"That doesn't sound like you, Buffy. What's wrong?" I asked, watching her fidget.

"You're aware Royal Centre was destroyed, right?" She cocked an eyebrow at me. "That's the capital for all of Hell. Where do you think we sell most of this type of thing?" She shook her head. "All the other places went there to make orders and deliver. Now there's nowhere to facilitate trade. Stuff like this," she gestured to the piles of stone all around us. "We're better off waiting until a new trade hub and commodities market has been set up. Otherwise, we risk having to sell it dirt cheap."

"You're thinking small, Buffy." I got to my feet and found myself towering over her. I hadn't meant to do it, more that I'd wanted to walk around while I talked. It was a nervous habit, but I hated sitting still when I talked to people. I always felt better when I was on the move.

"Thinking small?" she asked, and there was an edge of anger to her voice. "How so?"

"What would Mammon do in this situation?" I held up my gauntlets. "In a situation where there was no more commodities market."

"I'm not following," she said, shaking her head. "If she was smart, she'd get all the materials and then have her way with the market when it opened, using her resources to make sure she made tons of money."

"Well, yeah, she probably would do that," I admitted, taking a deep breath. "But we could *create* the market. You said yourself, this is all building materials, and that all of it went through Royal Centre. I assume that's because it was at the center of the trade routes, but that doesn't matter to us." I pulled out the Nexus Gateway Conduit. "We can deliver anywhere instantly."

Buffy's eyes practically turned into dollar signs as she looked at me. "You're right. We could become the center because we can deliver things quicker. Hell, *we* could become the center for all delivery, and once we did that, it'd be over." She threw her arms around me. "I'm so wet right now."

"Whoa," I said, taken aback. "That wasn't…"

"Not for you," she shook her head, disengaging from me. "I have so many plans to draw up." She nodded once before holding out her hands. "We'll need people. Lots of people. I can hit up the merchant's guild…" she stopped. "Though most of that is likely gone now. A lot of them were probably in Royal Centre. Ah well, I'll make it work." Buffy spun on her heel. "Angel, I need someone to bring Arthur the list once I compile it. Can you handle that?"

"Um… sure thing," Gabriella said, she nodded, and it was then I'd realized she was back. She'd just been standing in the background waiting patiently. "I'm good at running errands."

"Excellent," Buffy said, smiling as she turned back to me. "Give me the conduit. I'm gonna hit up the merchant town. I think I can convince them to help us. They can't match what we can do with the conduit."

"We'll need to get a few more of those made too. Can you relay that to Sally?" I asked, but Buffy held up her hand.

"That's not going to happen right now. Let me talk to the guild, get their blessing, and move from there, okay?" Buffy waggled her fingers at me expectantly.

"Right, sorry. I'll let you do your thing." I handed her the Nexus Gateway Conduit. "Do your thing and make us rich."

"On it," she said, turning and heading toward the gate without so much as a look in our general direction.

"Thanks for getting her Gabriella," I said, smiling at the angel.

"You're welcome, Arthur," Gabriella said, smiling at me. "We have about twenty minutes before your meeting with Gwen, by the way. You may consider getting cleaned up first." She pinched her nose. "You kinda smell."

"Right…" I looked back at the Coti. I could pull it out, but I'm sure it'd take at least ten minutes, and that'd cut into shower time. "Okay, let's do that."

6

All showered and dressed, I followed Gabriella toward where I was supposed to meet Gwen, but when I found her, I was surprised to see Mammon and Saramana sitting there too. As I entered the makeshift conference room in the middle of the big building near the center of town, I found myself confused as to the sudden audience since Gwen normally handled these sorts of things.

"Wow, you got him here on time," Gwen said, looking at Gabriella and smiling. "I'm actually quite proud of you."

"Thanks," the archangel said, nodding furiously. "I told you I'd do a good job."

"So, um, what's this about?" I asked, gesturing at the table where the three women were seated.

"What this is about is that Royal Centre has been destroyed and Lucifer is on the loose," Mammon said, swallowing hard. She didn't look at me and instead turned her attention toward the huge paper laid out on the table. "Near as we can tell, she hasn't gone on a murderous rampage, so you must have stopped her."

"I did for now." I shrugged. "We have a truce because, basically, she wants her hammer and I want her armament."

"You can't give her the hammer," Mammon said, leaping to her feet so suddenly, her chair clattered to the ground. "If you do, we'll never be able to stop her from killing us all."

"Sam thinks it's a good idea," I said, moving closer so I could see the paper.

"Samael has bad judgment," Mammon replied, simply. "She gave Dred his first armament."

I was about to respond to that, to defend Sam, when Gwen stood and put her hands out.

"Be that as it may, neither of those are topics for

this discussion." Gwen took a deep breath, causing her breasts to strain against her tight white button up. "What is the topic of this discussion is how to move forward given what we know. I've asked Saramana to sit in. Buffy was supposed to be here, but she said you gave her a task. She explained it to me, and I agree, but I wish you'd have talked it over with me." She waved a hand before I could explain myself. "It's a good idea, so I don't want to get into an argument about it."

"Right, fine," I said, feeling like I was seconds away from getting attacked. "What, specifically are we going to talk about? I have fields of stone to clear."

"So that you can repair Clarent?" Gwen arched an eyebrow at me. "Yeah, I know about that."

"Well, then yes. Exactly." I tried to ignore the sudden flare of embarrassment I felt over breaking the one item that had made me special. "I guess I should have told you."

"Again," Gwen said, meeting my eyes in a way that made me squirm. "This isn't a discussion about what you should have told me about. I trust your judgment, Arthur. I trust you're doing what you think you should."

"So, what are we supposed to talk about?" I asked, unsure of what was going on. "The town seems to be coming along, and Buffy has the trade thing happening."

"We have some problems," Gwen said, gesturing to Mammon. "Why don't you start?"

"Most of my wealth was destroyed in the blast at Royal Centre. I still have the lands you freed as well as Blade's End and Lustnor, but those two towns were stripped to the bone. There are a few people there for day to day, but not a lot beyond. In short, I'm poor." She looked at her feet. "I'd used most of what I had available to cement my position in Royal Centre, which in retrospect was dumb."

"Okay, I can see how that would be bad but—"

"Arthur, she means we now have to take care of both of those cities with no resources. That's the major issue. There's no one to trade with. No food to buy. No workers to work the land. It's a big problem." Gwen sighed loudly. "Unless you want to leave her people to starve."

"No, I don't." I fidgeted. I hadn't thought of them at all, but with Mammon part of our coterie now, we were responsible for her people too. "What do you think we should do about those towns?"

"You're actually asking me?" Gwen said, slightly taken aback. "Is this a trick?"

"No," I said, shaking my head. "I have some ideas, but I want to hear yours first. You're the one with your fingers on the pulse of our situation."

"Ah," Gwen said, and she seemed amused, which was odd. "Let's table that for a second because I think Saramana can lead us into that."

"I thought you were leaving," I said, turning to the head of the Carpenter's Guild. "We already talked about everything…"

"That's just it. I have no way to actually get back." She bit her lip. "I need someone to let me use the Gateway to get home, but once I do, well, we'll need more of the gateways to keep commerce going…"

"Buffy is supposed to be setting something like that up already." I shrugged. "Just have her take you when she heads to your city."

"We already set that up," Gwen said, waving off my comment.

"So, what's the problem then?" I shook my head. "I'm just sort of confused, I guess."

"Why is that? Don't you want to be involved?" Gwen asked, peering at me. "I thought you would."

"I want to be involved, but this is your area of expertise… Oh." I nodded. "I see what this is."

"Do you?" she asked, a sly smile crossing her lips. "Do you really?"

"Yes, you wanted me to see that what you do is important. I do." I nodded once. "If you didn't take care of all this kind of stuff, I'd have to do it, and I clearly have no idea how."

"Good." Gwen pointed at Saramana. "In exchange for helping her, we're going to sign an exclusivity contract, which means two things. One, her town will have the first choice of our exported lumber. In exchange, we'll get a certain percentage of every project that uses our lumber, which since we'll control most of the shipping via our conduits, allows us to drive our competitors out. We'll make a fortune."

"That sounds like a Mammon idea," I said,

glancing at the Princess. "Which annoys me because I sort of like it."

"It was my idea," Mammon conceded with a shrug. "In fact, Gwen and I are going to go to every trade town and sign similar agreements. We'll also get you a damned mason." She shrugged. "Once we do that, we'll be swimming in money and talent."

"Well, that all sounds great, so, um, let's get to it?" I shrugged. I felt sort of irrelevant.

"We will," Gwen said, pointing at the paper. "Right after we decide what we want to do. Should we build this town up? Move to Lustnor or Blade's End? Should we build smack dab on top of Royal Centre?"

"Let's stay here." I pointed toward the window. Through it, we could see the Darkness on the horizon. "We're close to that, but at the same time, it allows us to harvest Dark Blood easily, which will let us empower our weapons and armor for the coming battles. We can expand backward toward Lustnor with ease. Blade's End is on the other side of the world, and so is Mammon's lands. They're not in imminent danger of Darkness attack since they've been freed, so we can mostly ignore them."

"Are you sure you want to stay here?" Gwen watched me carefully. "It's the most dangerous place."

"If we move back, we'll be conceding the territory to the Darkness. We can't give them an inch, let alone miles. The moment we move back, they'll retake this." I shrugged. "Lustnor is too far for us to build our stuff there and then travel here. I think it's better all-around to stay here and expand backward." I took a deep breath. "Unless the Royal Centre is a serious idea. I just don't feel like it was."

"It's not really. Getting the ability to rebuild there will be endless red tape," Saramana interjected. "I keep telling them that, but they keep ignoring us. Besides, if we ever want to lock down Lucifer again, it has to be there. That's where the ley lines are the most powerful."

"Right, so that's out." I took a deep breath. "Are we good then?"

"There's just the matter of Mammon's people. We have to supply them." Gwen watched me. "I'm worried if we pull them here, we'll just create resentment with the shortages, and we have no idea what the refugee situation is going to be like. Royal

Centre may have been destroyed and along with it, many people, but there are those refugee camps in the forest. Those people will come here. We're the closest and besides you're here. We need to be ready for that."

"Can we get some people to work the farmland then?" I looked back out the window. "I'm going to clear it all." I made a fist. "I need to get good enough to extract Stygian Iron to remake Clarent. There will be a lot of grinding to make that happen."

"Saramana, do you think you can help us with that?" Gwen asked, turning to the guild head. "I'm sure everyone is going to be hurting, but I'm sure you'll have some pull."

"Not with Randi. She's a total bitch and runs the farming sector. She always hated being ignored, but with Royal Centre not here, we'll have to sweet talk her. It won't be easy." Saramana put her hands on the table. "Everyone will be trying to process new contracts or make her stick to the Royal Centre decrees, but without the city to enforce anything…"

"No-man's-land. Just the way I like it," Mammon said, licking her lips. "Look, I'll take care of getting us everything we need." She came around the table and stood in front of me. "You just figure out how to deal with Lucifer." She poked my chest. "In a way that doesn't involve all of us dying. You saw what she did while trapped by our most powerful wards. That was without her hammer."

"Right, I'll deal with the Devil," I said, taking a deep breath. I wasn't sure how to do that, but at the same time, there was plenty else to do. Sure, I needed to find the hammer, but I needed Clarent to do that first. If I didn't have my sword, there was no way we'd beat the Darkness.

"I guess that's all," Gwen said, looking past me to Gabriella. "I want hourly updates on Arthur's progress clearing the stone. Make sure no one bugs him without my approval." I was about to object when Gwen looked at me. "You have the tendency to get distracted." Then the succubus clapped her hands. "Dismissed."

"Dismissed?" I asked, somewhat annoyed at her. "What the fuck?"

"What, Arthur?" Gwen said, meeting my eyes. "Is there something else you want to ask me?" The way she said it was a challenge, and I realized, she was still ten kinds of pissed off at me for dismissing everything she did around town. I also realized it was probably better to avoid this fight if I could. See, I learn things.

"No, I'll be outside picking up rocks." I shrugged. "You girls have fun."

7

"I made this for you," Annabeth said, walking up to me as I worked on clearing the fields directly behind the Graveyard. It'd taken me the better part of a week to clear all the Coti from town, but today was the first time I'd moved beyond the walls.

Now that I was looking at the seemingly endless stretch of field in front of me, I was beginning to lose the will to go on. For one thing, My Proficiency had stalled at twenty percent. Ever since then, it'd taken a lot more effort to move it even one point, and now, after nearly half a day, I'd barely managed to raise it from twenty-four to twenty-five.

I had, on the other hand, experimented with some of the other stones, and found that they had risen pretty quickly until about ten or so proficiency before hitting a similar wall, so there was definitely something I was missing. Still, I was half inclined to go around and try to find all the different ones, but that also wouldn't get these fields clear, and in addition to my needing to level up my skill with the gauntlets, we did need the land for farming, assuming we actually recruited farmers.

"You made me something?" I asked, wiping my brow with the back of one hand as I turned toward the sculptor. She was carrying what looked like a picnic basket in one hand. "You made me lunch?"

"No." She frowned and turned her eyes to the picnic basket. "I'm just delivering this. Would you like me to cook you something?" She seemed a bit surprised at the possibility, though I couldn't tell if it was in a positive or negative way.

"I just presumed." I shrugged and took a sip of water from my canteen. Despite there being no sun, I could feel the heat of the day baking into my flesh. It didn't help that I was surrounded by dusty fields.

"Ah." She looked at the basket in her hands. "I can see how you might think that since I'm bringing it to you." She set the basket down on the ground beside me. "It's just a breadless sandwich and some stewed rice."

"You know, it's not really a sandwich if it doesn't have bread. That's kind of the whole thing." I waved off the comment and moved toward her. "Thank you though. I appreciate you bringing it out to me. I'd probably have forgotten to eat if you hadn't."

"I doubt that. Gabriella would have made you eat." Annabeth looked around. "Where is she anyway?"

"I'm not sure." I rubbed my chin and looked around. "She left a little while ago saying she was bored. She doesn't really stick around to watch me work. Between you and me, I think she enjoys defending the city with Sheila. The two of them have been patrolling for monsters more and more."

"Well, she was raised as a warrior. She probably doesn't know how else to contribute." Annabeth stood there for a moment fidgeting with her hands. "Anyway, I should get back to work. I'm trying to sculpt some statues to help with the farms. Sort of like scarecrows, but you know, with benefits." She met my eyes as she said the words.

"Well, I won't order you to stay and chat with me,

though I wouldn't mind the company while I eat," I said, flopping down beside the basket. "I'll understand if you're too busy. The last thing I want is for Gwen to yell at you."

"You just don't want her to yell at you," Annabeth teased, but sat down next to me, anyway. "Besides, we can all take a break sometimes." She opened the basket and pulled out what looked like a cabbage-wrapped burger, only I knew we didn't have cabbage which meant only one thing.

"Devil's lettuce?" I asked as she offered me the sandwich. "I hate that stuff."

"Am I going to have to force you to eat your veggies?" she replied, raising an eyebrow at me. "Because I'll be honest, I don't care what you do in that regard."

"Well, then I'm not going to do it," I said, taking the sandwich from her and eyeing it suspiciously. The problem was, I knew from experience that if I unwrapped it, the juices from the meat would get all over my hands. I didn't really want to have to clean up after lunch, so I just sighed and bit into it. The flavors of horseradish and onions hit my mouth like a roundhouse kick.

"Want half?" I asked after I'd chewed for a moment. "I know you don't really eat the lettuce, but it's not really so bad."

"You just looked like someone stabbed you in the throat," she said, shaking her head. "I have tea, I'll be fine." She patted the canteen at her hip. "I ate already anyway."

"Fair enough," I said, taking another bite before washing it down with a gulp of water from my own canteen. "So, what did you make me? You said you'd made me something or am I misremembering?"

"Oh, that's right," Annabeth said, reaching into her satchel and pulling out a small figure. She held it out to me allowing it to dangle between her fingers. "It's a charm I made for mining. I'm not quite sure if it'll help, but I figured it couldn't hurt."

"Thanks," I said, wiping my left hand on my pants before taking the proffered necklace. The little man on it looked surprisingly similar to me, only he had a pick raised high overhead like he was about to bring it down on a bunch of rock.

"You like it? I couldn't figure out how to sculpt magically removing rock from the ground, so I just went with the basics." She looked at her feet sheepishly.

"I love that you made it for me, Annabeth. You really didn't have to do that." I smiled at her and slipped it over my head. The figure was heavy against my chest, and while I felt no effects from it, I sort of hoped it would work. Normally, I'd check with Clarent, but since I was without the sword, I couldn't. Man, I had relied on Clarent so much without realizing it. Now that I was without it, I found even basic tasks difficult if not almost impossible, and this was one of them.

"I'm glad," she said, nodding to me as I took another bite of my not-sandwich. "I could try to make some others if you want. I'm not sure if there's a god of mining or anything." She shrugged. "Maybe I should visit Ruby's Gleam. I bet they have lots of mining sculptures." She looked at the sky in thought. "I'd have to get Buffy to take me, and she and her goblin friends sort of hate doing things when I ask them."

"What's in Ruby's Gleam?" I asked, sort of confused. I'd not heard of the towns in all the meetings about the status of trade routes and whatnot. Like we'd thought, most of the trade towns weren't taking to the idea, but since we had the only mode of transportation that didn't take days or weeks, we were making headway among most of the other small towns. The problem was the guild towns. They weren't interested in helping since they sort of blamed us for the destruction of the Royal Centre.

It hadn't really been our fault, but it was hard to change their minds. So far, the Carpenter's Guild was the only one that had signed on, and the others weren't looking like they were going to come around anytime soon.

Worse, there were a lot of refugees. Stained, those people who had been visibly marked by the guilds as unworthy, were coming in every day, and while the grunt labor was helpful, without Clarent, we couldn't give them useful skills, nor see if they already possessed them. With most of the Stained too scared to tell us if they knew how to do anything, it was doubly upsetting.

"Ruby's Gleam is the Miner's Guild town. It's not one of the major guilds really, more of a subsidiary of the Blacksmith's guild." She rolled her eyes, and I was inclined to agree.

"Yeah, they're especially not happy since the head

of their guild died in Royal Centre. Have they replaced her yet?" I asked, wishing that the lady hadn't died. It sort of put a freeze on negotiations since there wasn't a provision for making an alliance without a guild head. No, until they finished the new selection process, there was no use dealing with them.

"Not yet. They're still trying to figure out the best way." Annabeth shrugged. "You know, now that I'm thinking about it, while I'm not sure how much it'd help you, perhaps going to Ruby's Gleam for a day or two would be a good idea. You don't know anything about the materials here." She gestured at the surroundings. "I know that sometimes when I got stuck trying to sculpt a material, learning about what made it tick helped me to get better."

"I hear what you're saying, but I'm not so sure." I looked out at the fields. Maybe she had a point though. I'd pulled several of the higher difficulty Coti out of the area, and it'd barely made a blip, making me think that either the grinding was truly insane, and going to get worse, or that I was going about it incorrectly. Maybe a trip to the miner's guild would be a good idea.

"Well, if you change your mind, let me know,"

Annabeth said, getting to her feet as I finished my sandwich. "I'd be happy to go along with you."

"Are you heading back to town already?" I asked, sighing as she turned to go. "I was really enjoying your company."

"You were?" she asked, turning back to regard me like I was playing a trick on her. "Why is that?"

"I don't know. I just like you." I shrugged. It was true. Ever since we'd gone through the crafting contest, I'd found myself enjoying her company. "I enjoy spending time with you. It makes me happy." I scratched my head. "Can't really explain it more than that."

"I should really get back to work." She looked at the sky, and I could see the wheels in her brain turning. "We both should."

"I know," I said, getting to my feet. I resolved to finish the rice later. The sandwich was already sitting heavily in my stomach, and I was worried I might be sick if I ate more before going back to work. Besides, it'd keep for a snack later. "Maybe we can have dinner together though? You know, catch up?"

"I would like that a lot," she said, stepping toward me and giving me a peck on the cheek. "I'll let Gabriella know to schedule us some time for dinner."

"Thanks," I said, feeling ridiculous that I had to schedule dinner with Annabeth with Gabriella, but if we didn't, the time slot would be used for something else, probably a boring meeting. "Actually, after you see her, can you send her my way? I want to have the whole Ruby's Gleam thing arranged." I sighed, looking at the fields. "Because what I'm doing now isn't working."

"I'll send your secretary over," Annabeth said, smirking at me. "Now back to work. I don't want to hear you're behind and have to miss our date."

8

I was halfway through clearing the second farm plot when Gabriella called to me. Wiping the sweat from my brow, I looked up to see her coming toward me with both Buffy and Annabeth in tow.

"Arthur!" Gabriella cried, waving one hand frantically.

"I see you. What's up?" I called back, taking a swig from my canteen. The water had warmed in the hot, humid air, but it felt good to drink something anyway. Still, a nice break in the shade with a frozen lemonade would be great.

I was pretty sure that was out of the question though. I'd barely started this second field, and according to the schedule Gwen had provided me, I needed to be working on the third section by the end of the day. Already, I could see the few Stained who had come to our town for refuge tilling the dirt with hand plows under Crystal's careful supervision.

It was probably better that they were doing it by hand. If they had some kind of rototiller, I'd have never stayed ahead of them. Even still, I knew if I didn't finish this plot soon, that'd happen anyway.

"So, we have a bit of a dilemma," Buffy said as the three of them stopped next to me. The goblin took one look at me and scrunched up her nose. "You need a shower."

"That's the dilemma?" I asked, confused. Part of me wanted to sniff myself to see if she was right, but I opted not to. I'd been working in the fields all day and had been sweating like a pig. I probably did smell.

"No," Buffy said, shaking her head and causing the gold hoops in her ears to jingle. "The dilemma is that while I can spare the time to take you to Ruby's Gleam, I can't stay there and show you around. The commodities market is going well enough, but transporting all this stuff?" She sighed. "On one hand it's lucrative because we can sell some super speedy deliveries for extra, but at the same time, that means we need to deliver them, and we still only have one Nexus Gateway."

"Oh. So how am I supposed to get around there?" I asked before stopping. "Is that the dilemma?"

"Bingo," Buffy said, nodding once. "The only option is to let Annabeth go with you. She knows the area well and has contacts there. Plus, she knows about these materials better than I do. At least intrinsically. I just see them in dollars and sense, she is like some kind of stone hippie."

"I am not a stone hippie," Annabeth said, stepping past Buffy and meeting my eyes. "I'd be happy to go with you, but if I do, I won't be able to work on the pieces to make more Nexus Gateway Conduits. As it stands, I've only completed enough to try two times."

"Fixing Clarent is more important than creating the conduits, so we'll just have to be delayed on the conduits. Besides, Sally and Sam have to do their parts, and last I checked, Sam was still in bed," I said, waving off her comment before turning to Buffy. "Or am I missing something?"

"Nope." Buffy shook her head. "That's the only

reason I'm even contemplating this. Both Sally and Annabeth are ahead, especially since you were able to sort out which Etheric Fire would most likely turn into S Grade, but Sam is still out of the picture. It's not even like we can get someone else to do it because she's the only one who knows the recipe." Buffy tapped her foot, clearly annoyed with how reality was putting a damper on her grand plans to buy the whole world.

"Right, so when do we leave?" I wiped my forehead again. "I do need to finish this field and shower…"

"We don't have time for either of those things." Buffy smacked the place on her wrist between her two gold watches. "You have another six minutes in the window before I'm busy for the rest of the day. Unless you want to fuck up the whole schedule, but keep in mind, I may not be here for you to force to break the schedule. You'd probably have to wait until I got back. That could be either tomorrow or the next day depending on how things go."

"I guess that will have to do." I finished the water my canteen. "Gabriella, can you have Crystal instruct some of the Stained to move the rocks they can by hand? I think I've gotten most of the hard stuff removed from this plot."

The archangel looked up surprised, and I got the impression she hadn't been paying attention to our conversation. Her cheeks flushed. "Sorry, I missed that, Arthur. What do you need?" She smiled nervously.

"Have Crystal get rid of the rocks with some of her team. She can repurpose the Goblin Extractor to help with the really bad ones if need be," I said, gesturing to the plot. "I'm going with Annabeth to Ruby's Gleam. Also, please tell Gwen even though I assume Buffy already has."

"I have," Buffy confirmed.

"Will do!" Gabriella squeaked before marching off determinedly toward Crystal.

"Well, come on. Time's money, and it's flowing down the drain while we stand here yapping." Buffy let out an explosive breath and without waiting for us to follow headed toward the Nexus Gateway.

"Well, sorry about dinner," I said, holding my hand out to Annabeth. "Raincheck?"

"Raincheck?" Annabeth said, taking my hand as we followed the goblin toward the portal. Buffy had already flicked it on, and the portal gleamed in the distance like the shimmering tear in reality it was. "You're not buying me dinner in Ruby's Gleam?" She cocked an eyebrow at me.

"That's a good point," I said, turning to Buffy as she waved at us frantically, gesturing for us to go through. "Say, Buff, what's my per diem?"

"Your per diem?" she asked, confused. "You don't have one."

"What about food and lodging?" I asked, meeting her eyes. "How much do I get for those things?"

"Nothing," she said, shrugging. "Or less than that, actually. We don't have it to spare." She rummaged around in her pocket for a moment and produced a piece of paper with scribbles I couldn't read on it. "Give this to the innkeeper at the Bloated Barnacle, and he'll give you food and lodging. Don't go anywhere else. We have a deal worked out with them for lower prices as long as we don't patronize other establishments."

"Okay," I said, taking the paper and pocketing it. "Sounds great."

"Also, you'll have to sign some autographs and take a picture. You know, 'The Builder eats here,' sort of thing." Buffy gestured toward the portal. "Now get going. I need to be in Blade's End to pick up more Etheric Blood in the next ten minutes."

With that, the goblin hustled us through the gateway. The familiar sensation of being torn down to the subatomic level by mystic forces filled every ounce of my being to the brim with pain, but I tried my best to man through it. As we appeared on the other side of the portal, I found myself looking at a rocky expanse that looked to have quite literally been carved into a mountain. We stood in a small section that was gated off with massive stone doors.

"We were told to expect you," said the large-breasted dwarven woman at the gate as she came forward, a beer in one hand and an axe in the other. She took a huge gulp of the frosty black brew and looked us up and down. "You're so tiny."

"Tiny?" I asked, glancing at Annabeth who was busily ignoring the dwarf. I don't mean to say that she looked like a midget either. This guard looked exactly like a dwarf straight out of Lord of the Rings, beard and all. To be honest, the beard combined with her overly large bosom made some very strange thoughts rattle around in my head.

"You're so scrawny." The dwarf circled me and smacked me on the ass. "Just skin and bones. Don't they feed you?"

"I eat okay," I said, rubbing my ass. It stung from where she'd smacked me. "So, um, are you going to let us inside?"

"That depends, dearie," the dwarf said, moving back toward the gate with a wicked gleam in her eye. Then she paused meeting my gaze as she took a long sip of her giant beer, nearly draining half of it. I expected her to continue when she had finished, but instead, she just kept staring at me.

"On what?" I asked, feeling uncomfortable. Beside me, Annabeth fidgeted.

"On what exactly you're doing here," she said, smacking her axe against her shoulder before draining her beer. Instead of putting it down, she turned to a barrel just beside the gate and stared at it contemplatively. "Little help?"

"Are you just going to stand here and get drunk?" I asked, wishing Annabeth would help me out because I was totally lost. "We need to go inside and learn about mining." I shrugged.

"Little help?" the dwarf repeated, shaking her empty glass at me. "Only have two hands, and I can't put down my axe or my beer. You understand, right, dearie?"

"Jesus tap-dancing Christ," I said, getting annoyed with how little they seemed to care about helping me, but before I could say more, Annabeth hurried forward.

"I'd be glad to help," she said, giving the dwarf an apologetic look. "But yes, as we said before, we're here to learn the secret of rocks and metal, and as we all know, the dwarves are the best at both."

"I can't hear you, dearie," the dwarf said, holding her empty glass out as Annabeth approached. "I'm much too thirsty."

Annabeth gave me a helpless shrug before turning to the barrel. She put one hand on the spigot and gestured to the dwarf. "Put your glass under?"

"Much obliged," the dwarf replied, smiling so broadly I could see her white teeth despite the red expanse of her beard. "I work up a mighty powerful thirst talking to people while I'm guarding."

"I can see how that'd be frustrating," Annabeth

replied, turning the spigot on. Dark bubbly liquid flowed into the dwarf's glass, and as it did, the dwarf gave a delighted squeal.

"You're a princess and a scholar," the dwarf said when the glass was full. Then she took a huge swallow, practically draining it again. "So, yes, what is your business here?"

"We want to learn about mining," I said, touching my chest while making an effort not to get pissed off. "That's why we came. I was told we were expected."

"You are expected, but that doesn't mean I can just let you in. If I did, what would they say to me? Why they'd say, that's Mina Bloodbeard, the dwarf who let a man into our henhouse without even asking the right proper questions." She peered closely at me, green eyes flashing as she took another sip of her beer. "Though now that I look at you, I don't think our women will have much to worry about. I think even the children could break you over their knee if you got handsy." She watched me for a long moment. "But hear me when I say this: By my great grandmother's black beard, if you do anything untoward, I will chop off your dick, mix it into my momma's famous chili and then feed it to you." She finished her beer. "Are we quite clear, Builder?"

"Yeah, I'll keep my hands to myself," I said, shaking my head. "Promise."

"Now, I didn't say that," the dwarf replied, setting her beer on the small table beside the gate and ambling toward me with swaying steps. She stopped in front of me and gave me another once-over. "You're a bit scrawny, but I'd be willing to give you a toss. Probably have to have you on top though. Otherwise, ye'd break." She gave me a wink. "Yer tall, so maybe yer tall down there too."

"That's a very kind offer…" I said, taking a deep breath and looking to Annabeth for help. Only she was very pointedly ignoring me while pretending to study the impressive carvings on the door. I hadn't quite noticed them before, but as I saw her looking, I realized they depicted a giant dragon sleeping on a horde of gold.

"Oh, I understand." Mina smacked me on the thigh hard enough for me to wince. "Don't wanna say anything in front of yer lady friend." She leaned in then, covering her mouth conspiratorially, which was doubly strange because she was about crotch level. "But you should know, once you go dwarf, you won't ever be the same again." She looked up at me, eyes a bit brighter than she should be as she slowly licked her lips. "Now then, inside we go. And remember what I said, hands to yourself." She smacked me on the ass again. "Now get a move on." She did it again. "Hurry, hurry."

"Ouch, stop," I said, covering my ass with my hands as I headed toward the gate while Annabeth waited for me unhelpfully. While her words had somewhat intrigued me, I found it incredibly hard to believe the dwarf was that good in bed.

"Stop what? Just givin' you a little taste of what you can expect." The dwarf grinned widely. "Little pain never hurt no one." She sniggered. "Now get inside." She smacked one meaty fist down on the button beside the door.

The huge stone slabs creaked and groaned as they opened, revealing a long, dark hallway lit with glowing red torches, making me think we were about to descend into Hell. You know, if we weren't already in Hell.

As we stepped inside following Mina Bloodbeard down the narrow corridor, I noticed the doors were opened with a set of springs. They had been coiled up before but were now fully extended to hold the huge stone doors open. It seemed a bit of an odd design since if the mechanism failed, it would cause the doors to open, but then again, I guess you didn't want to get trapped inside a mountain.

Still, as I turned my eyes back to the cavern, half caught in the marvel of all the dwarven pictographs lining the walls like hieroglyphics, I kept seeing that same dragon from the doors. What's more, the pictures seemed to be showing how the dwarves had battled it over and over again only to have their lives ended with a fiery, bloody death.

"So, uh, what's with the dragon?" I whispered, leaning in close to Annabeth in an effort to not have our guide hear. I wasn't quite sure why I kept it from her, only in that it was probably common knowledge, and I didn't want to seem dumb.

"Yeah, about that," Annabeth said, shrugging. "There is a dragon who lives in the heart of the mountain. It was once part of the dwarven city, but you know dwarves and their gold, and if there's one thing dragons like, it's gold."

"Wait, there's an actual dragon living in this mountain?" I exclaimed aloud, suddenly concerned. I mean, I'd dealt with dragons a couple times before, but they'd always been on my side. I'd seen the creatures decimate entire armies of Darkness warriors. If there was one here that didn't bode well.

"Of course, there's a dragon," Mina said, glancing at me over her shoulder. "Why else would we agree to help you?" She began to laugh.

"What do you mean?" I asked, raising an eyebrow at the dwarf.

"You're supposed to get rid of it in exchange for our help." The dwarf smacked her hands together. "That was the deal your goblin struck since she didn't want to pay with money. The only other option is services." She gave me a lascivious grin. "And not that kind either, though they might render you a bonus."

As I watched the dwarf eye fuck me, I felt my stomach sink with dread. If what Mina said was true, Buffy had signed me up to fight a dragon without so much as telling me. That was total bullshit, and when I got back, she and I were going to have a word. After all, we'd dealt with dragons before, and even had a way to tame them.

"No wonder she didn't want to come," Annabeth murmured, and a quick glance in her direction let me know she'd been as surprised as me. "Next time I see that goblin, I'm gonna wring her damned neck."

"You and me both," I said while the dwarf leading us into the depths of the hellish mountain stopped in front of a huge stone door and picked up what looked like a pair of black sacks.

"Now, if you'd be so kind as to put these bags over your heads. You won't be able to look at the inside of our beloved city without first speaking to the princess." Mina smiled. "Standard procedure of course."

9

While part of me wanted to go back to the Graveyard and yell at Buffy, most of me didn't see the point. For one, that wouldn't change the fact that the dwarves wanted us to kill a fucking dragon. For two, well, I knew my pleas would fall on deaf ears. If there was one thing I knew about Buffy, it was that she valued money above all.

Not only were the dwarves offering to help me learn whatever I needed to do, but there were countless other rewards outlined in the contract I couldn't read.

"So, you're saying that we'll be entitled to all of this metal if we slay the dragon and recover the treasure?" Annabeth asked. She was sitting next to me at a large wooden table, her elbows propped up on it as she studied the contract. "As well as a percentage of said treasure?"

"Yes," the dwarf at the head of the table said. "I swear it on the silky beard of my grandmother, Queen Amaya."

"Right, I dunno what the beard thing means, but I get it, princess. We kill the dragon, you help us." I sighed. "There's just one problem. How do we kill the dragon?"

"That's easy, ya daft boy," the princess scowled at me before looking toward Mina. "I thought he was supposed to be smart."

"I thought so too, but alas, the cute ones never are." Mina shrugged. "Guess that's why you just look at them."

"I suppose you're right," the dwarven princess said, stroking her blonde beard as she leaned back in her chair. Then she kicked her booted feet up on the table and held out her hand. "Bring me my pipe. I'm not nearly high enough to deal with his idiocy."

"Coming, princess," Mina said, turning toward the back counter of the room where drinks, snacks, and various other items were arranged. We'd been offered none of them, which struck me as a bit lacking on the hospitality side. Then again, they were dwarves, and manners didn't exactly seem to be their strong suit.

"You didn't answer my question about the dragon," I said while Mina busily packed a bone-white pipe full of a gray mossy substance.

"By the hair on Satan's black hairy ass, you stab it in the face." The princess snorted. "How else would you kill it?"

"And why haven't you killed it yet?" I asked, glancing at Annabeth who merely shrugged. Part of me wished I'd read up on how to kill dragons, but I just hadn't had the time.

Instead of replying, the princess took her lit pipe from Mina and took a long drag on it. Then she exhaled a cloud of blue smoke into the air as her eyes glazed over. "That's a long story, starting with the grandmother of my grandmother's grandmother." She turned her glassy eyes to me. "And it involves a lot more talking than I'm willing to do without an ale or three." She sighed. "But the long and short of it is, well, it's a really big dragon. Has teeth the size of a grown woman and breathes flame strong enough to melt the skin off your bones." She clapped her hands together while shifting the pipe from the left side of her mouth to the right. "And I don't mean your flimsy whimsy human bones either. I mean dwarven bones."

Then, like she felt the need to demonstrate, she put her hand into the candle burning on the table between us. I instinctively cringed away, but I needn't have bothered because her flesh didn't burn. Hell, it didn't do anything at all.

"Well, um, what have you tried so far to beat it?" I said, my eyes not leaving her hand as she played with the fire.

"I'm not done yet," the princess snapped, pulling her hand back before drawing on her pipe. She blew a ring of smoke into the air. "This dragon has got scales hard enough to blunt the sharpest sword and can see in the dark." She waggled her fingers. "Which I suppose is why it keeps all the lights off, and its hearing? Better than its vision." She smiled then, revealing a mouthful of bone white teeth. "And don't get me started on its sense of smell. Puts the other senses to shame."

"Sounds like we're pretty much fucked," I said, turning to Annabeth and raising an eyebrow. "Unless you have any ideas."

"I could try to sculpt something." She flushed. "I know it's probably not helpful, but I'm not exactly combat trained."

"That's okay, dearie," Mina said, placing a mug of dwarven ale in front of the princess. "Just give it the old one, two." She threw a pair of punches at the air. "That's what I'd do."

"Well, why don't you come with us then?" I asked, a bit more hope in my voice than I'd have liked. I mean, I was pretty sure I was as good as dead, but this way at least I'd take a dwarf with me. Besides, if it came to it, I didn't need to outrun the dragon. I just needed to outrun the slowest person, and I had no doubt both Annabeth and I were faster than the short-legged Mina.

"Alas, she would, but the contract clearly states we're not to render aid of any kind." The princess pointed to the contract in Annabeth's hand. "You'll find it in section six, subsection F, clause three." She shrugged. "Besides, Mina is the smelter who will be training you, should you succeed. She's the best we have."

"I thought she was just a royal guard?" I said, confused. After all, Mina had been watching the gate, not smelting.

"That she is. One of our best guards," The princess nodded. "You'll be very impressed with her should you not die a horrible fiery death."

"All dwarves take a turn at the guard station. Helps us not to take those guarding us for granted, dontcha know?" Mina added helpfully. Then she gestured at the table. "I'm also a chef."

"And a sommelier," the princess said, draining her mug. "Speaking of which, my thirst hungers."

"Coming right up, princess," Mina said, voice so cheery I thought I was going to lose it. This whole scenario was beyond ridiculous.

"How is being a sommelier helpful in any way?" I asked, getting to my feet. "I feel like you're just fucking with us."

"It's a very valuable skill in the Underdark where the black grapes grow." The princess looked at me like I was the crazy one. "We need someone to pair the wine made therein with our fantastic array of cheeses."

"Cheeses?" I asked with a sigh. "Let me guess, she knows how to make cheese too?"

"Not really. I spent a summer trying, but I just couldn't find my whey." Mina snorted. "Get it, whey?" She waggled her eyebrows.

"Right," I said, looking to Annabeth for help, but she was back to studying the contract in earnest. It made me wish we had Buffy, Mammon, or Gwen to help us. No, instead, they'd sent the wandering sculptor and me to deal with these crazy people. "Guess we'll get on with the dragon then. Where is it?"

"First you must enter through the stone gates of blood at the bottom of the mountain. There you will descend through the belly of the beast into the lava plains. Should you survive that, you must cross the gemstone bridge before you reach what was once known as Wrath's plateau. The name will make sense when you get there." The princess waved a hand as if to say 'it is what it is' before continuing. "Beyond that, you will find the wall of fire, and be forced to travel across the burning desert within while falcons circle overhead to reach our castle where the dragon sleeps."

"Are you out of your fucking mind?" I said, getting to my feet. "How do you expect me to do all that with only a sculptor to back me up?" I glanced at Annabeth. "No offense."

"None taken," she said, staring at the princess wide-eyed. "I agree with you. I'm the worst possible person to help you with this." The sad thing was, as much as I wanted to comfort her about it, she was agreeing with me. Besides, doing so would only hurt my argument, which was the last thing I wanted to do right now.

"Hey, if you're mad about the terms, tell it to your goblin." The princess finished her pipe and laid it on the table between us. "The original contract offered a contingent of blood smiths led by one of the royal family, a hobbit guide, and an aged sorceress, but the goblin took them out in exchange for an additional six percent."

"Six percent you say," I deadpanned, ready to kill Buffy dead.

"Six." The princess met my eyes. "Now if you don't

have anything else, Mina will put the bags back over your head and lead you down to the gates."

I turned, glancing at the bags hung on the wall behind us. I did not like this place one bit, but there was no use arguing. We'd gotten royally fucked by Buffy. All I could do was lie in the bed she'd made for me.

"No, go ahead and bag me," I said, sighing.

10

As we stood before the Stone Gates of Blood, Annabeth squeezed my hand. Mina stood just a few feet away, watching us with a bored look on her face while I tried to psyche myself up.

"I'm glad you're here," I said, turning to look at Annabeth and trying to smile. It was true in so much as I was glad I wasn't going alone. "But you can still back out."

"No." Annabeth shook her head. "I recognize I'm not going to be as helpful as Sheila or Gabriella would have been, but at the same time, I still want to help, even if all I can do is die alongside you." She returned my smile. "Please don't make me do that though."

"I'll do my best." I swallowed hard and looked back to the stone doors. They were perhaps ten feet tall and black as night. The entire face of them was carved with a humongous twelve-armed dragon. In each hand he held a screaming dwarf while he blew a gout of fire into the sky. Spines covered his back, jutting from his armored plates like katanas.

"Can you two go inside already? I have a date with a beer." Mina shuffled behind us. "It's more of a threesome really."

"Aren't you going to open the doors?" I asked, turning and looking at the dwarf. It was hard to see her since she was backlit by red-flamed torches, but even with darkness shrouding her features, I could see her scowl at me.

"That wouldn't do you any good," Mina huffed, coming forward. She shouldered past the two of us and squatted down next to a silver bowl I'd not seen before. "To open the door, you must put blood in the bowl." She drew her thumb across her throat. "And only those who contribute blood can enter." She stood and looked at me. "Honestly, this is pretty standard stuff. How do you not know this?"

"Did you know this?" I asked, ignoring the dwarf

and her illustrious beard and looking at Annabeth. "Because I didn't."

"I did not." Annabeth took a deep breath and exhaled slowly. "I'm not all up on dwarven stuff. The last time I came, it was with the dwarven master Inoia. We didn't have to deal with all this nonsense."

"Wait, you know Inoia?" Mina asked, and the tone of her voice had taken a dark edge. "That bitch owes me fifty coins." Mina held out her hand. "As her apprentice, you're obligated to pay on her behalf."

"There's no way I'm paying that." Annabeth laughed so loud, I couldn't help but smile. "Inoia is a drunk and a cheat. Of course, she owes you money. Good luck collecting on that debt. You'd sooner squeeze blood from a stone." Annabeth snorted. "And even if you want to try to make *me* pay it, you'd have to go through the sculptor's guild, and something tells me you've tried that already."

"Worth a shot," Mina groaned before producing a knife. "Now who's first? I always like the cutting part. Don't worry, I'm an expert surgeon."

"Of course, you are," I said, rolling my eyes as I

extended my hand to her. "How much blood is needed?"

"Not so much," she said, snatching my wrist and pulling my hand toward the bowl. She stabbed my index finger with the point before squeezing my finger as hard as she could. Pain shot through me, and for a second, I thought my finger was going to pop like a balloon. A single blood drop welled on the tip. As it slipped off my flesh and splattered against the empty bowl, creaking filled my ears.

The sounds of gears and pulleys ratcheting to life echoed throughout the cavern as the doors slowly began to open. Only instead of revealing a doorway, they revealed a blood red sheet of rippling energy. Sparks leapt from its surface to bounce off the opening doors with a snap, crackle, pop.

"Let me guess," I said as Mina released me and grabbed Annabeth's hand. "That's to keep out those who don't give blood."

"Yep," Mina said as she repeated the process on Annabeth. When her blood splashed into the bowl though, I noticed she began to glow with soft red light.

"Whoa, you're glowing," I said in astonishment.

"You are too," Annabeth said, nodding to me. "Didn't you notice?"

I looked at my own hand and found she was right. A similar glow had enveloped my hand, and I had half a mind to pretend I was an apparition. I didn't, but let me tell you, it was only because I was sleeping with the girl next to me and wanted to continue to be able to do so. The last thing I needed was for her to think I was a dork. Then again, she had wanted to sleep with me, so how sound could her judgment really be?

Mina crossed her arms over her huge chest as she looked at the two of us. "You should take this more seriously."

"You're right," Annabeth said, nodding sagely to the dwarf. "Next time I'm about to walk through the Stone Gates of Blood to almost certain doom, I'll remember to be calm and collected." She smacked her head with one hand. "Silly me."

"Good. I'm glad you're treating this as a learning experience," Mina intoned, smiling like a teacher with a prized pupil. "Now, off with you. As I said, I have a couple lovely blondes and a nutty brunette waiting for me." She made a shooing motion.

"Guess now is as good a time as any," I said, putting my gauntlets on before pulling my sword free of its sheath. I took a deep breath, focusing on the sword, and as I did, I decided it was time to give the thing a name. After all, it was, for all practical purposes, my main weapon now.

"Seure," I whispered, and as I said the word, I used it to summon this sword's version of armor. As the ethereal energy coalesced around my body to form plate mail that was both light as a feather and stronger than steel, I couldn't help but miss Clarent a little.

Still, Seure would do just as well as Clarent when it came to actual fighting especially after I'd used it for a bit. The main difference when it came to actual fighting ability had more to do with me being used to Clarent. After all, I'd trained with Clarent for a long time. I was used to it. This new weapon, Seure, while incredibly similar, still felt a touch off.

There was nothing for it. After all, the whole reason I was here was to get help finding Stygian Iron so I could reforge Clarent.

"Ready to kick some ass and chew bubblegum?" I

looked to Annabeth as the last of my armor settled into place.

"Chew bubblegum?" the sculptor asked, face scrunched up in confusion. "What's bubblegum?"

"Doesn't matter," I said, taking a step toward the portal. "Because we're all out."

11

Stepping through the shimmering expanse of red energy was sort of like stepping through a spider web. The magic seemed to cling to me, sticking to every part of my body as it ripped off the glowing red sheen I'd gained by sacrificing my blood to the bowl gods.

Only, once I finished brushing myself off and stood there in the darkness of the other side, I realized how terrible of an idea this was. For one, just a few feet away was a series of black stalactites and stalagmites, but beyond it, I could see only a greenish mound.

"Um... where's the beast?" I asked, staring at the huge mound of dirt directly in front of us. It was, quite literally, the only other thing here of note. "Wasn't there supposed to be a beast?"

"I have no idea," Annabeth shrugged next to me, taking a step closer and using the torch she'd stolen before jumping through the portal to peer into the darkness beyond the massive stalagmites. Stealing the torch had pissed Mina off, but I was glad Annabeth had taken it because otherwise we'd be trapped in pitch black darkness. "Do you suppose the mound does something? Maybe it summons the creature?" She waved her torch around a bit. "The wall ends about fifteen feet back, so… unless it does, we may be trapped in here."

"Well, if that doesn't sound ominous, I don't know what does," I replied, willing a bit of energy into my sword. Blue light began to emanate from the blade, and I used it to light my way while shimmying through the gaps in the rows of stalagmites.

As I moved forward, I reached out and touched the stone wall to my left. Only, instead of feeling like rock, it felt like damp scaly flesh. Heat radiated off of it, and I swear, it nuzzled my fingers a little.

"Maybe we don't go in there," Annabeth said,

moving up beside me. "The air feels like wet breath."

"Annabeth, I hate to say it, but I'm not sure where else to go," I replied, pointing inside the maw with my sword. "There's nothing else here."

"What if this cave is the beast and—"

She probably would have said more, but a thick pink tentacle exploded from the mound, striking her in the chest with enough force to knock her off her feet. She hit the ground with a bone-shuddering thud, and her head rebounded off the rock. She lay there dazed as the throbbing blue-veined tentacle wrapped around her leg before pulling her deeper within the cave.

I leapt forward, grabbing Annabeth by the arm and trying to haul her backward, but a fat lot of good it did. My feet didn't so much skid on the smooth stone floor as go out from under me. I fell hard on my ass as the tentacle dragged us toward the mound despite my best efforts to stop it. Try as I might, it was just too strong. No. I'd have to try something else.

"You can't have her," I cried, slashing at the tentacle with my sword. It struck with a clang that reverberated in my ears, and a flash of sparks from the impact both blinded me and ran down my arm, but that was about all it did.

I reared back, ready to try again while bracing my feet on the ground and pulling with all the strength I could muster. Only before I could bring my sword down again, the stalactites overhead began to descend. Not quickly, but fast enough for me to avoid being taken if I let go and left Annabeth. Only I couldn't do that.

There was no way in hell I was leaving her to be eaten by this. I called upon my magic, allowing it to flow off the edge of the weapon as I got ready to blast the mound. Darkness filled my vision as the jaws slammed shut behind me like a steel trap. The smell of rotting meat hit my nostrils and turned my stomach as I unleashed my blast, but if the jet of sapphire plasma sort of evaporated upon contact with the mound.

"Fuck!" I looked around, trying desperately to orient my vision to the murk, but thanks to the flash of energy from my attack, I couldn't see much despite the glow of my sword, which was also when I realized we'd somehow lost the torch.

Letting go of Annabeth for a second, I scrambled to my feet on the spongy earth and called upon the power of the red gem in the hilt of my sword. Hellfire sprang to life in my free hand, and I flung it at the tentacle instead of the mound. The fireball hit the tentacle with an explosion of force that threw me from my feet.

The tentacle jerked backward, releasing Annabeth and disappearing into the mound as the whole cave rumbled violently. The smell of burning flesh filled my nostrils, and warm, musty air clung to me, making me feel sticky and gross.

Ignoring the spasming cave, I took a quick glance around, and when I didn't see the tentacle anymore, I knelt down beside Annabeth. Her eyes had rolled back in her head, so all I could see were the whites. The tentacle had released her, but she still seemed to be unconscious. That was no good because I had no idea how to heal her if she didn't wake up on her own.

"Please wake up," I whispered, moving between her and the tentacle and raising my sword to protect her should it attack again.

When it didn't immediately attack, I reached down

with one hand and shook her gently, trying to rouse her. She didn't respond. Worry crept up my spine as I looked around but saw no signs of an exit. The ground rumbled again, and the tentacle pulled back into the mound.

I grabbed Annabeth, ready to shield her when the ground beneath my feet opened. We pitched downward into the murky darkness, and as a terrified scream ripped from my lips, the ground slammed into me with bone-shuddering force. Only instead of exploding like a bag of jam, my body bounced into the air. My arms went out, windmilling in the empty air as I fell again and hit the ground once more. This time I didn't bounce nearly as high, and by the third time, I didn't even leave the ground.

I lay there, trying to figure out how to breathe as my body howled in agony while thanking my stars for my armor's supernatural durability. I got to my hands and knees and spit out a mouthful of blood before pulling myself to my feet and looking around. The 'room' was lit by what looked like effervescent neon yellow cilia extending from the walls.

"Guess this is what they meant by the belly of the

beast," I mumbled, ignoring the waving cilia as I stared down the long dark tunnel ahead of me.

I tested the ground, wondering if it would bounce when I walked, but while it was spongy, it didn't have that much give. No, it'd probably only made me bounce because I'd fallen really far. It made me feel lucky because otherwise, I'd have just been dead.

"Annabeth, are you okay?" I asked, making my way over to her unconscious form. Only, as I approached, I realized she was definitely not okay. Her left arm lay twisted awkwardly beneath her, no doubt broken by the fall.

Hopefully, she would heal soon because I had no idea how to help her. I mean, I could have made her a split or something, but admittedly, even after spending a lot of time in Hell, I wasn't exactly sure what the limits of her demonic healing would be. The last thing I wanted to do would be to try to help her and have the bone heal wrong or something. After all, she was a sculptor, her hands were, quite literally, her livelihood.

"I wish Sally was here," I mumbled, taking a deep breath and resolving to have her teach me some basic first aid and physiology when we got back because I had no way of knowing whether her arm would heal in a few minutes or if it'd take hours.

The only thing I could do would be to protect her until she awakened. Then I could ask her what to do, assuming she knew.

"Guess I'm carrying you," I said, bending down to grab her. As my hand touched her body, she twitched. I pulled my hand back and stared at her. "Annabeth, are you okay?"

She didn't respond.

"Annabeth?" I stared at her for another moment, and when she didn't move, I knelt down next to her. As soon as my hand touched her skin, she jerked way more violently than before.

I scrambled backward, sword gripped tightly in my hands as eight spindly green appendages that reminded me of scorpion legs stretched out from beneath her.

"Stop!" I cried as her whole body was hoisted into the air. The legs began to move, carrying Annabeth's body down the tunnel. I wasn't sure where it was taking her, but something told me it wouldn't be anywhere good.

Not wasting a second, I ran after Annabeth but found it surprisingly hard to keep up with the creature. Its nimble three clawed feet picking along the slimy ground like it was made to do this, which it probably was.

My chest was heaving with effort by the time I caught up to the bug. Up ahead, the path we were on looked like it was about to drop off. The creature stopped short of the edge and slowly lowered itself to the ground. Then it sort of flipped, tossing Annabeth to the ground beside it.

A creature resembling a humongous green scorpion stood beside Annabeth. Its actual body wasn't big, only about the size of a football, but that didn't mean its huge, lantern-sized claws and stinger weren't terrifying.

"Don't touch her!" I snarled, stepping toward it with my sword raised and calling upon my magic. If it so much as twitched, I was going to blast it to smithereens.

It turned and regarded me with a thousand magenta eyes. It opened its mouth and let out a high-pitched warble, shattering my eardrums and making me fall to my knees, clasping my head.

As my sword hit the ground beside me, the scorpion lunged at me. I dodged just as it landed on the spot, and I snatched up my fallen weapon.

The creature's claws tore gouts in the fleshy floor beneath as I came to my feet covered in sticky slime. The scorpion whirled around, tail rearing back to strike as I pounced, using the muscles in my legs to propel myself high into the air.

As it buried its stinger in the spot where I'd been only a moment before, I came down on top of its body with all the force my bulk could muster. The creature's legs buckled, snapping with a sound like breaking twigs as I drove my sword through its body, pinning it to the dirt. Its carapace smacked into the ground as I unleashed a blast of sapphire energy while on top of it. The scorpion exploded like a goo-filled melon.

The smell of sulfur filled my nostrils as I scrambled backward, worried the creature's foul guts might be poisonous, or you know, dissolve my flesh like acid.

Thankfully, that acid thing didn't happen.

Chest heaving, I took a deep breath, my eyes still watering as I turned toward Annabeth so I could make sure she was okay.

She was not okay.

A dozen more scorpions surrounded her. They regarded me curiously as though they couldn't quite figure out what I was doing there. To be fair, the feeling was mutual.

I had half a mind to try to run away, but there was no way I was leaving Annabeth behind. No. It was time to fight them all off. Taking a deep breath, I gripped my sword tightly.

My muscles tensed as I got ready to attack them with wild abandon. Only before I could, the middle one knelt down. Its spindly legs folding up beneath it like an accordion. I stared at it in confusion as the others followed suit.

"What's going on?" I asked even though I was sure the creatures couldn't understand me.

"Hello." The word warbled inside my brain, and I got sort of dizzy as its head moved outward from its body on a long stalk that hadn't been visible before.

Had it been retracted inside its carapace? "Can you understand me?"

When I didn't immediately respond, it turned toward the others and sort of shrugged. They shrugged back.

"It's not a demon. Maybe it's too young to understand?" one of them asked, the sound like a trumpet blast in my brain. "How old do humans need to be before they can talk?"

"No. It seemed like it was talking a moment ago," the creature furthest to my left said as it stepped past the others, examining me with its magenta eyes. "I think it's just dumb." It looked me over again. "I say we eat it." Those words made a chill run down my spine. If there was one thing I certainly did not want, it was to be eaten by a bunch of giant scorpions.

The others nodded, clearly taken with the idea. Well, that was no good. No good at fucking all. Pushing down my fear, I took a deep breath, trying to calm myself.

"Sorry," I said aloud, and all of their eyes fixed on me at once. It got eerily quiet as they watched me stand there holding my sword in a white-knuckled grip.

"You can talk?" the one who had hello replied in my head, only this time the words had a confused lilt to them. "Why did you not respond earlier?"

"Erm… well, see here's the thing, people don't usually speak directly into my mind…" I shrugged because I didn't have a better answer.

"How can that be? Are you broken?" the one who had wanted to eat me asked, its voice grating on my brain. "If he's defective, we should definitely eat him. Keep the species strong and all that. Why we owe it to the entire human race to eat him."

"I'm not defective. My species is just different," I replied, waving my hand frantically. "We talk out loud. Not mind to mind."

"Okay," one of the middle ones said, coming forward. "Why are you here?"

"He's after the children," another hissed.

"Look what he did to Jenny," the one to its left chided. "He killed her for no reason!"

As they all began to nod in agreement, the far-left scorpion spoke up. "I still say we eat him."

"Wait," I said, holding my hands in the time out sign even though I wasn't sure they'd understand the gesture. "That one is named Jenny?" I pointed to the crushed scorpion.

"Yes," they said at once, and it was like a cacophony of horn blasts in my mind.

"Okay…" I mumbled not sure what to do with that. "Um… sorry about Jenny."

"Don't be. She was sort of a bitch," the one in front chirped, and the others reluctantly agreed.

"All right," I said, taking a deep breath and meeting the scorpion's million magenta eyes as best I could. "What is your name?"

"You may call me Bill." He turned and pointed to the left one who wanted to eat me. "That's Ted."

Ted nodded at me like he hadn't just suggested eating me.

"Okay…" I mumbled for the second time in as many minutes. "Those are kind of odd names for scorpions."

"They aren't our actual names," Ted said, shaking his head like he still thought I was dumb. "Those are your mental equivalents of our names. You would not be able to pronounce our names."

"So, you mean it's my fault you're named Bill and Ted?" I asked, raising an eyebrow. I wasn't sure how I felt about that. It seemed kind of… invasive. Then again, if it kept them from eating us, I was okay with it. "

"In a word, yes," Bill said, nodding. "Would you like me to introduce the others?"

"No. I already feel like my brain is going to explode," I said, shaking my head.

"We get that a lot," said Ted.

Bill elbowed him with one spindly appendage. "No, we don't. He's the first of his kind we've ever seen."

"Why do you always have to be so particular?" Ted squealed, glaring at Bill. "Besides, you're ruining this excellent adventure."

"Excellent adventure? More like Bogus journey," Bill snorted, stepping away from the other scorpion and rubbing his multifaceted eyes with his two front appendages.

"Whatever," Ted added, glaring at Bill as the huge scorpion moved closer to me.

"Anyway, we have a small issue. See our job is to feed the monster." Bill pointed to the cliff as two of the scorpions began dragging Jenny's corpse over to the edge. They tossed her off the cliff with about as much concern as I'd have given an empty soda can.

"So, what's the problem?" I asked, raising one eyebrow as I made a mental note to trust these scorpions a whole hell of a lot less far than I could throw them.

"Well, I'm going to go out on a limb here and assume you don't want us doing that with your mate over there." He nodded toward Annabeth.

"Um, yeah, please don't do that," I replied, wondering if I should grab Annabeth's arm or something just to make sure they didn't try.

"Hence our problem." Bill drummed his front legs on the ground. "The beast will likely not even notice he's consumed Jenny. Not enough meat on her chiton." Billy shrugged. "At least, he's never noticed before."

"What happens if you don't feed him?" I asked as a bad feeling settled in my stomach.

"Then this chamber fills with stomach acid." Bill shrugged like it wasn't a very important concern even though it sure seemed like it was to me. "You must escape before that happens."

"Wait, you're going to help us escape?" I asked.

"Of course. We're not murderers. We're only supposed to feed dead things to him. You'd give him a stomach ache." Bill looked at me, and I got the sense he was smirking. "He'll try anyway though. He's dumb like that, which is why he has us."

"Okay," I said, rubbing my face with my hand. I wasn't quite sure if I could trust the scorpion, but if it kept me from being dissolved in acid, I was all for taking the chance. "So how do we get out of here?"

"There are only two ways out. One is to enter lava plains down there." The creature pointed over the cliff again. "The other is to go the back way, but that is not without danger. It is guarded by the seven, each of whom is deadlier than the last. Both will lead you to Wrath's plateau."

"Seven, is that all?" I replied, swallowing back my

concern. Seven seemed like a hell of a lot, especially given Annabeth's current condition. Still, I was pretty sure I'd rather fight seven dudes than carry her through the lava plains. That sounded like a recipe for disaster.

"I think so," the scorpion began moving toward the cliff. "But who knows, could be more."

12

The trip to the scorpion's back way was, how can I put this delicately, uneventful. Why? Because the scorpions bound us to their backs with sticky goo and carried us down. Admittedly, it was a little disconcerting because crimson lava bubbled and popped in the superheated pit below us, but hey, nothing is perfect, right?

After only a few minutes, the scorpions stopped on a narrow ledge with a solid gold door the size of a garage door embedded into the side of the cliff. Throbbing inflamed veins spread out along the area surrounding the door, giving me the impression it wasn't particularly awesome to have a massive entrance implanted in your esophagus.

Anyway, after the scorpions hummed a weird tune that sort of reminded me of the itsy-bitsy spider, the door swung open to reveal a yellow, effervescent tunnel that smelled like raw fish. The walls inside looked ragged and raw, and for the first time, I wondered if this tunnel had been crafted by the dwarves. It seemed likely being that this was the way to their stronghold, but then again, I didn't expect the belly of the beast to really mean being swallowed a giant hell beast, so there was that.

"This is as far as we can go, Builder." Pat gestured for me to enter. "Good luck."

"Thanks for everything." I slung Annabeth's still unconscious form over my shoulder in a fireman's carry. "But are you sure this is a better way than going down to the lava fields?" I pointed down below.

"Are you lava proof?" the scorpion asked, tail bobbing in a way that let me know he was curious.

"I am not," I conceded, wiping my brow with my hand. It was hot as balls here.

"Then you must take the back route past them." The scorpion pointed at the door behind me with one huge claw. "It is, as you say, what it is."

"Fair enough. Just thought I'd ask." I waved to him and stepped inside. I'd barely made it five feet when the door slammed shut behind me, leaving me trapped alone in the corridor with only an unconscious sculptor for company. The ground beneath my feet oozed and pulsed as I padded forward, wishing not for the first time, every inch of the place wasn't covered in slime. At least, I hoped it was slime. For all I knew, it was saliva or something worse…

I took a deep breath that tasted of day-old gym socks and made my way forward until I came to a sheer drop off. About half a meter past the edge was what looked like a ruby-colored stepping stone. I squinted, trying to see beyond it, but had no such luck. Nope, the only way forward seemed to be that stone.

"Well, here goes nothing," I told Annabeth's unconscious form as I shifted her weight so I could try jumping it. Normally, I'd have not even bothered, but since my armor granted me increased strength, I was sure I could make it a foot and a half.

Hoping I wasn't making a huge mistake, I stepped across the gap and onto the ruby. It was only a couple feet in diameter, and I stood there for a moment, steadying myself. As I once again shifted Annabeth's weight over my shoulders, an emerald stone appeared about three feet in front of me, but the pathway remained otherwise dark and gloomy despite the glowing yellow walls. It sort of reminded me of walking through an unlit hallway as the lights came on one by one. Only, you know, with stepping stones above a pit of absolute darkness.

"You know, I think this would be easier if you were lighter," I mumbled before jumping across the gap.

As my feet hit the emerald step, a jade platform appeared a few hundred feet above my head. I stared at it, trying to figure out how the hell I was going to get up to it when a braided gold rope ladder tumbled downward. It came to rest with a thud right next to me.

I grumbled, "Not that I think you're fat or anything, Annabeth. It's more that I don't really want to carry you through the whole dungeon. You understand, right?"

"Thought so." I grabbed ahold of the ladder and tugged on it. The ladder seemed sturdy enough. "Guess we're climbing up. Hang on, okay?" I grabbed the rung and climbed onto the ladder, putting all my weight on it. When it didn't immediately tear free, I breathed a sigh of relief.

I began the tedious climb upward. I had to stop every few moments to either catch my breath or adjust Annabeth, so she didn't fall. Sweat dripped down my body as I pushed myself up, one rung at a time while careful to go slow enough to keep from rocking the ladder.

Even still, it took forever. In fact, despite my increased strength, by the time I put my hands on the platform and hauled myself onto it, my muscles had turned to jelly.

I shoved Annabeth onto the platform before climbing up there myself and laying down next to her unconscious form. I lay there panting, my chest heaving with effort as I stared at the unending darkness above, trying to regain my breath. If I had to carry her the whole way, we definitely weren't going to make it. At least, not anytime soon, and I didn't exactly have much in the way of supplies beyond my canteen.

"Maybe I can just look around a bit while you rest here?" I turned toward Annabeth as I spoke and saw a woman standing there with a golden dagger clutched in one hand.

"Fancy meeting you here, Builder," she said, gesturing at me with her dagger before dropping into a curtsy. "I'll be honest, it's been ages since I've had a visitor." She touched her face with one hand as she rose to her feet. "Tell me, does my makeup look okay?"

Her skin had the tight, pale texture of a corpse left in the morgue for a month, and blue veins throbbed beneath her porcelain flesh. Her eyes reminded me of the milky marbles of an unseeing cadaver, only hers were fixed upon me. Her white as snow hair was piled upon her head in tight buns with a pair of black as night horns jutting from the center. So yeah, she was the picture of fucking loveliness.

"I think it's great," I said, swallowing hard as I looked at her. I wasn't sure what or who she was, but at the same time, she scared the bejesus out of me. Not because she felt particularly powerful. No, it was more because she was basically one of the walking undead. "Mortician chic is definitely in this year."

She took a step toward me, and her bare, alabaster

feet barely made a sound. Her shimmering blue dress whipped around her even though there was no wind in the cavern, and I got the impression she was trying to decide whether or not to take me seriously.

"Let me help you up. When you're ready, we can begin our battle. I should warn you, I'm tougher than I look." She reached her left hand out toward me, and as I took it, she gripped my hand with enough strength to make my bones creak beneath my gauntlet. I tried to squeeze back, but it was hard enough to keep from crying out.

"Thanks," I wheezed when she released me, and I barely resisted the urge to wring out my hand. If she had a grip like that, I wasn't exactly confident in a test of strength. Pretty sad considering how decrepit she looked.

"Don't mention it, but you really should work on your handshake. Your grip is a bit weak." She smiled at me, revealing a mouthful of rotted teeth. "Now, do you know the rules for our little contest?"

"Um… no." I shrugged sheepishly. "I don't even know what our contest entails."

The woman stared at me for a long time, probably

trying to decide whether or not I was serious. After what felt like hours, she rubbed her chin thoughtfully. "Something tells me you really don't have any idea what we do here." She gestured around the tiny platform.

"Uh… yeah. I have no idea at all. I was brought here by some scorpions." I shrugged. "I'm just trying to get to the dragon at the end of the tunnel, but then my friend got hurt." I nudged Annabeth with my toe, but she barely moved.

Before I could blink, the woman dropped to her knees and poked Annabeth's nose with one spindly finger. "She's still alive, but if you wish for her to help with the contest, that can be arranged." She waved a hand at Annabeth, and a soft purple glow surrounded her body before fading away.

"What did you do?" I asked, gripping the hilt of my sword and ready to go to town on the woman if she'd hurt my friend.

"I tried to heal her." The corpse bride looked at me, brow knitted in confusion. "That really should have worked." She leaned in closer to Annabeth. "Oh well, I guess you'll have to fight to the death without her." She shrugged.

"Die!" Annabeth cried, her fist lashing out in a blow that slammed into the woman's face with an earsplitting crunch. The zombie stumbled backward, landing hard on her butt and gripping her nose.

"Fiend!" the woman shouted through her hands as black ichor dribbled down her face.

"Sorry, but if you mean to kill us, I can't show any mercy," Annabeth said, scrambling to her feet. "Even if you did heal me."

"Wait, you knew what she was?" I asked as Annabeth dropped into a fighting stance beside me that reminded me of one of those Shaolin monks. It was weird because I'd known she was trained in hand to hand combat and often sparred with Sheila, but I'd never really considered her a warrior. Now though? Well, I was glad she knew what she was doing.

"No, but I heard her say we were fighting to the death," Annabeth said as the woman sprang to her feet.

"You will pay for this. Now, ready yourselves for the end." The zombie woman slashed the air with her dagger. The movement was so fast, I felt the wind move even from where I stood beside Annabeth, but at the same time, I could still follow it enough to know I could probably fight her off. It was weird, a few weeks ago she'd have scared the daylights out of me, but now? Now, I almost wanted to fight her.

"It's two against one," I said, gripping my sword tightly. "Those are bad odds."

"You're right," the talking corpse said. "You should have brought more—"

Annabeth cut off her words with a roundhouse kick to the zombie's face. The creature staggered sideways, her dagger slipping from her hand and hitting the ground with a clang. Before I could blink, Annabeth followed up her kick with a barrage of punches, peppering the zombie's torso as she tried to cover up.

The zombie reeled back as another devastating kick caught her in the solar plexus. It was followed by an upward elbow that sent her reeling backward toward the edge of the platform. Her arms shot out, grasping at the air for balance right before Annabeth decked her in the face.

"That was freaking awesome!" I exclaimed, staring open-mouthed as the zombie tumbled backward off the platform.

"When you wander Hell by yourself, you learn a thing or two about fighting." Annabeth fidgeted slightly as she scooped up the woman's fallen dagger. "She seemed really powerful, so I figured the best way to beat her would be with a surprise attack. I doubt that trick would work a second time."

"Either way, it seems like it worked," I said right before a bone white hornet the size of a small car rose from beyond the edge of the platform. "Fuck."

"You'll pay for that," the wasp buzzed as its decayed, multifaceted eyes fixed on me. "Both of you."

It came at Annabeth stinger first, and she dodged to the left, barely avoiding the acid that the wasp shot from its ass. The smell of burning plastic filled my nose as the stone began to bubble and smoke.

I lunged for the flying insect, swinging my sword at the creature's torso while it was focused on Annabeth. With little apparent effort, the wasp darted away before spinning and coming at me. I crouched down as it approached, and at the last second, launched myself into the air like I'd done with the scorpion. I landed on its back as its razor-sharp wings cut into my armor and sending sparks cascading over its back.

Trusting my armor could handle it, I drove my sword into the section of carapace beside the left wing with all the strength I could muster while unleashing a sapphire blast of energy. The wasp screeched in pain as the wing blew right off its back in a cloud of green ichor.

Unfortunately, I'd forgotten one thing. By blasting its wing off, the creature could no longer hold us aloft. We plummeted from the sky, falling straight past the platform and into the dark abyss beyond. I jerked my sword free in a spray of slime that covered my chest and arms in foul-smelling goo and leapt from its back, using all my strength to propel me through the air.

As I slammed into the wall, I drove my sword into the wall as hard as I could, managing to stop myself from falling to my certain doom. Even still, the force of the impact rang down my entire body. A cry of pain slipped from my lips as slick, yellow blood flowed from the wound in the wall.

I hung there, sword dug into the wall, and watched the broken wasp disappear into the darkness below.

I rested there for a moment before reaching upward and using my gauntlets' power to tear gobs of flesh from the surface. It was hard since I'd never done it before, but once I tried a couple times, I got the hang of it. The key was to try to pull the veins just below the surface out.

Ichor sprayed over me as the first vein tore free from the flesh. As it hit my hand, I dropped it and tested the crater I'd made in the wall. It'd work well enough. Now, to make a couple dozen more. If I could get up that far, I could leap to the ruby platform and make my way back up the ladder.

I spent another few minutes, ripping more hand holds out of the beast's flesh. Yellow slime rained down around me the entire time, but I soon had a set of handholds leading back up to the platform. Now, I just had to climb my happy ass back to the top. Awesome.

13

By the time I'd made it back to the platform, I found Annabeth sitting Indian-style with her stolen dagger lying flat across her knees like she was some kind of meditating monk. Six animal-headed corpses surrounded around her.

"Nice of you to drop by," she said, raising one slender eyebrow at me as I collapsed onto the jade platform, my chest heaving and my muscles reduced to quivering bowls of Jell-O.

She got up, padding over to me as she waved her bloody dagger at me. "This thing is awesome by the way. The moment I touched it I got stronger and faster than I've ever been before. And look what else it does." She pointed it at the far wall and let loose a blast of energy that blew a crater-sized hold in the gooey flesh.

"So, I got to climb back up here while you got a cool weapon," I muttered, rolling onto my back and staring up into the darkness above. "Seems fitting."

"Well, it's a good thing I did, Arthur. I got attacked by six more guardians. Without this dagger, I'd have never been able to take them on." She smiled. "You know, just to put things in perspective."

"What perspective is that, exactly?" I asked, willing myself into a sitting position and barely succeeding. I pulled out my canteen and unscrewed the top when I realized I hadn't bothered to refill it before we left. I stared longingly at the empty canteen before sighing and putting it away.

"The 'I got tons of awesome loot' perspective of course," Annabeth said, offering me her own canteen.

"You keep it," I said, waving her canteen away.

"Are you sure?" She frowned. "You're all sweaty, so I'm sure you're thirsty."

"I don't want to drink all your water. I'll be fine," I said, letting her help me to my feet. "Wow, you do seem a lot stronger." I looked her up and down. "It's all from the dagger."

"No, I got some other stuff too." She touched the amulet around her neck. "The second one dropped this, and it gave me the strength of ten demons." She held her hand out. "The third one dropped this ring, and it made me super-fast."

"Well, I guess we know which of us is taking on the dragon," I replied. Part of me was annoyed I'd had to deal with the stupid wasp lady while Annabeth had gotten a bunch of loot, but at the same time, I knew she needed it. Besides, I had Armaments to find.

"Um… Maybe we cross that bridge when we get to it?" Her face paled. "You don't seem pleased. I thought you would be."

"I'm plenty pleased, just tired." I took a deep breath. "So, what do we do about that?" I gestured toward the center of the platform where a keyhole had appeared. "Did you find a key?"

"No." She shook her head. "None of them dropped one either." She shrugged. "I could try sculpting one, but I don't really have any material for that…"

"Did you search their bodies?" I asked, looking at the corpses and hoping the key hadn't been on the zombie wasp. If it had been, well, I guess we'd have to try her method, even though it didn't give me high hopes.

"Um… no." Annabeth swallowed and looked at her feet. "Was I supposed to do that?"

"That's like the first rule of adventuring. Always check the bodies for loot." I smiled at her. "Which was the last one you killed?"

"Um, that one." She pointed to a moose-headed creature on the far end of the platform. "The bastard didn't actually drop me any gear." She kicked at the dirt in his general direction. "Cheapskate."

"Maybe he did, and it's still on his person?" I moved over to the corpse and began going through his robes while trying to ignore the fact I was pillaging a dead body. Thankfully, it only took me a few seconds to find the chain of a necklace around his neck, and as I pulled it free of his armor, I found a large jade key on the end of it. "Bingo!"

"Well, I've learned a valuable lesson," Annabeth

said as I moved toward the keyhole in the center of the platform. "Always loot the corpses."

"It's a good lesson to learn." I placed the key delicately in the keyhole, and it began to glow like it was filled with nuclear radiation before exploding into a cloud of emerald sparks that rained down around us before petering out on the stone.

"Was that supposed to happen?" Annabeth mumbled just before a wrinkly old dwarven woman with a long black beard and a completely shaved head descended from the darkness above on wings of glittering gold. She was wearing a blood red armor and had a huge double-bladed axe over one shoulder. As her booted feet touched down, she grinned at us, revealing a toothless, gummy mouth.

"Welcome, travelers," she said, voice like the whipping desert winds. She looked us over with eyes that were little more than complete and utter darkness. "Do you know who I am?"

"Um… no," I replied, feeling my cheeks heat up. "Is it that obvious?"

"It is." She grinned at me and rocked back on her heels expectantly. "So, you should ask who I am."

"Okay, I'll bite," I said, suddenly worried this was the guardian that the scorpions had told me was a bitch. "Who are you?"

"I am Sathanus." The dwarf's grin turned fierce as she looked me up and down. "But you may know me as Wrath." She pointed her axe at me, and literal flame exploded from beneath her feet, turning the jade platform where she stood into slag. "Why have you come into my sacred tunnels?"

"Wait, you're Wrath?" I said, suddenly excited even though from the look of things I ought to be scared. "Like the Princess of Wrath, Wrath?"

"Yes!" she boomed, taking a step toward me, and when I didn't take a step back, she stopped. Confusion spread across her face as she looked me over once more. "Why do you not fear me, human?"

"This is great!" I said, turning to Annabeth and grinning stupidly. "Can you believe our luck?"

"Do you have a definition for luck I'm not aware of?" Annabeth asked, and as she spoke, I realized her face had paled, and her knees were shaking. She was definitely scared, but I couldn't figure out why. I mean, this was the Princess of Wrath, after all. Surely, she'd help me. After all, I was the Builder!

"Mortal," Sathanus, Princess of Wrath snapped, drawing my attention back to her. "Explain yourself this instant." She pointed her axe at me again. "Or else."

"I'm the Legendary Builder." I jabbed my chest with my thumb. "I needed to find you so I could get your blessing and Armament." I nodded. "Then we can fight the Darkness!"

"You're the Builder?" Sathanus snorted. "That's impossible. You're much too scrawny, you don't have a beard." She looked me up and down. "And you do not have Clarent."

"I broke Clarent," I said sheepishly. "I was helping Mammon, and it shattered. That's actually why I'm here. I need the dwarves to teach me to mine Stygian Iron so I can repair it, and they requested I come fight a dragon down here in exchange for their help."

"You mean to tell me you're here to fight the dragon who rules my roost?" She glanced from me to Annabeth and back again. "And all you brought is a girl who is equipped with gear she found from my minions?" She shook her head. "You are on a fool's errand."

"Why is that?" I asked, suddenly confused. "I found you. That's already the best thing that's happened today."

"Wait, you wanted to find me?" Sathanus shook her head, cheeks flushing. "No one ever wants to find me." She smacked her chest with one hand, and a resounding clang echoed through the cavern. "I am the raging fire that burns the whole town, the enemy who sneaks up when you least expect it to drive a knife into your gut, the—"

"The Archangel of Wrath." I finished, interrupting her. "I've got it."

She stood there for a moment looking at me. "I do not understand why you've sought me, Builder." She shook her head. "It is unwise. After all, there is a reason I have been sealed down here since your species was born."

"Maybe she's right, Arthur," Annabeth said, moving closer to me and taking my hand. "Perhaps we should just go."

"At least one of you has sense." Sathanus's eyes flitted to Annabeth. "Good woman you have there. You should listen to her."

Instead of responding immediately, I reached into my satchel and pulled out the book Gabriella had given me. *The Once and Former Builder.* I flipped it open, and like I'd thought, there was a new section showing the archangel in question. I didn't have time to read it now, but that was okay.

"You're in my book." I showed her the page. "That means we can help each other." I smiled at her. "It also means I am who I say I am."

"Why am I in your book?" the dwarven archangel asked, moving closer and peering at it. "And why is there a picture of my pants on the next page?" She gestured at her lower half, and I realized she was correct. The pair of armored pants listed as her Armament looked like the ones she was wearing. They were the color of flesh spilled blood and made of linked hoops of chain.

"That is the Armament you can provide me to defeat the Darkness." I smiled at her, glad I didn't need to craft the item. Getting the materials to craft the *Unrelenting Grips of Greed* had been damned near impossible.

"You want me to give you my pants?" Sathanus asked, taking a step backward, face scrunched up in confusion. "What will I wear then?" She shook herself. "Unless you mean for me to be naked?" She took a step backward. "Look, I'm flattered, really, but…"

"Huh?" I said because I'd already been envisioning myself with another Armament. With hers, Mammon's, and Lucifer's I'd have three, and while that wasn't Dred's five, it was a hell of a lot closer than I'd been yesterday. "I don't think it's supposed to be your pants." I gestured at her legs. "Those would never fit me."

Sathanus grew very still. "Are you saying I'm fat?"

"What? No, not at all." I shook my head, wishing I had Clarent. If I did, I could have just looked at the tooltip attached to her pants and known if they were the right ones. Still, I was willing to bet the Armament wasn't meant to be her actual pants. "I'm saying look at you and me. I'm much taller than you, and your legs are big enough to crush my skull like a melon. There's no way I could wear them."

"You *are* calling me fat." The Archangel of Wrath glared at me. "And short."

"Look." I rubbed my face with my hands. This

conversation was not going where I wanted at all. "Unless you plan on taking off your pants here and now and giving them to me so I can try them on and find out if they fit, I think we can safely assume it's not them. You must have another set of pants somewhere that will actually fit me." I tapped the page. "The reason I say that is because there's no recipe to craft the pants. There would be if it were something I could make."

"Does he make any sense to you?" Sathanus asked, directing her gaze to Annabeth. "Because I'm as confused as a nun in an orgy." She shook her head. "I do not much like being confused. It makes me angry, and let me just say, people tend not to like me when I get angry."

"I think what Arthur is trying to say," Annabeth said, putting a hand on my shoulder, "is that each of the archangels can provide an Armament to the Builder. Those Armaments give him the power to defeat the Darkness. You can provide him with the Armament of Wrath. Judging by what I see in the book, it's supposed to be a pair of pants."

"I already understand you want my pants," Sathanus said, shifting from foot to foot. "But I'm not giving you my pants." She flushed again.

"We don't think the pants in the picture are the ones you're wearing," Annabeth said, tapping the page. Then she stopped and stood there, and I could have sworn a lightbulb turned on above her head. "What are your pants called?"

"They're called pants. Well, greaves actually. I know they're not technically greaves, but that sounds more fearsome." Sathanus struck a pose with her axe. "There's Sathanus, Archangel of Wrath in her Greaves of Certain Doom!" She nodded. "See, it just sounds better."

"I agree," Annabeth said, nodding furiously before turning to me. "And Arthur, what are the pants in the picture called?"

"The Merciless Greaves of Wrath." I scanned over the stat block written beside it.

The Merciless Greaves of Wrath

Type: Leggings

Durability: 5,300

Defense: 1D10

Enchantments: Armament of Wrath

Ability: Reflection– Creates an aura around the user that

reflects seven times the damage dealt to the user back to the damage dealer.

"I guess they reflect damage back at the attacker?" I said, shrugging. "Creates some kind of aura." I scratched my head. "Do the ones you're wearing do that?"

"Oh!" Sathanus said, nodding like it all made sense. Only not the good kind of sense. The kind of sense that occurred when you realized you'd fallen ass first in a nest full of fire ants. "Well, that isn't happening. There's no way you're getting those."

"Why not?" I asked, watching her closely while she muttered under her breath.

"The Merciless Greaves of Wrath are with my treasure over yonder." She gestured into the darkness with her axe. "It is guarded by a dragon. You would have to slay her to retrieve them." She stroked her magnificent black beard. "And you are much too scrawny and beardless to succeed." She sighed. "We've been through this."

"So, the dragon I was already going to kill has the greaves?" I asked, suddenly excited. "That's great!"

"I think your Builder is broken," Sathanus said,

looking at Annabelle and gesturing at me with her axe. "He thinks he can defeat Envy."

"Wait, Envy is the dragon?" I asked, suddenly confused.

"Dragon is more a placeholder term, I'll admit." Sathanus shrugged. "But yes, Leviathan, Archangel of Envy is the guardian of the treasure. She coveted my treasure and took it from me, and now she roosts on top of it, rolling over in gold and bathing in it." Sathanus got a far-off look in her eyes. "She doesn't even want it. She just wants it because I had it and she didn't. Honestly, it's a little pathetic."

"Maybe I can convince her to help me and get two armaments for the price of one?" I asked, looking from Sathanus to Annabeth and back again.

"To be clear, you wish to convince an archangel consumed solely by envy to give you things? I think you might be overconfident because you have bargained with Mammon, but you do not understand the difference between her and Leviathan." Sathanus rubbed her bald head. "Envy wants things just because another has them and for no other reason. It is why she hasn't left this place in millennia."

Sathanus sighed. "The moment she knows you want the Greaves, you will never get them. It will make her want them all the more because the idea of you having something she can't will make her insatiable."

"Still, we have to try." I took a deep breath. "If you help us, and we succeed, we all get what we want, right?"

"Admittedly, I'm intrigued. I am not sure how Envy will deal with the Builder, especially one marked by Greed. That may make her want you more, though I am not sure you want her to want you." Sathanus inhaled sharply, her nostrils flailing. "However, it costs me little to send you to the bitch." She nodded. "I shall help you." Her eyes narrowed. "But if you fail, know that I will visit such exquisite torment upon you, it will make you wish you had never been born."

"You know, you would catch a lot more flies with honey instead of vinegar. Maybe don't jump right to the whole death and dismemberment thing." I shrugged. "Just as an FYI."

"Here's the thing, Builder," Sathanus replied as she thrust her axe into the sling on her back. "If you tear off a fly's wings. It will eat whatever you give it."

Her hands snaked out as she spoke, wrapping around our wrists, and before I could even squeak in protest, she jumped off the platform, taking both of us with her. My heart jumped into my throat as I seized onto her arm.

Her gilded wings flapped mightily as Sathanus zoomed upward into the air while wind buffeted all around us.

I'm not sure what my face looked like, but my fear must have been evident in my features because the archangel's smile faltered as she stared at me.

"Are you afraid of heights or something?" Before I could tell her it was more from being dragged off the cliff, she nodded once. "It is no matter if you are. We are almost there anyway."

She was right. A second later she landed on a raised platform made of solid gold with a glimmering liquid metal portal at the far end.

"What the hell just happened?" I asked as she released Annabeth and me. "Where are we?"

"We are at the gateway that leads to the castle

where Envy hoards my treasure." Sathanus beat her wings, floating up until she was eye level with me. "Just cross the Burning Desert, and you'll be at the castle." The Archangel of Wrath leaned in close, so her eyes were inches from mine, and I could feel the anger rippling off her. "Do not fail me. You have given me hope. Take it away, and I shall be incredibly displeased."

She was gone so suddenly, it spooked the hell out of me. I stumbled backward in surprise as Annabeth sucked in a breath beside me.

"Remind me to never offer to accompany you anywhere ever again," Annabeth said, looking at me as she tried to regain her composure.

"Aww, I thought you liked spending time with me?" I asked, holding out my hand to her. "Or am I mistaken about that?"

"I like spending a vastly different kind of time with you." She took my hand. "This is not what I had in mind." She shook her head. "I figured we'd have a nice dinner followed by, well, you know." She gestured at me. "Not crawling through a dungeon and dealing with dwarven archangels."

"You make a fair point," I said as we walked toward

the portal. "I'd much rather do your thing instead of my thing."

"Well, let's get this over with then." Annabeth gave me a determined look. "Because afterward, I plan on you making it up to me good and hard."

"I look forward to it," I said as we leapt through the portal.

To be honest, I wished I hadn't because travel through the magical portal felt like having my insides sucked out through a straw.

A moment later, I landed on the other side on my hands and knees, sweat dripping down my body with Annabeth beside me. As my stomach slowly unwound itself from the knot it was in, I sat up and stared at the surroundings.

We were in a chamber no bigger than a barn. Only the walls were made of fire, and above us, giant predatory falcons flitted through the air. Their gazes settled on us as Annabeth pulled me to my feet. Fear vaulted through me, making my mouth dry and my knees shake. Those birds were freaking huge. No, huge was a massive fucking understatement. These birds were big enough to carry off Godzilla.

"I suggest we run away," Annabeth said, gesturing at the circling birds above with her golden dagger.

"Noted," I replied and took off running through the burning doorway as the first of the falcons dove toward us with its huge claws extended.

14

I darted to the left, not sure of what else to do as the falcon's mammoth claws gouged into the red sand beneath my feet. The creature was so close, I could have reached out and touched it if I'd been so inclined. Which I wasn't because I was too busy scrambling to my feet as the massive bird turned toward me and regarded me with its beady eyes. It took one menacing step forward as battle cries from other birds sounded off to my right.

The bird's beak slashed at me, cleaving through the air as I dove forward, scrambling between its legs before its claws could turn me into minced meat. I'll admit, heading toward its talons wasn't my brightest idea ever, but I was sort of banking on something I'd heard as a little kid. If you could pour salt on a bird's tail, it wouldn't be able to fly. So how did that help me? Well, I was sweaty, and sweat was water and salt right?

Trying to ignore the voice in the back of my head telling me I was an idiot, I jumped on the bird's back. It bucked like a raging bronco, its head swiveling around to glare at me as it flapped its massive wings. Seizing its tail feathers as tightly as I could, I barely had a moment to contemplate how wrong my old wives' tale was when the thing sprang into the air.

It soared high above the ground, banking and weaving through the sky as I hung on with all the strength my tired muscles could muster. Thankfully, my adrenaline was pumping full steam ahead. Otherwise, I wasn't sure if I'd have managed to last long at all. I gritted my teeth together and pulled myself forward onto the creature's back, one handful of feathers at a time. At least they were nearly as big as tree branches, so it wasn't too difficult to grip them.

When I was nearly to its neck, I stopped because I wasn't sure if the thing could turn around and stab me with its wickedly sharp beak. I lay there, clinging to its back as I forced myself to take a couple deep breaths. Now that I didn't actively fear for my life, at least not in the 'oh god a giant early bird is going to get my worm' way, I noticed there was a lot of structure beyond the barn of fire we'd just left. In fact, in the minutes I'd clung to the falcon we'd crossed what seemed like miles of Burning Desert, which was awesome except for one minor problem.

Annabeth was back there with the other falcons. Panic exploded through me as I tried to figure out how to get down so I could go back for her. Maybe I could survive the jump? Only, I knew that would be impossible. If I had wings, I might have survived the drop, but I had no doubt that the second I was airborne, the falcon would snatch me. Then I'd be as good as dead.

No, I'd just have to wait until we got some place safer and then try to make my way back. I just had to hope Annabeth would still be okay then.

"Neat trick," Annabeth called from beside me, her wind-muffled words driving away the dread steadily building inside me. I looked in the direction of her voice and saw her riding her own falcon. Her hands were gripping feathers on either side of its head.

She jerked it hard to the left, causing her raptor to angle toward me.

Not one to be outdone, I gripped my bird in the same way and pulled as hard as I could to my right. The falcon squealed as it flapped its mighty wings, jerking us hard to the side and moving toward Annabeth. I tossed a glance at her, and she smiled at me and nodded like I was a new pup who had just learned to play fetch.

"So, what's the plan?" I yelled, hoping my voice wasn't drowned out by the wind whipping by us and the beating of huge falcon wings.

Annabeth must have heard me because she pointed off into the distance. I craned my head toward the spot she'd indicated and saw what looked like an ebony castle. I wasn't quite sure how large it was because we were so high… in… the… air…

My heart leapt into my throat as I realized I could easily fall to my doom. I took a deep breath and tried to keep from freaking out. Then I shut my eyes and took a long slow breath. When I opened my eyes a moment later, we were nearly to the castle.

I pushed as hard as I could on the bird's head, and we fell into a dive that nearly had me calling for my mommy… which I totally didn't do despite what you may have heard from a certain sculptor.

A second later, we were on the ground, and I realized the castle wasn't as big as I'd thought. It was only about fifty or so feet tall. The blocks were made of what looked like obsidian and had a sort of flaked look to them that reminded me of the way people used to make spearheads by chipping away at the rock.

I sat there on the back of my falcon, partially waiting for my heart to stop trying to flee my body, and partially waiting for Annabeth to land as she circled above me in a slow dive. After what felt like an eternity, she touched down beside me and shot me a wry grin.

"Well, we're here." Annabeth gestured toward the castle, which was sort of funny because as soon as she released her hold on the giant bird, the creature bucked her off. She hit the ground with a thud, laying there for a moment dazed as the falcon eyed her. It snorted, scratching at the ground beside her with one massive claw before leaping in the air, and I'll admit, I was a little surprised it hadn't slashed her into ribbons.

Either way, after Annabeth got to her feet and glared at the retreating falcon like she was double-dog-daring it to come back, she motioned for me to get down. I was a little hesitant. What if my bird didn't decide to just leave? I took a deep breath and leaned in close to the beast.

"I promise if you don't try to eat me, I won't fly on your back again. Deal?" I asked as I tentatively released it. When it didn't throw me to the dirt immediately, I took that as a good sign and jumped off its back.

The sand was warm beneath my feet even though it was the color of freshly spilled blood just like the ground had been in the place where we first arrived. I was about to make a remark about it when my bird slashed at me with its huge golden beak. I dove forward as the blow tore into my armor, throwing sparks across the ground. I hit the dirt in a roll, trying to ignore the rage welling up inside me because my stupid bird had decided to try to eat me.

I came to my feet and sprinted toward Annabeth. She stood just inside an archway that was just big enough for a man to walk through, which was good because I was pretty sure the falcon wouldn't be able to come after me. I just had to get there.

"Come on!" she cried, unleashing a blast at the huge falcon with her dagger. I didn't see the effects of the attack, but the shriek that followed nearly shattered my eardrums.

As I burst through the entrance, I tried to stop myself, but my momentum carried me forward, anyway. I collided with the far wall and split my lip on the sharp stone.

The bird stomped one clawed foot on the sand outside with enough force to shake the ground beneath my feet. The falcon screeched behind me, making the hairs on the back of my neck stand up straight before shoving one beady eye against the entryway and glaring at me. It was unnerving. Almost like it was telling me that if it ever saw me again, it would eat me. Then again, it could have just been in my head.

"Well, that was close," I breathed, wiping my face with one hand. I could still hear the falcon outside, but that was fine with me. Outside was where it belonged.

"Too close," Annabeth agreed as I looked around

the room. The walls were made of that same chipped black stone, and blazing blue torches flickered on the walls, casting dancing shadows across the space.

"So, left or right?" I asked, glancing in either direction. Both led off through archways similar to the one leading outside, but I couldn't see down either of them because they were so dark.

"Let's try left," Annabeth said, moving toward the closest torch and grabbing it like she meant to pull it free of its sconce. Only as she touched it, all the torches went out, and the sound of hissing gas filled the air. I spun, intent on going for the doorway leading back outside, but as I did, a wall of rock slammed down in front of us, sealing us inside.

As I summoned magic into my sword to give us some light in this godforsaken darkness, I heard something thudding to our left. I whirled in time to see the passageway blocked to our left. Cursing, I spun back around in time to see Annabeth collapse to the floor as green gas sprayed from a vent behind the torch she'd grabbed.

I moved toward her, intent to grab her and pull her to safety, but the moment I got close, my vision went hazy. My sword hit the ground with a clang went out, and darkness surrounded me. I held my breath, trying to pull myself backward, but my body felt so heavy I couldn't make it move.

My legs went out from under me, and I fell, only I didn't even feel myself hit the ground.

15

Cold water startled me awake, and as my eyes fluttered open, I found myself staring at a goblin so covered in jewelry I could barely make out her flesh. Her arms were covered in bangles, wristbands, and bracelets. Her ears were dotted by studs and had golden hoops punched through the outside. She leaned in close to me, causing her much too big golden chainmail shirt to jangle noisily.

"How could you be so stupid as to try to steal from me?" the goblin asked, getting all up in my business. She smelled like sweat, metal, and oil, and as she regarded me like something she'd scraped off the bottom of her shoe, I tried to figure out just how fucked I was on my fuck-o-meter. As the goblin continued to glare at me, I was pretty sure it was somewhere between totally and absolutely.

"We didn't try to steal anything from you," I said, trying to move away. Only it was no use because I was tied to a stone chair with so much rope I'd have never been able to wiggle my fingers, let alone break free.

"Liar!" she screamed, her left hand jutting out to point at Annabeth. "She tried to steal my most prized torch." The goblin hugged herself. "Of all the torches. Why did you have to go for that one? The others I could have possibly forgiven, but *that* one? No chance." She shook her head, eliciting another jingle-jangle from her clothing, and I got the impression her pockets were stuffed to the brim with more gold.

"We weren't trying to steal it," I said carefully. "We knew it was your favorite, so we were bringing it to you." I shot her my best smile.

"More lies!" the goblin screeched, turning her back on me. "How could you have known it was my favorite? *I* didn't even know it was my favorite until you tried to take it from me." She craned her head back around and fixed me with her gold-flecked green eyes. "Riddle me that!"

"I'm guessing you're the Archangel of Envy," I said, meeting her eyes, but it was like trying to stare down a toddler that was seconds away from throwing a fit in the middle of the goddamned store because you would not let her have candy. Only this time, there was no distracted parent on a cell phone to save me.

"How do you know that?" she asked, spinning back around with such fury that gold coins flew from her pockets and scattered across the ground with a clang. Her eyes went wide as she looked to and fro before pouncing on the closest coins. She covered them with her arms while eyeing me carefully. "I see you watching my gold. Well, you can't have it, it's all mine."

"I don't want your gold," I said, watching the goblin.

"Why not?" she asked, stopping so suddenly it was damned near creepy. Her hand hung there, clasping the coin she'd picked up as she slowly turned her gaze down to it. "Why don't you want it? Is there something wrong with it?" She eyed the coin suspiciously, causing more coins to fall to the ground. "You didn't answer me. Why don't you want my gold?" She crossed her arms over her chest. "Everyone wants my gold."

"I can assure you. I absolutely do not want your gold," I said, taking a deep breath and looking around the room. Aside from the goblin and Annabeth, there was no one else in here. Hell, there was nothing at all in the room save brick walls. It made me want to look behind me to see if we were in some kind of cell, but since there was so much rope binding my head to the chair, I couldn't do that.

"You're not talking sense." The goblin sidled up to me and held out a single gold coin to me. "I might be persuaded to give you one if you tell me why you don't want it." She watched me for a second before her eyes flickered to the coin in her hand. "But not this one." She shoved the coin back in her pocket and began rummaging around. "None of these ones, but a different one maybe. These are too special to part with." She looked back up at me, watching me with fevered intensity. "Tell me." She grabbed me by the shoulders and shook me so hard the entire chair rocked from the effort.

"I just didn't come here for gold. I—"

"So, you did come here to steal something!" she said leaping onto me and pressing her face against mine. "I knew it." Her eyes narrowed. "Tell me what it is."

"I came here for you," I replied.

"Well, you can't have... wait, you came here for me?" the goblin pulled back a couple inches and looked at me carefully. "Why would you come here for me?" She cocked her head to the side. "No one ever wants me."

"I do." I nodded quickly. "That's why my friend and I came here. We were trying to find you." I took a deep breath as she turned to regard Annabeth.

"I do not believe you," the goblin said, but she sounded unsure. "I think you're tricking me, trying to get my gold." She gave me a sly look and tapped her forehead. "I'm onto you, don't think I'm not." She leaned back in then placing her mouth near my ear. "But tell me why you want me. I must know." She pulled back again. "Or are you just tricking me?" She tapped her chin before leaping off of me, causing more coins to spill across the ground, only this time she ignored them. "I think you're tricking me." She began to pace in front of me. "Are you tricking me?" she looked up at me. "Well, are you? I must know. Tell me the answer."

"I'm not tricking you. I was really excited when I found out you were here. It's one of the reasons I came all this way." I nodded, trying to convince her. The sad thing was, it should have been easy to do because it was true, but something told me she wasn't playing with a full deck.

"One of the reasons?" she asked, raising a pierced eyebrow at me. "What were the other reasons?" She pointed a spindly, bejeweled finger at me. "Were the others to steal from me?! Admit it, thief!"

"You need to chill with the thief stuff," I said, taking a deep breath and exhaling slowly. I didn't know what this was exactly, but Envy was clearly broken in a way that made no sense to me. Was it because she'd spent so long down here with just her gold for company? I wasn't sure, but while Sathanus has seemed a few cookies short of a jar, the Archangel of Envy seemed like someone had left only crumbs in hers.

"But you're a thief, aren't you?" the archangel watched me carefully. "Aren't you?"

"I'm not a thief. I don't want your stuff." I sighed. "We've been through this. I came here for you." I nodded. "Understand?"

"Don't patronize me, boy," she spat, stamping one foot on the ground and causing more coins to fall to the ground. "To do so would be to invite doom. You do not want to invite doom."

"I don't," I said, wondering exactly what she was going to do to me.

"Why not?" She stamped her foot again. "I give really great doom. You'd like it. Well, not like it exactly…" She trailed off into mumbling. "God, you're blowing it. Just be natural. Get him to reveal what he plans to steal. He must want to steal something. No one would come here for you. No, no, no."

"I'm the Builder of Legend," I said, and at my words, she stopped and looked at me, understanding dawning across her features.

"Ah ha!" she said, pointing at me once more. "So that's why you're here, is it?" The goblin crossed her arms over her chest. "Well, you won't get any materials from me. They're all mine. Every last brick is mine. Every twig, every bit of moss. Mine, mine, mine."

"I said, I don't want that stuff." I sighed, not sure how to make her understand. "Look, can you untie me?"

"So that's what you want? To be untied?" She took a step toward me and flicked her hands out, causing long black talons to sprout from her fingertips. "Maybe we can work out a deal," she added, leaning close to me. "Where you get nothing! Bwa, ha, ha!" She stopped her maniacal laugh and touched my calf with one talon. "How do you feel about that?"

"Honestly, just meeting you is all I wanted," I said, shutting my eyes. Envy was way too insane to deal with, and Dred only had five Armaments. Maybe I didn't need Envy's armament. Maybe I could just figure out a way to get home and run the fuck away. No. That was wrong. I was the Builder, it was my job to fix whatever this was.

I opened my eyes and found the archangel's face to be only millimeters from my own. Her huge eyes stared right into mine.

"Give it back," she said, and her voice was cold and

angry. I felt her talons on my throat then as she pressed her thumb into my flesh. Not hard, but enough to let me know she could skewer me with ease.

"Give what back?" I asked, very carefully.

"Give back what you wanted!" she snapped, salvia flecking across my face. "Now!"

"I can't give it back. It's just a feeling," I said, taken aback. "Do you honestly expect me to give back that I wanted to meet you? That's like, not even possible."

"That's exactly what a thief would say," she snarled, wings rising from her back. They were unlike anything I'd seen before, resembling the wings of the green dragons I'd seen in Blade's End. They were sort of bat-like in shape, but the flesh was green and gold with giant golden prongs on the ends. Only the gold didn't look natural. It looked like prongs had been dipped in gold. More piercings covered the wings themselves, so that when she unfurled them, it was nearly blinding in the torchlight.

"Fine, you can have it back." I sighed.

"I don't believe you," she said, and as she spoke, she seemed to grow in size. Her face elongated and her eyes turned into serpentine slits. "I think you still want to meet me." She leapt off the ground. "This will not do." She began to pace again, but this time, as she did, her body seemed to stretch, and her legs seemed to divide, so that in only a few moments, she practically filled the room with her serpentine bulk.

"Trust me. I wish I'd never met you," I said as she turned back to me, eyeing me with a face that was more lizard than anything else. I couldn't even tell how it'd happened. One moment she was a goblin, and the next? The next she was a huge fucking serpent with a billion arms and legs. What made matters worse was that as her bulk pressed against the walls of the room, I got the distinct impression she hadn't stopped growing, and if that was true, we were at risk of being crushed.

"How can I know you mean that?" she hissed. "Do you even know what it's like when someone tries to take something from you?" Her huge head surged forward, and her black tongue flicked out, tasting the air like the snake she was. "Do you?!"

"Yes, actually." I swallowed and shut my eyes. "I'm

an orphan. I lost my parents when I was really young. So yeah, I kinda know what it feels like." I narrowed my eyes at the giant serpent. "And, you know what, fuck off."

"Interesting," the archangel said, turning its head so it could look at me with its huge green and gold eye. "I get the impression you're telling the truth." It seemed to settle. "I suppose you do know what it's like." Her mouth widened, revealing fangs the size of my arm. "All the more reason for me to devour you whole. You know what it's like to steal from people, and yet, you still came here to do the same!"

As she reared back, jaw unhinging so she could swallow me whole, part of me wanted to give up and let her eat me, but most of me? Most of me was pissed off this was how I was going to die.

"I want you to remember this moment, Leviathan," I said, glaring at her as she lunged forward, gobs of saliva spattering across the floor. "Because when the Darkness comes, and it will come, it will take everything you have. Know, that had you acted differently right now, you might have been able to save that which was truly precious to you."

16

"What do you mean?" she hissed, mouth so close to my face I could feel the heat of her breath wash over me as she spoke. "Who would dare steal from me?" Leviathan reared back, fangs glinting in the light as her hooded cobra's head unfurled. "Tell me!"

"The Darkness," I said, still glaring at her. I wasn't sure what was going on with the archangel, but I was done with this conversation. "Now either eat me, you bat shit crazy fuck, or let me go so I can save everyone and everything." I tried to nod toward her. "Including you and your stupid gold."

"I'm not following," the massive creature said, and as she spoke, her body reverted back into the diminutive goblin. It happened so suddenly, it actually took me a few minutes to realize it'd happened. One moment she was a giant serpent, and the next, well, she was a winged goblin. "Explain what you mean by Darkness." She glanced around before peering into a particularly dark corner. "I don't see anything there."

"Do you really not know what the Darkness is?" I asked, raising an eyebrow at the goblin as she slowly approached the corner and waved her hand through it.

"The absence of light," Leviathan said, turning to regard me. "You think me a fool?"

"No, not actual darkness." I sighed. "*The Darkness.*"

"You're not making any sense," Leviathan replied, wings folding up into her back as she approached. "Why won't you tell me so I can understand? Just give me what I want!" Her hands clenched into fists. "Why do you deny me?"

"I'm trying, I just…" I stopped, watching the goblin. "What would you trade in exchange for the information?"

"Trade?" she asked, watching me closely. "You wish

to trade with me? Do you even know me?" She smacked her chest with one hand causing her golden chainmail to jingle. "I am the Archangel of Envy!"

"Right, and you're supposed to safeguard us against the sin of wanting someone else's possessions, qualities, or luck." I nodded toward her. "How are you doing with that?"

"I have not been the person you speak of in a very long time." She shook her head. "I can hardly remember a time before I was here with my hoard." She looked around. "If I were to leave, that tricky dwarf would take it all, and I'd never get it back."

"Let's assume that's true," I said, taking a deep breath and exhaling slowly. "Let's assume the dwarf does come and take all your gold."

"She will! I've known her for eons. She wants nothing more than to take what is mine!" The goblin nodded furiously. "I see it in her eyes when she comes to tea."

"Right, okay. Part of me wants to inquire about the whole tea thing, but I'll wait until later, okay?" When Leviathan nodded, I continued, "Think about all your gold, gems, whatever it is."

"Okay?" she asked, walking over to me. "I am picturing all my pretties."

"Do they make you happy?" I asked.

"Yes!" she cried, dancing. "I love knowing I have so much stuff because if something happens, I'll be set. World ends, got my stash." She nodded again. "Only problem is protecting it. Can't trust anyone…" she trailed off into muttering.

"And wouldn't you be happier if you, um, didn't have to protect it?" I smiled. "Wouldn't it be nice to leave this tomb because that's what it is, a tomb."

"It is not a tomb." She crossed her arms over her chest, but her tone was a touch uncertain. "I still live."

"Do you really? What was the last thing you did?" I asked.

"I found you! Before that, I counted my coins, and before that, I counted the rubies." She looked suddenly horrified. "I probably should count the rubies again. What if one disappeared?"

"How could it possibly disappear? You're a giant fucking dragon, and you're clearly so strong you've kept out the Archangel of Wrath and her army of dwarves," I cried, suddenly exasperated. "You'll be fine until the Darkness comes to eat everyone."

"There you go with that Darkness thing again." The Archangel Envy stared at me for a moment. "I will agree to your trade. Tell me how to stop this Darkness from taking what's mine, and I will grant you what you wish." She took a deep breath. "But only if you agree to return it when you're done. I can lend but not give."

"That sounds reasonable. When the Darkness is defeated, and I'm dead, you can have whatever you want back." I nodded to her. "Do you agree?"

"I agree, but you must swear a blood oath on it." She held her hand out. "Do you swear to that?"

"Yeah, sure," I said, trying to give her my hand. "You're going to need to unbind me for that."

"Oh, right, sorry!" the goblin nodded, looking down at my hands where they were tied to the chair. "Just one hand though. I don't want you tricking me."

"Fine!" I growled. "Do the left one. I'm right-handed, and I need to be able to use my sword."

"Your sword?" she asked, slashing open the bindings along my left arm with her claws. The moment they fell free caused my entire arm to tingle. "What sword?" She glanced around. "You don't have a sword."

"I just meant in general. Not a specific sword. I'm right-handed." I shook my head. "Let's get on with this. What do we do?"

"I will cut your hand, drawing blood. I will then cut my own hand, and we will shake. The bargain will be sealed in blood so if you don't follow through lots of bad things will happen." She cut her hand, causing blood to well up in her palm. "Would you like me to list them?"

"No." I didn't either. If I heard what they were, I might not do it, and I had to do it. After all, what choice did I have with this batty goblin? "Go ahead and cut me."

"As you wish." She drew one talon across my palm, splitting the flesh like a ripe peach. It hurt so much I nearly screamed, but I bit my lip and focused on a happier time. Like when I'd been trapped for a year fighting wind monsters. "Ready?"

"Yeah," I said, holding my hand out, and as she took it, the entire room seemed to shake. Green electricity exploded from our handshakes and rippled across my flesh, and as it did, I realized this might be a bit more than I'd first expected.

"There, the bond is complete!" Leviathan nodded. "Now, tell me what you want so we can come to the terms of our agreement."

"I feel like this is happening backwards, but okay." I took a deep breath. "First, I want you to untie my friend and me. Then give us the stuff back you no doubt took."

"I didn't take anything. You just left me gifts." She crossed her arms over her chest. "But fine. You can have them back, Indian giver."

"Next, I want you to provide me with your Armament so I can stop the Darkness." As I spoke, she gave me a confused look.

"I really don't know what you're talking about," she said, shaking her head. "Please just tell me because I can't bargain like this. You keep speaking of things I'm not familiar with."

"Okay, look," I took a deep breath in an effort not to lose it and start screaming. "There's a picture of the armament in my book. I'll show you. Give it to me, and when I die, you can have it back. Okay?"

"Okay…" she said, reaching down the front of her chainmail and pulling out my book. "What page is it on?" she began thumbing open the book. "This is all blank. Are you lying to me?"

"No." I held out my hand, and as I did, I realized I wasn't bleeding anymore. In fact, instead of any sort of wound at all, I now bore a scar on my palm in the shape of an ouroboros, the serpent eating its own tail.

"No?" she gestured at me with the book. "Why is it blank?" She stamped her foot. "Why is this all so difficult?"

"You're the difficult one!" I snapped back before I could stop myself and immediately wished I hadn't because I was still tied to the chair and she could turn into a Godzilla-sized serpent. "Just give me the book, and I'll show you. Only I can make it work."

"You've enchanted it?" she asked, handing me the book. "You must show me how you did that." She tapped her cheek. "Another bargain for another time."

I ignored her as she continued to ramble on as I flipped through the book. It was a lot more difficult than need be because I wasn't left-handed. Still, I finally found the page with Envy pictured upon it. Only as I scanned the text, everything became clear.

"You have amnesia?" I asked, turning to look at her?

"I don't know what that is, but I probably do. I have everything." She looked at the book. "Unless it's something I don't have, in which case I want it!"

"Right," I said, turning my eyes back to the page and reading through the bullet points beneath her picture.

Leviathan– Archangel of Envy.

- Tasked with keeping the sins of Envy at bay.
- Fell during Lucifer's rebellion against the high court
- Struck her head on the ground below and was badly damaged in the fall
- Side effects include long-term memory loss, amnesia, and psychosis

"Anyway, this says you have long-term memory loss and amnesia, which is why you don't remember the Darkness." I tapped the page. "If you let me, I can bring you to the edge of Hell and show you the Darkness."

"Why would I want to do that?" she asked, peering closely at me.

"Let me ask you a different question," I said, suddenly feeling bad for her. "As an aside."

"It doesn't hurt to ask, but I may not answer." She stared at the book before pointing to the other page where her armament was listed. "What's that?"

"The Armament," I said, waving my hand. "But let's just table that too for a second. I still want to ask you something."

"No. I want to know why you have a picture of my belt," she said, lifting up her chainmail to reveal a six pack of abs and a pair of golden trousers cinched together with the belt that was pictured on the page. "See. It's the same."

Now, I couldn't actually be sure if that was true because I couldn't see the tooltip for it, but unlike with Sathanus's pants, this belt did look like it would fit me. It was also much too big for the goblin woman who looked like she'd wrapped the chain around her waist twice and then knotted it instead of using the buckle.

I glanced back down at the page and nearly had a heart attack when I read the description.

The Remorseless Chain of Envy

Type: Belt

Durability: 2,300

Defense: 1D6

Enchantments: Armament of Envy

Ability: Spell Steal– Allows the user to temporarily mimic an ability from an opponent once the ability has been used in combat. Only one ability can be mimicked at a time.

I took a moment to shove down my inner greedy pig because I realized I needed to get the belt from her and letting her know I wanted it wouldn't work. The ability to steal an ability from an opponent was too powerful to pass up, and it might make the difference during the fight with Dred and the Darkness. Still, there might be another way. If what the book said was true, maybe I could heal her. Then dealing with her wouldn't be so damned impossible.

"It's a neat belt," I replied, looking back up at her and shrugging, "But anyway, I had a question for you."

"What's your question?" she asked, dropping her chainmail down over the belt and looking at me.

"What if I said I could fix you, or at least, I was pretty sure I could fix you?" I pointed to the book. "It says you hurt your head when you fell from Heaven."

"You could fix my head?" she gave me a confused look. "What's wrong with it?" she tapped her skull, eyes starting to widen in panic. "You mean something I own is broken?"

"Yes, well, sort of. I'm not sure, but I know someone who would be able to help. As I said, I'm the Builder, so even if she can't help you right now, I'll make sure I find a way to help you." I watched her. "Will you let me help you?"

"And what would you want in exchange?" she asked, rubbing her head with one hand. "To fix my head, so what's mine isn't broken anymore."

"I just want you to come and see my friend, Sally. Would that be okay?"

"If I do that, Sathanus will come and steal all my things. I don't know if I can risk it." The archangel of Envy began to pace in front of me. "But if I stay, my things will stay broken, and that's no good at all."

"What if I get Sathanus to agree to come too? That way you can watch her the whole time?" I offered.

"What's the catch?" Envy asked, moving closer to me and peering into my face. "There's always a catch."

"There is a catch. You need to let me take a couple things to her as a show of good faith—"

"I can't let you take what's mine, thief," she cried.

"How about you give it to me then, that way, when I die, you get them back?" I showed her my hand where she'd marked me. "How's that sound?"

"That seems fair," she said, nodding once. "Go and speak with the dwarf. If what you say is true, and she agrees to the journey, I will accompany you as well."

17

"The architecture is really amazing," Annabeth said as we followed Leviathan through the winding halls of the palace. Truth be told, I wasn't that impressed because while I was sure the pillars and whatnot were nice, there was so much stuff piled everywhere, I mostly just wanted to leave.

As we passed by a literal wall of old magazines and kitten calendars, I found myself hoping there would be no wind to knock the thing over. The absolute last thing I wanted was to be buried alive in filth.

"Thank you," Leviathan replied, turning to look at the sculptor. "I especially like the high ceilings. Let's me hold more things." The goblin picked her way through the very narrow pathway through all the junk as we headed toward a room at the far end.

"That's an excellent point," Annabeth said, and I glared at her.

"Don't encourage her," I whispered. "She could turn into a giant serpent and eat us if she thinks you're coveting her stuff."

"I can appreciate things other people have without wanting them for myself, Arthur," Annabeth said with a shrug. "Besides, what I think she really wants is to be valued and is using stuff as a surrogate for that."

"What are you two mumbling about?" the goblin asked, turning to look at the two of us. "Are you plotting something?"

"We were just thinking how lovely your home is, and how nice it is for you to show us your collection. You're really a very nice person, and I'm glad to have met you," Annabeth said, smiling at the goblin. "Why, if you would let me, I'd like to carve you a gift sometime."

"You wish to give me a gift?" The goblin watched us. "For being nice?"

"Yes," Annabeth said, nodding. "I'd love to sculpt you something because I know you'd cherish it."

"I would cherish it. I cherish all my treasures." Leviathan took a deep breath. "Perhaps we can talk about it after we have summoned Sathanus, although I'm not sure why you need a pair of pants to do it." She raised one foot in the air. "They're long, won't fit me, so I don't see what use they'd be to her. She's not much taller than me." The goblin glared at me then. "Unless she wants them because they are mine." She pointed a finger at me accusingly. "Is that what this is about? Are you trying to help her steal my pants just because she knows I like them?"

"No," I said before she could wind herself up more. "I'm one hundred percent not trying to do that."

"Then explain yourself!" she crossed her arms over her chest.

"As I said," and before I could say more, Annabeth put a hand on my shoulder in an effort to calm me down. We'd had this conversation six times already, and I was really starting to get pissed off. "The pants have a special spell I can use to summon her. At least I think they do. If they don't, I have no idea how to find her without crossing the Burning Desert, and call me crazy, but I absolutely don't want to do that."

"Those birds aren't very nice," Annabeth agreed.

"There are birds?" Leviathan asked, turning on her heel and making her way forward. "Will I get to see them? I can't actually remember the last time I saw a real bird."

"I think you'll get to see lots of things you'll like when you come back with us," Annabeth said, moving between the goblin and me. "You'll make lots of memories you can keep forever."

"I like the sound of that." She tapped her head. "I don't remember too well." She smiled and glanced back at us. "But you think you can fix me?"

"I think there's a good shot," I said, trying to give her a reassuring smile. Truth be told, I wasn't sure if she could be fixed. I had no way of knowing what was damaged in her head or anything of the sort. All I knew was that Sally was a healer, and if I had Clarent, I could augment her abilities. Still, it might beyond the reach of even the best healers in Hell. Even with my abilities.

The plan also relied on me reforging Clarent, and I'd been unable to even start on that. I had yet to actually succeed in getting the Stygian Iron for Sam. Still, I was about to have not one, but two Armaments. That was worth a few minor delays, assuming, of course, I lived through the day.

"We're here!" Leviathan said, stopping suddenly in front of a series of dressers stacked precariously one on top of the other. She dropped down to her knees and pulled open the bottom most drawer, causing the entire structure to sway dangerously.

"Be careful," Annabeth said, eyes going wide as she watched the stack of dressers. "That may not be safe."

"Of course, it's safe," Leviathan said, tugging on a pair of scarlet chainmail pants. Only they were caught on something in the drawer. "Just needs a little effort." Her flesh began to glow with soft emerald light, and as it did, I felt my left palm heat up. I looked down at it just as she tugged the pants free.

As she held up the pants to me with one hand, the tower of dressers fell. I instinctively cringed away, one hand going to my sword.

My fingers wrapped around it as Leviathan flicked her wrist casually at the fallen dressers, suspending them in midair. They hovered there for a second as all the knickknacks and clothing that had fallen out of them went back into the drawers. Then the dressers settled back down in their tower.

"So, how are these pants supposed to work?" The goblin held them out to me. "They don't seem very special."

I reached out to take them, half expecting her to pull them away and freak the fuck out, but she didn't. Instead, she let me take them. The moment I did, I realized the problem. These felt exactly like how *The Unrelenting Grips of Greed* had felt before I'd gotten Mammon's blessing. There was no magic in them or anything. Still, I was determined to try to call Sathanus because option B, heading outside and finding her before coming back here would piss me the fuck off.

"Hmm," I said, staring at them and trying to envision the dwarven archangel. "Nothing seems to be happening." I glanced at Annabeth as I pulled out my book, hoping there might be something helpful inside. "Do you wanna try?"

"Try what?" she asked, taking them from me. Only, as her fingers wrapped around the pants, the light from her dagger, amulet, and assorted pieces of loot she'd gotten from the guardians in the cave along the way here flared to life.

"What's going on?" Envy screeched, throwing one arm up and backing away as crimson light bathed the room.

"Why have you summoned me?" Sathanus's voice boomed as she appeared overhead, her golden wings holding her easily aloft. Her gaze flitted from Annabeth to me before settling on Leviathan. "You!"

"Hello, sister," the archangel of Envy said, crossing her arms over her chest and looking up at her with an unimpressed sneer. "It's about time you showed up. We've been waiting for you forever, and you know how valuable my time is to me."

"Waiting for me?" the dwarf said, dropping down in the narrow pathway behind me. "And what is all this junk? You've turned my palace into a mess."

"Just stop," I said, making a time out gesture with my hands before things could spiral out of control. I wasn't quite sure how Annabeth had summoned her here, but I was guessing it was because her items were from Wrath's minions, and that had somehow powered the armament enough for her to sense it. Then again, I wasn't going to waste time trying to get an explanation.

"You're not the boss of me, Builder. You don't get to tell me what to do!" Sathanus snorted, reaching back for her axe. "Now step aside so I can teach the goblin some manners."

"If you could beat me, you'd have done it already." Leviathan rolled her eyes. "Now, come along like a good girl. The Builder has promised me things, and I want them."

"What is she talking about?" Sathanus asked, her bushy eyebrows knitting together in confusion. "What have you promised her?"

"That you'd come with us to our camp outside." I pointed at Envy. "You have to know she got hurt. I want my healer to fix her."

"What you want to do is impossible." Sathanus looked past me at Leviathan, and something like concern flickered across her features. "Do you not think we've tried that?" She huffed. "Do you think we're all that stupid and never thought to try to heal her ourselves?" She narrowed her eyes at me. "Well?"

"I think I'm the Builder, and so once I get Clarent repaired, I can find out if the skill exists to fix her. If it does, we can find someone to learn it." I glared right back at the Archangel of Wrath, which yes, was probably a bad idea. "Did you have that when you tried?"

"No!" she hollered back at me before she realized what she'd said. Then she blinked a couple times and rocked back on her haunches. "That is an excellent point, actually." She looked at Envy. "Very well, I shall accompany her to your village." She actually smiled, and I saw hope glimmer in her eyes. "Tis the least I could do."

Only as she said it, I realized I'd been tricked. Wrath hadn't wanted me to get rid of Envy, she'd wanted me to help her. Or at least, she'd hoped I would. How did I know that? Because I could feel it through the bond I had with Envy. It was weird to feel the goblin's emotional reaction it, along with the knowledge that the dwarf could have thrown her out if she'd wanted to. No. Envy had spent all this time waiting for the day of reckoning to come, and it never had. Interesting.

"Great," Annabeth clapped her hands. "So, all that's left is for Arthur to remake Clarent and we can help her."

"Yup," I said, hoping Annabeth was right. "But we can go to the village now, if you like."

"I don't want to go right now," Envy said, biting her lip. "Not until I know you can fix me." She swallowed. "I'm scared I'll go all that way and then have to come back still hurt."

"I could stay with you here," Sathanus said, surprising me. "Keep you company until he gets back. Would that be okay?"

"I think I would like that," Leviathan said, taking a deep breath. "As long as you don't try to steal all my stuff."

"I won't steal your stuff, Levi," Sathanus said, turning back to me. "What do you need from us to be successful?" The way she said it, let me know she knew I knew, and we could drop all the pretenses.

"I need you to mark me so I can use these pants." I held up the pants to her. "Then I need Envy's belt. Finally, I need something to present to the dwarves so they'll help me."

"I can only grant two of those things to you," Wrath said, and before I could say anything, she punched me hard in the left shoulder. Pain shot through me right before my arm lit up like it was on fire. I cried out, reaching for my shoulder with my right hand as the imprint of a red hammer began to glow through my clothing in soft red light. "That is my mark. It will fix your problem with the greaves as well as with the dwarves. It is written into their laws to help anyone bearing my mark." She smiled. "And if it doesn't work, call upon me, and I shall come to your aid." She licked her lips. "I almost want that to happen."

"Right, okay," I said, still rubbing my shoulder. It hurt, but not nearly as much as when I'd gotten Mammon's mark. Which was a little odd because that'd hurt so much, I thought I'd die. Was it because she'd had to infuse the gauntlet with power and these pants were made already? Then again, Leviathan had obviously marked me during our pact…

I glanced down at my book, wanting to flip through it and check for answers when Wrath's voice brought my attention back to her.

"Sister, will you allow the Builder the use of your

belt? It is the only way he will have the power to help you in his quest," Sathanus, took a step forward until her body was practically pressed against mine. "He'll return it when he's done."

"He already promised me that," Leviathan said, pulling her shirt back up to look at the belt. "But I'm not sure I can do it."

"You can," Sathanus said, moving past me, and practically knocking me into a pile of candelabras. Annabeth wisely stepped aside as the dwarf approached. "I know you can, Levi."

"Can you do it for me?" the goblin swallowed hard and shut her eyes. "Just take it off before I realize it's gone. I can't do it myself."

"Sure," Sathanus said, and as she reached out to undo the knot, Leviathan began to grow.

"Hurry," The archangel of Envy hissed, her eyes narrowing into serpentine slits. "I won't be able to hold back the serpent for long. She doesn't want you to take what's mine."

"As soon as I get this to you, run!" Sathanus said, fingers moving quickly to unbind the knots. "I'll hold her off until you can escape."

"We can't run all the way back, we'll never make it," I said as the dwarf pulled the belt free and offered it to me.

"You can because I know what this belt does. Take my teleport ability and use it to escape." She shoved the belt into my hands as Leviathan transformed, her massive body exploding into being as she reared back, eyes fixed on the belt.

"Mine!" the huge serpent screeched. She struck, mouth agape. Sathanus jumped in front of her, catching the massive serpent's strike on her axe and holding her back.

"Go!" Sathanus cried as I slipped the belt around my waist. The moment I did, I felt the raw pulse of Leviathan's power. She aimed to have this back if it meant killing us all, but what's more, I could see the pieces of her mind, and how they could be put back together. I just couldn't do it now.

"Arthur?" Annabeth asked, grabbing my arm as I shut my eyes and focused on Sathanus. Every ability she'd used in front of me spilled out in front of me, and I quickly grabbed hold of the teleportation one. No sooner had I done it when Leviathan threw her across the room. She slammed into an old chandelier before plunging into a pile of shoe boxes.

"There's no place like home," I muttered, clicking my heels together as the massive serpent struck once more.

18

We vanished as Leviathan's jaws closed around us. I stumbling backward into the dwarven princess's room, one arm up to shield myself while Annabeth moved to deflect the blow with the chainmail pants she'd been holding. Only the attack never came as we landed in a heap on the ground.

"What have you done?!" the princess cried, leaping to her feet and coming toward us, beer in one hand, axe in the other.

The entire room shook violently as she moved, causing the contents of her mug to slosh onto the ground. Pictures fell off the wall and shattered on the stone floor in front of us. Steins of beer fell over, spilling their contents onto the ground and bits of dust and debris fell from the cavernous ceiling.

"We hit a small hiccup," I said, trying to push myself to my feet, but with Annabeth laying on top of me, it was no use.

"Why is my entire mountain shaking?" the princess snarled, her eyes filled with a strange combination of fear and anger. "How can this be? It hasn't erupted in over ten millennia."

"It's not going to erupt," I replied as Annabeth finally managed to climb off of me. "That's Leviathan and Sathanus fighting. I think it will subside soon, but either way, you have to help us." I pulled down the collar of my shoulder, revealing the Mark of Wrath blazing on my left shoulder.

"That wasn't our agreement," the princess said, but it didn't seem like there was a lot of fight in her words. Still, that didn't stop her from coming over to me and glaring down her nose at me. "Our agreement was for you to get rid of the dragon who resides within our former stronghold." Another tremor shook the room. "There was supposed to be treasure, not earthquakes."

"Yeah, I said there was a hiccup," I replied, taking

Annabeth's hand and letting her help me to my feet.

"Put them on," she said, shoving the Merciless Greaves of Wrath into my hands. "I dunno what's going on down there, but you may need the boost in power if Leviathan breaks through."

She needn't have bothered saying anything. The moment I touched the greaves, I felt the pulse of Wrath's power. It reminded me of a pressure cooker right about to blow its lid and start screaming. The thing was, I could also tell that her battle with the Archangel of Envy, for better or worse, was winding down.

"What kind of hiccup?" the princess asked as the room shook again, causing the barrel of ale in the corner to fall over and roll against the far wall. That had been worse than the others. What was going on down there?

"Can you hear me?" Sathanus's voice broke into my mind.

"Y-yeah, I can hear you," I said aloud almost too stunned by the intrusion to reply at all.

"That doesn't make any sense, nor does it answer

my question," the dwarven princess said, glancing back at the barrel as an aftershock shook the room.

"Good!" Sathanus thundered. "I think Levi is tired out, and she'll nap for a while on account of the statue I broke over her head. I'm coming to you."

There was a flash of light in front of my eyes like a thousand fucking daggers stabbing me in the brain. The greaves in my hand turned superheated, and as I tried to scream and drop them, a burst of plasma exploded from the mark on my shoulder. The whole of the room shimmered with silver light like it was covered in a glowing spider's web. The crimson flash of energy tearing through me hit the web like a bowling ball, tearing a hole through the threads.

"Ahhh!" I cried, shutting my eyes and trying to think of something, anything but the heat pouring off my shoulder. I stumbled backward, one hand reaching out to the wall for balance, but my fingers melted through the stone, tearing molten gouts in the wall as I slid to the floor.

"Wasn't sure that'd work." As the dwarven archangel's voice filled my ears, the pain vanished. My eyes fluttered open to find her standing in front of me while the remains of the tattered silver web fizzled and went dark. "Changed my mind about staying with Levi now that you're safe, well, relatively speaking anyway. Besides, me staying there is just gonna piss off her dragon half." Sathanus shrugged and moved to wipe some dust off her acid-pocked armor. "When she wakes up as a goblin, she might be more amenable to waiting."

I wasn't sure if that was true, but most of me didn't care. I had shit to do, and dealing with the psychotic Leviathan now that I had the armament and mark was the last thing I wanted to do.

"W-who are you?" the princess asked from behind Sathanus, and as I looked, I saw the dwarf standing there open-mouthed. So far, the dwarven princess had been pretty unflappable, but Sathanus's presence had definitely flapped her.

"I am Sathanus," the Archangel of Wrath said, whirling to glare at the dwarven princess. "Archangel of Wrath and mother of your entire race." She pointed to the ground. "Now kneel and show me respect."

The princess dropped to the ground, prostrating herself before the archangel, and for a second, I wondered if it had been of her own volition or if

Sathanus had made it happen somehow. Judging by the absolutely perfect stillness displayed by the princess, I was betting Sathanus had done something.

"Good," Sathanus said, clearly amused. "Do not speak until spoken to because I'm about to tell you what you will do." She gestured back at me. "The Builder has received my Mark, and in so doing has broken the ties your foremothers placed upon me. I can now leave this mountain and go wherever I please. I will be doing so." She inhaled sharply. "Perhaps after I have a drink." She reached down beside the prone princess and pulled the mug out of the girl's hand. Then Sathanus gulped the contents down.

"Wait, Arthur freed you?" Annabeth asked, and her voice was barely a whisper. As I turned toward her, the Archangel of Wrath did the same.

"Yes." Sathanus nodded before tossing the mug over her shoulder. It hit the ground with a crash, shattering into a billion shards of glass. "I was bound below, but now that I have shared my mark with one who is not bound, the binding is broken." She smiled evilly as the last glowing remnants of the web finally died. "What? You thought I was helping because I'm nice? I'm the Archangel of Wrath, dearie." She raised her axe and took a tentative swipe through the air. "Now then, I have some murder and mayhem to unleash upon those who imprisoned me, so if you'll excuse me." She gave me a salute with her axe.

"Wait!" I cried, holding out my hands, which admittedly was a bit awkward since I was still holding the greaves. "That wasn't part of our deal."

"You're right, I did promise to make them help you, didn't I. That seems like a perfect punishment for them," she said, glaring at the princess. "Do whatever Arthur wants, and I won't slaughter your whole race for pissing me off. Remember, I made you. I can unmake you just the same." Wrath vanished, leaving us standing there like idiots.

"What did you do?" the princess snarled, leaping to her feet and charging me like an undersized bull. She poked me hard in the chest with one stubby finger. "How could you release the Archangel of Wrath? What the fuck is wrong with you?"

"Would you believe me if I said it was an accident?" I asked sheepishly. "Besides, none of this would have happened if you'd told me, or better still helped me." I gestured angrily at her with the greaves. "I came here to get material to fix my sword, and you sent me on a long ass quest." I glared at her. "Tell me, will your treasure matter even one iota when Dred comes to kill you all?"

"Your job was to get rid of Envy, not free Wrath," she retorted, completely ignoring my point. "I'm guessing ye didn't get rid of her either since Wrath said she knocked Envy out." The Princess harrumphed hard before throwing her hands up. "And now I have to help ye because if I don't, she'll kill us all." She gave me a glare that could melt stone. "So, thanks for that, ye fucking fuck."

"You know, the language isn't necessary," I said, pulling on the greaves because I was tired of carrying them. I mean, I'd fucked up by releasing Wrath, but hey, on the other hand, what was the worst Wrath could do, right? Right?

"When I want shit from you, I'll squeeze your head," the princess snapped but made no move to stop me from pulling on the greaves. It was a bit strange because as I secured them with Envy's belt, I felt a surge of energy run from Mammon's gauntlets on my hands, through the belt around my waist, and into the greaves.

The entire room slowed down. I could see every last dust mote in the air. Hell, I could hear every sound in the room, and what's more, I could pick out each and every source. The whole thing only took a split second, but as it did, I felt the power of the three armaments I wore and knew that if I wanted to, I could kill everyone in this town, and it would be easy. No, it would be less than easy. After all, they'd offended me, and they owed me things. I could take those things, make them mine. I knew how to use them better, anyway.

I shook myself, trying to push back the thoughts as my whole world tilted sideways. My hand went to the hilt of my sword, and before I realized what I was doing, my blade was drawn. Sapphire energy cascaded off the blade as my gauntlets began to glow with soft silver light, my belt lit up like an emerald sparkler, and my greaves filled with crimson energy.

As I took a step forward, the temperature in the room dropped, and frost was left behind in my wake.

"No. You will be nice." My words came out in an icy mist as I pointed my sword at her. "I came to ask for your help, to ask you to teach me the ins and outs of mining so I could get the material myself, but I've changed my mind." The princess finally seemed to realize I'd moved, and her eyes filled with terror as she looked down at the glowing sword pointed at her chest. "See, I've been going about this all wrong." My free hand curled into a fist as a surge of anger came over me. "I've been trying to work with all you people, trying to work the system, but the system isn't working. It's time for all that to end."

"Arthur, what are you doing?" Annabeth asked, confusion filling her voice.

"I want Stygian Iron, and I want it now. Give me what you have, or I'll take it. You won't like it if I do." I sheathed my sword and ambled over to the table. Voices continued to cackle in my skull like a flock of crows, but at least we were in agreement. We wanted something, and they'd give it to us or else. My gauntlet-covered hand closed around a mug of ale, and as I raised it to my lips, I glanced back at the princess.

"Why are you still here? Go get my metal before I get *really* angry." I made a shooing motion toward the princess, but her eyes were still tracking my movements, still following me to the chair. As she completed the motion, the wind displaced from my motion hit her full on, throwing her back through the door and into the hall. As she hit the far wall outside, I turned to the empty seat next to me. "Come, Annabeth. Have a seat."

19

"What do you mean that's all you have?" I asked, glaring at the small handful of black ingots Mina had offered me. I wasn't quite sure where the princess was, but I hadn't seen her since she'd left to get the metal a couple hours ago. Since then, Annabeth and I had been waiting here trying to make the best of things. It hadn't been so bad because the dwarves had finally given us food and drink, though I wasn't sure what Annabeth had said to the two guards outside to get them to do it.

"Stygian Iron is nearly impossible to extract from the ground, and even harder to purify into ore." Mina pointed at what had to be less than a hundred grams of the stuff. "This is all we've got."

"What about armor, weapons, cookie sheets?" I growled, slamming one fist onto the table. I got to my feet and came around the long table. Clearly, she wasn't taking me seriously. I wanted something from her, something I deserved, and they weren't giving it to me after I'd been nice enough to let them live. "This can't be all you have. This is a mountain full of dwarves. Go bring me all the metal. Now." I glared at her as my hand inched toward my sword. "Or next time I won't be so nice."

"We figured you'd ask for stuff like that," Mina said, placing a handful of pictures on the table in front of me. "We have nothing made of Stygian iron. The items you see pictured have some designs painted with it, but there are scant amounts of it. Even if we took it all, it wouldn't even be a third of what's on the table." She gestured at the dark pieces of metal. "There really isn't any. We're not hiding it from you. The absolute last thing we want is for Wrath to come back more pissed off."

"So, this whole trip has been worthless," I said, gripping the table so hard, the wood started to creak. I needed the metal to reforge Clarent, and while I wasn't a blacksmith, I could tell what we had wouldn't do the job. We'd need a lot more than this. "Why didn't you tell me before I spent the last few hours sitting here? My time is fucking valuable."

"Your time hasn't been wasted," Mina said, hands going up defensively, and as I looked at her, I wondered if she expected me to attack her. "I can help you get more iron." She showed me a copy of the contract I'd brought with me. The one that showed the node for Stygian Iron. It was where I'd planned to go once I'd learned how to pull the stuff out of the ground.

"How can you help me get it?" I gestured at the paper in her hands. "That metal is at the bottom of a goddamned volcano, and I don't know how to get it out."

"That's why I'm here. I know more about Stygian Iron mining than anywhere on the planet." She pointed at those ingots. "Who do you think got those?"

"Arthur, before you get angry, I think you should consider her offer. If she comes with us, maybe it will work out," Annabeth said, putting a hand on my shoulder. Her touch had a calming effect on me, which was weird because I hadn't realized how angry I'd become.

"Fine," I said, holding out my hands to the two of them. "Let's go."

Mina stared at me dumbly but made no motion to come to me.

"Just do it," Annabeth said, pocketing the few ingots of Stygian Iron before taking my hand. "Arthur can teleport."

"How?" Mina asked, taking a tentative step forward. "How could he possibly do that?"

"I used the Armament I got from the Archangel of Envy to borrow the ability from Sathanus," I said, tapping my ouroboros belt buckle with one finger before reaching out to her again. "I can teleport until I decide to replace it with a new power."

"Seems handy," Mina said, but I got the impression she still didn't believe me. Either way, she took my hand.

"It is," I whispered, concentrating on the coordinates for the Stygian Iron deposit. I had a vague idea where it was, and as I felt Wrath's power come over me and mix with that of Envy's belt, I could clearly see the mountain in my mind's eye. It was huge and covered in snow, but from the look of things, it didn't appear dangerous or active. Now the cone of the volcano was solid rock. "When was the last time this volcano erupted?"

"Mount Asmosuvius hasn't erupted in a long time. We shouldn't have to worry about that," Mina said, nodding once. "Though that is one of the reasons we haven't managed to extract the material."

"Because it could trigger an eruption?" I asked, concerned. "Should we try elsewhere?"

"There's nowhere else to try. There is Stygian Iron spread throughout the whole of Hell, but each deposit will only yield an ingot similar to the ones you have. We could spend weeks mining them and barely increase what you have by a third. This is our best bet, assuming you're strong enough to get it." Mina took a deep breath, and for some reason, the way she had said it bugged me.

"I guess we'll see," I grumbled, reaching out to the spell stored within my belt and triggering it. There was a flash of lightning in my mind, and then we were standing atop the peak.

Cold cut through me like an arctic blast, and as I

stood there, trying to acclimate myself to it, Annabeth cried out.

"It's so cold!" Annabeth screeched, wrapping her arms around her body. "I think I'm going to die." Her teeth chattered as she spoke. Beside me, Mina was also shivering, her knees knocking together so hard, I began to wonder what was going on.

Sure, it was cold, but not to the degree they seemed to be experiencing. No, it was more like when I went outside in my boxers on an October morning. Cold, sure, but not unbearable.

That's when I realized the ice beneath my feet was starting to melt. Steam curled upward from it, and I could feel something deep below calling to me, something familiar that made my heart hammer. It was weird because I could have sworn I felt Gwen with me, felt her wrapping her arms around me and keeping me warm. Only, how could that be possible?

I wasn't sure, but now wasn't the time to find out. No. Right now I needed to figure out how to help my friends. "This won't work," I said, glancing at Mina and Annabeth before grabbing their hands.

In an instant, we were back inside the dwarven

stronghold. The sudden change in temperature was unnerving, but nice in a weird way. It was sort of like stepping into a warm lodge after an afternoon skiing.

"Mina, get us proper supplies for the trip," I said, kneeling beside Annabeth and running my hands up and down her arms in an effort to warm her up. "Are you okay?"

"I will be," she said, nuzzling toward me for warmth. "Oh, you're so warm." Her breath was hot on my neck as she spoke, and then she wrapped her arms around me, pulling my body against hers.

"Don't mind me," Mina said, getting to her feet and stumbling toward the door. Her beard was covered with frost, and she was breathing hard, but at the same time, she seemed way better off than Annabeth. "I'll get the gear and meet you back here in a few minutes."

It wasn't a few minutes. It was more like an hour, but when Mina returned, she had a lot more than warm clothes. While Annabeth changed into her new duds, I opted only to take a warm cloak because they didn't have anything that'd fit me.

Besides, I'd felt warm enough thanks to the heat surge in my chest, whatever that was.

"What is all this?" I asked, glancing at the three backpacks the dwarf had brought. They were laden with gear.

"Food, water, tent, sleeping bags, few pairs of socks." She nodded to me. "Mine also has some miscellaneous mining tools, and I'll be bringing my lucky pick." She tapped the weapon as it hung from a loop on her belt. "Admittedly, since you can run us back and forth, we don't need to stay out there, but at the same time, I wanted to be prepared." She offered me a stoppered black bottle. "Drink this."

"What is it?" I asked, eyeing it carefully as I took it from her.

"A warming potion. Should help keep away the worst of the cold. You'll need it especially if all you're taking is a cloak." She shrugged. "Or don't and freeze to death. It isn't like I care. If you die, I'll just slit you from throat to crotch and crawl inside you for warmth."

"Fair enough," I said, popping the top but before I could take a drink, Annabeth snatched it from my hands.

"Let me try it first, that way if something happens to me, you'll know." Then before I could tell her I didn't want her to risk herself for me, she took a long gulp of the liquid. Her skin began to glow faintly red before the effect faded. "Ugh, it tastes like cod liver oil."

"I've never actually had that before," I said, watching her. "Do you feel okay otherwise?"

"Yeah," she stuck her tongue out like she was trying to look at it. "I think you're safe."

"Of course, he's safe. If we did something to him, Wrath would smite us. As a rule, I don't want to get smote." Mina shook her head. "Now let's go, daylight is burning, and it will be colder at night. Much colder."

"Got it," I said, taking my own drink. The vile liquid seemed to touch every part of my soul as the taste of fish, liver, and the all-consuming anger of Hades itself slid down my throat. Then I was suddenly warm. So warm, it was actually uncomfortable.

"Good, let's go. It's starting to get a might hot in here, and I absolutely don't want to take off my clothes in front of you." Mina gave me a sour look and held out her hand to me.

"That's where you're supposed to say 'no offense,'" I replied, taking her hand while offering my other one to Annabeth who took it.

"That so," Mina said, looking me over. "Interesting."

With that, I stepped back through the void and onto the frozen mountain.

20

The ice crunched beneath my feet as I cinched my cloak tighter and made my way around the volcano. The top wasn't actually that big, maybe a hundred feet or so in diameter, but it made up for that in wind. Because we were a bit lower than the lip, the wind sort of funneled down into the crater, making it so most of the snow was over a foot deep.

We'd spent some time clearing away a small patch, and now Annabeth and Mina were busy setting up camp, giving me time to try to locate the Stygian Iron deposit. There was just one problem. Even with the *Relentless Grips of Greed*, I couldn't tell where the big nodes were. All around me, tooltips popped up indicating Stygian Iron, but since I had no way of knowing which one was the biggest, I was worried I'd have to pull them all up.

Before, I could sort of go by the difficulty and depth to ascertain how large the source might be, but all of them were at max difficulty. What's more, there were a lot of other high difficulty ores sprinkled about. I wasn't sure what any of them were, nor what they were used for, but something told me they'd be valuable too. Still, that was something I could discuss with Mina.

As the marker for the next Stygian Iron node appeared in my vision, I moved toward it, taking a quick glance at the tooltip.

Stygian Iron

Material Type: metal

Grade: S (Average)

Depth: 6,000 meters

Difficulty: 10

Proficiency: 0/100

Overall Proficiency: 10/100

A type of hellion iron typically used in the construction of powerful weapons and armor.

It was just like the others, giving me no indication as to how much of it there actually was. Still, I marked it anyway by planting one of the stakes in the snow over the top. Mina had asked me to do that, and I was hoping that, by the time I was done, we'd be able to come up with a game plan.

It took the better part of an hour to mark all thirty-six nodes. As I headed back toward the small camp the girls had made, I could see smoke rising into the air from a fire. I glanced up at the peaks rising above our small crater, worried the rising heat might melt the snow and cause an avalanche, but they were situated out away from the peak, making it likely that if the snow did come crashing down, it'd miss us and roll on down the mountain.

"Want something to drink?" Annabeth asked, offering me a cup of steaming liquid as I approached. "It's dwarven tea."

"Sure," I said, taking the cup and blowing on the steam. Truth be told, I didn't need it because I didn't really feel cold. I knew part of it was due to the potion and the cloak, but a lot more of it came from the pulsing heat in my chest. That had been part of the reason I'd walked around the crater. I'd hoped I could find what was making it go crazy, but unfortunately, the pulse seemed strong and steady no matter where I stood on the mountain.

The tea itself was good, if a bit strong, reminding me of the horrible stuff my boss had always liked at the Seven Eleven. Way too many spices and a bit too sweet. Still, it was something, and since I didn't know when my next break would be, I was inclined to stand by the fire and take a minute.

"That log should burn for about four hours," Mina said, tapping her covered wrist. "I have a timer set to alert me about a half hour before so I can put the next one on." She glanced at the sky and stared at the swirling mass of colors overhead for a minute. "We should plan on vacating before the second log burns."

"Why?" I asked, watching her carefully. "That's the second time you've brought it up, and I find it hard to believe it is a temperature thing." I gestured to where she had a few more bottles of the warming potion. There was even another bottle with a yellow label and the words XD on them. "You have lots of potions."

"I'm worried about the guardian, not the cold." She wrapped her arms around her chest. "Not that the cold is a picnic."

"What guardian?" I asked, my interest piqued. It was a little weird because instead of being scared or worried, I felt a rush of adrenaline at the thought of a fight. Only that wasn't like me. Normally, I was a bit more cautious, a bit more careful. That wasn't me anymore, or at least now. Now I wanted the guardian to come so I could show it who was the boss.

"There's an old legend about a guardian who comes in the dead of night." Mina gave me a sheepish shrug. "Not sure if it's real or not, but I don't really want to find out."

"You're scared of an old wives tale?" Annabeth asked, looking up from her spot a little ways from the fire. She looked like she was sculpting something out of a giant block of ice, though I couldn't quite tell the shape.

"Those stories come from somewhere," the dwarf said, trudging over to me. "You wanna stay and check it out, be my guest, but I'd rather sleep the night in my warm bed." She moved like she was going to smack me on the back, but then thought better of it. "Anyway, let's go look at the nodes you marked."

"Alright," I said, walking off toward the closest one. It was only a few meters away, but I quickly found the dwarf had a lot harder time moving through the snow than I did thanks to her short legs. "Want me to carry you?"

"I certainly do not!" she hollered, already red-faced as she kicked a path through the snow.

"Fine," I said, shrugging as I turned from the spot I'd marked and glanced at the tooltip the gauntlets conjured up.

Stygian Iron

Material Type: metal

Grade: S (Average)

Depth: 5,768 meters

Difficulty: 10

Proficiency: 0/100

Overall Proficiency: 10/100

A type of hellion iron typically used in the construction of powerful weapons and armor.

The node was still there, and while I hadn't expected it to move, I had to be sure.

"Say, how do you mine Stygian Iron?" I asked, watching her try to use my footsteps as a way to get to me. Only her legs weren't long enough for that either, and she fell face first into a snow drift. When she came up, her beard was a sheet of sleet and ice, and her wool cap was frosty and white.

"Normally, you don't," Mina said, finally reaching me and staring at the stake. "You get trace amounts of it with other ore. The best way to think about it is like a giant claw that grips other kinds of metal." She tapped the stake. "I'm guessing there's a deposit of some other kind of metal here too, right?"

"Yeah," I said, glancing at the tooltip to be sure.

Red Steel

Material Type: metal

Grade: A (Average)

Depth: 5,768 meters

Difficulty: 8

Proficiency: 0/100

Overall Proficiency: 10/100

A type of hellion metal typically used in the construction of projectile weapons.

"Something called Red Steel," I said, scrunching up my face. "Although I'm fairly certain steel is an alloy."

"Red Steel is quite valuable. It's normally used to make arrowheads and the like because while being incredibly light, it's incredibly durable and can be sharpened to a razor's edge. It almost never dulls afterward." She looked at the marker for a moment. "My guess is that the Stygian Iron is wrapped around the Red steel, or at least a lot of it is."

"So, what would you suggest?" I asked, wondering if it would be possible to untangle the two metals underground. I didn't have high hopes for that though. Something told me they'd only become separated in the refining process.

"I suggest you pull the Red Steel up if you can. Most of the Stygian Iron will come up with it. Then maybe you can pull up what's left with your magic or we can move to the next node." Mina shrugged. "Red Steel isn't hard to mine usually, so you ought to be able to get it with your nifty gloves." She gestured at my gauntlets.

"Seems reasonable, but I'm still not familiar with the Red Steel," I said, reaching out toward it with my power. It was way down there, and it took a bit longer than I was used to for my power to grab ahold of it. Only as I tried to tug it free like I had with most of the other stones, the thing barely moved. What's more, it was so difficult stars practically flashed across my vision.

"The thing about Red Steel is that it sort of wants to come up out of the ground. It is often shaped with a fat blunt end on one side that tapers off, giving it little hang-ups. Typically, when it's mined, we drill down to it and attach an anchor to the chunk. Then we use Earth magic to sort of squeeze the ore up while pulling on the chain. Only, the ground here is too hard to do that, being frozen and all. It's why we've never mined here."

"That and the guardian, anyway," I murmured as I thought about what she'd said. The words made sense with what I could feel through the gauntlets. I could feel a massive lump beneath the surface that sort of reminded me of a pimple. Only it was way the fuck down there.

"That too, yes," Mina agreed as I let go of the Red Steel. She'd said the ground here was too hard to dig, and while I agreed with her in principle, I wasn't trying to dig the ground. I was trying to pull something through it via magic. That might prove to be impossible, but I had an idea.

Concentrating on the Red Steel once more, I focused on the earth beneath it and above it. The whole thing appeared in my mind's eye as I pushed power into nudging the rock above the steel out of the way while pressing on the earth below. My chest started to heave, and sweat dripped down my face as I forced more power into it, and the weird thing was, it worked.

As the Red Steel shifted upward, the displaced earth was drawn in by my power and sucked underneath it, making the whole thing seem just this side of possible.

Sucking in a deep breath, I reached out with the power the Archangel of Greed had given me and infused it with that of Envy and Wrath. As I did the heat in my chest began to pulse once more. The ground beneath my feet began to steam again, and the snow began to melt as the metal was thrust up from the ground.

"Holy shit!" Mina said, staring at me open-mouthed. "You did that in only a few minutes." She moved toward the rock as I sat down on the snow, trying to catch my breath as the power I'd called dissipated. I was suddenly ravenous.

"This is really high-quality stuff." She held up the baseball sized nugget of Red Steel. "You see this blackened area around the bottom?" She touched the tail end of the ore where it looked like it'd been dyed black. "That's all Stygian Iron. Normally Red Steel tapers off pretty severely, so I'm guessing at least half of this area is Stygian Iron."

"Great," I said, getting to my feet. "How do we extract it from the Red Steel?"

"Oh, you'd need a really skilled Blacksmith for that." She shrugged. "You'd have to ask them, but even still." She glanced at the other markers. "Let's get the others done before we worry about the details."

21

I spent the next eight hours mining as well as I could, and it'd been pretty much the same routine the entire time. Mina would tell me how the dwarves typically mined a type of ore, and I'd try to mimic the system with my Gauntlets. Sometimes it worked, sometimes it didn't, but after eight hours we had what I thought might be enough even if it was only about half of what was here.

That said, I wanted to get it all just in case, but that'd involve spending another day out here, and as much as I wanted to press on, Mina was definitely starting to get worried. She kept glancing at the sky and hounding me. It was starting to piss me off. For one, I didn't have time to runaway and hide from a goddamned urban legend. For two, this mountaintop was mine. I owned it, and no ghost was going to scare me away before I was ready.

"Just one more," I said, looking at the marker for number seventeen. "That's just Red Steel, and I'm getting pretty good at it."

"No." Mina crossed her arms over her huge chest. "I don't want to get eaten by the guardian."

"There is no guardian," I said, and as I spoke, the heat in my chest pulsed. It'd been doing that more and more over the last eight hours, and now it felt like I had a sun beneath my ribcage. Thankfully, it didn't hurt, or I'd be worried, but either way, I was content to ignore it for one simple fact. It was definitely helping me extract the ore, and I knew that if we came back tomorrow, I'd have to start over building whatever charge had filled me.

"Spoken like someone too stupid to live," Mina replied, turning and moving back toward the camp. "Now come on. We only have a few minutes left before the second log goes out."

"Put the third log on, Mina." I gestured at the marker a few feet away. "I'll be there as soon as I get this one. Unless you have some way off the mountain that doesn't involve me."

"You're going to get us all killed," she cried, glaring at me with a mixture of anger and fear. I had the upper hand though. She couldn't teleport back without me. She'd just have to wait a few more minutes.

I turned back toward the Red Steel and looked at the tooltip.

Red Steel

Material Type: metal

Grade: A (Average)

Depth: 3,464 meters

Difficulty: 7

Proficiency: 10/100

Overall Proficiency: 12/100

A type of hellion metal typically used in the construction of projectile weapons.

"Well, that's interesting," I mumbled, circling the marker. All the Red Steel I'd pulled up before now had been difficulty eight and had been a lot deeper. Why was this one so much higher? I wasn't sure, but I felt a bit dumb as I looked at it. I should have started here. "Well, guess Mina will get her wish."

Using the gauntlet's power, I reached out toward it with my mind. As I grabbed hold of it and mimicked the extraction technique I'd used about a half dozen times so far, something punched me in the side of the head.

My temples exploded with agony as I went flying across the frozen plain and slammed into a rocky outcropping. Spots danced across my eyes as a shadow fell over me. As I tried to blink back my suddenly blurry vision, I found myself looking at a Ravager.

The damned thing was huge and black even compared to the ravagers I'd seen before. Its many limbs undulated with pure darkness as it leaned in close to me, chest eyes narrowed angrily. Its fetid breath hit me with enough force to melt the surrounding snow, and as I looked up at it, I saw purple energy glowing within it.

"You shall not have her. She is for the Destroyer!" it screeched, and the words raked across my mind like a cheese grater. My vision went black around the edges as it raised one clawed foot to stomp me into a pancake, and crazily, the only thing I could think was, "it can talk?"

The Darkness creatures I'd fought until now had hardly spoken a word. Hell, I hadn't even considered whether they could. Even when we'd captured ravagers, they hadn't exactly been brimming founts of conversation.

"Have who?" I asked, rolling to the side as the ravager stomped a hole in the snow where I'd been a moment before. Power thrummed through me as I pulled my sword from its sheath. My three Armaments began to blaze with light as I pointed my sword at the creature and unleashed a Sapphire Blast.

"You shall not have her!" it repeated, shrugging off my attack like I'd thrown a fly at it.

The ravager stomped toward me, and the whole world shook as the sky flashed and thundered. It was then that I realized I could see the crackling outline of a portal above. Only this one was different. Purple energy tethered it shut, and what's more, those same tethers were linked to the ravager.

"I don't know what you're babbling about." I dodged as another blow whipped by me with enough force to ruffle my hair. Even with the enhanced speed granted to me by the Armaments, this motherfucker was as fast as I was.

"Stop moving," it snarled, the words spraying fetid green slime across the snow that sizzled and popped. The smell of sulfur hit my nose as I called upon the strength of my Armaments, and as I did, I felt Sathanus take notice of the creature. It was weird, knowing she could see through my eyes, but I was sort of glad it had happened.

Why? Because she got pissed, and not in the 'oh no there's a Darkness Warrior' way, I'd seen before. No. This was an immense, gut-churning hatred.

The ravager swung at me again. As I tried to leap the blow, a tentacle exploded from its flesh, lashing around my ankle and flinging me to the side like I was the end of a whip. My entire body snapped painfully, and my sword slipped from my hand.

As it flew across the tundra, Sathanus appeared beside me and swung her axe. The blade hit the tentacle with a loud thwack that sent me flying off after my sword. My body slammed into the ground a few feet away, carving an agony-filled furrow into the snow.

"Release her!" Sathanus snarled, her massive wings unfurling to glint in the light. "Now."

"You shall not have her!" the ravager replied right before it stomped on the dwarf. Sathanus's free hand shot up, catching the huge foot and holding it aloft. Her muscles strained, cording with effort as the ravager used the combined force of its weight, its strength, and gravity in general to push down on the dwarven archangel.

The ground beneath her feet cracked, furrows rushing out in every direction, and as it did, the heat inside me pulsed. Purple fissures opened across the flesh of the ravager, and it screamed loud enough to shatter my eardrums.

"What's going on?" I cried, getting to my feet so I could help Sathanus. Only I wasn't sure how. Never before had I even seen a ravager get hurt. The only time I'd ever seen them die had been when I'd broken the Graveyard of Statues free, and the resulting explosion had melted them. Only there was no way to mimic that, was there?

"Arthur, I can't beat it alone," Sathanus said, conceding the test of strength with the beast and leaping to the side. The ravager's foot slammed down, burying itself to the halfway point in the stone.

"What can I do?" I asked, picking up my fallen sword. I wanted to fight the ravager, but I wasn't sure how. The damned thing was so big I could hardly hurt it with my sword. "I'm not sure how to stop it."

"Get my sisters. Bring them here." She glanced at me. "Envy first, preferably. She's bigger."

"Right, okay!" I said, not sure I wanted to leave Sathanus here by herself. Still, she was the Archangel of Wrath. If she couldn't hold this thing back, what chance did I have? That was also when I realized something. The greaves I wore meant it took seven times the damage from every hit it had dealt me, and from the look of things, it wasn't fazed at all. Damn.

"Now would be good," Sathanus said, slashing at the ravager again, and as her axe bounced off the creature's flesh in a flurry of sparks, I teleported.

I appeared back in the room where I'd last left the goblin. She lay in a pile of clothes that looked more like a nest than anything else, and as I approached, her eyes snapped open.

"You!" she screeched, leaping to her feet and coming toward me, only it seemed like she wasn't looking at me. No, she was looking off into the distance. As she reached me, she blinked a couple times, eyes finally focusing on me. "My sister needs me. Take me to her." The final words came out in a hiss, and I could already see her body elongating as I grabbed her arm and teleported back to the summit.

As we reappeared, the heat inside my chest became so intense, I could barely breathe. Sathanus was airborne now, busily slashing at the ravager's thick hide. More purple fissures had opened up along its body, and the portal above pulsed and sparked.

"What's going on?" I asked as Leviathan tore herself from my grip.

"Stole what's mine!" Leviathan snarled, her body elongating into her monstrous dragon form. She leapt for the ravager like she was going to smother it beneath her bulk. "Must give her back!"

I wanted to ask more, but now wasn't the time. No, now was the time to get Mammon and complete the triad. I vanished once more.

"Arthur? How'd you do that?" Gwen asked, her face

awash with shock as I turned to Mammon who was standing just a few feet away. The two of them were in the middle of what looked like a hotel room, and there was a half-eaten meal on the table as well as two empty bottles of wine.

"We don't have time for questions," Mammon said, grabbing my arm. "Let's go." She took a deep breath before turning her gaze to Gwen. "You too, Gwen."

"Wait, what's going on?" Gwen asked. "One second we were eating, and the next you were saying we needed to go, and Arthur would come." She met my eyes. "Just give me a second."

"Sorry," I said, doing as Mammon said and grabbing Gwen's wrist. "It'll make sense when we're there."

I vanished, and as I reappeared, my chest suddenly felt like it would explode. Gwen's scream filled my ears as darkness exploded across my vision. I felt myself falling into a blast furnace as heat ripped up through my chest. Beyond the heat, I could feel was Gwen's wrist in my hand. Her power pulsed like a live wire, far beyond what I'd ever felt from her or anyone save the archangels.

22

"Arthur, get up!" Mammon cried, and her voice was like a bucket of ice water. It washed away the flame threatening to consume me from within, driving the fire back enough for me to think, to move, to do something.

Gwen lay on the ground beside me, her mouth open, and her eyes distant. Purple flames writhed along her flesh, and as I moved toward her, I realized they weren't actually burning her. Relief swept through me as I turned toward Mammon.

"What the fuck is going on? She's on fucking fire!" I cried as purple wings burst from the ravager's back. The massive creature sprang into the air, chasing after Sathanus who had taken to the air. A quick glance around the battlefield revealed why. Leviathan had reverted back to her goblin form and lay unconscious on the tundra. It was back to a one-on-one battle. That should have scared me, should have made me want to run away, but I was too concerned for Gwen to do that.

"That's no ordinary ravager," Mammon said, her eyes full silver as she drew out her left hand, causing a silver cat-o'-nine-tails to appear in her grasp. Its silver-hewn form glinted in the light as her silver wings extended from her back.

"I got that," I snarled. "How do we stop it, and more importantly, what happened to Gwen?"

"She's a succubus," Mammon said like that explained everything.

Overhead, Sathanus dodged a series of tentacles too numerous for me to count as she plunged through the mass and smashed her axe into the underside of the ravager's chin. The blow snapped the creature's head back, but before she could capitalize on the blow, more tentacles shot out, knocking the Archangel of Wrath away.

"I know she's a succubus," I snapped, glaring at Mammon. I was torn between wanting to help them defeat the purple-winged ravager and wanting to teleport Gwen away. Only, I wasn't sure doing that would help. More importantly, though, I needed to know why Mammon had wanted Gwen here because it seemed like she'd known this would happen.

"Because right now, that ravager is the host for Asmodai!" Mammon pointed at the ravager. "And as you can see, the thing is doing a piss poor job of it." Her gaze flicked to Gwen. "Gwen will be better."

"I'm not following," I said as Mammon lifted into the air, intent on helping Sathanus.

"Arthur, we only have one shot to crack that son of a bitch open and pull Asmodai free of the darkness twisting her soul. Do as I say and we *might* live." Mammon reached out one hand toward the portal. "Cut those bindings open and throw Gwen inside. Doing so will cause what's left of Asmodai to leap from the portal she bound shut with her power into her new host."

"I won't sacrifice Gwen," I said, glaring at Mammon. "I can't do that."

"She'll be fine," Mammon lied before her face softened. "Well, mostly. Either way, it's our best bet at stopping this ravager. Those things are designed to take down archangels. Their powers nullify a lot of our strength. Our magic just slides off of them." She took a deep breath. "I have to go now, Arthur. Trust me. Do this, or we lose." She took off, hurtling toward the creature as it pounded on Sathanus, knocking the dwarf around like a ping pong ball.

"Fuck!" I cried, feeling suddenly helpless as I watched the battle because I knew Mammon was right. That thing had already taken down Leviathan, and from the look of things, Sathanus was going down next. Worse, I had the sneaking suspicion that while powerful, Mammon wasn't on the level of Wrath.

While I wasn't sure what had happened with Asmodai and the ravager, it was obvious this fucker was going to kill Sathanus and Mammon. It became even more obvious when Mammon smashed into the monster like a runaway train, and the blow from her cat-o'-nine-tails didn't even cause the behemoth to look up.

"Arthur, do it," Gwen said from next to me, and at her words, I felt the warmth within me pulse. She swallowed hard and sat up. "I can feel something in there calling to me." She pointed toward the portal. "It's so familiar." She took a deep breath. "I can't explain it, but I know what I need to do."

"We don't know what it is, Gwen." I took a deep breath, meeting her eyes. "I can't lose you. I won't—"

"It's not your choice," Gwen said. Flame licked up and down her body as she got to her feet and faced me. "It's mine." She stumbled slightly, and I reached out to catch her. The moment I touched her flesh, a firecracker exploded inside my chest. Warmth and pain beyond my imagining seemed to electrify me to the core of my soul.

She kissed me then, and the feel of her lips on my drove the pain away, drove everything away until there was literally nothing but the feel of her mouth on mine. She broke it a second later, and as she did, longing hit me like a kick in the crotch. I doubled over with the need for her, and as I reached toward her, wanting only to taste her one more time, to hold her one more time, she shoved me backward.

"Arthur, let me do something you'll respect for fucking once," she said, leaping into the air, her bat wings carrying her toward the bound portal. Only, as she flew toward it, the massive ravager caught sight of her.

It turned, ignoring Sathanus and Mammon completely as the two archangels hit it with everything they had. It darted through the air toward her on lavender wings, cutting through the sky so quickly, I knew it'd catch her long before she'd reach the portal.

"No!" I cried, initializing my teleport before I even realized what I was doing. All I knew was that it couldn't have Gwen. I wanted her, needed her, and what's more. She was *mine!* It could not have what was *mine!* That was unacceptable.

As the ravager hurtled through the sky, I reappeared right in front of it and drove my sword right into the center of its milky chest eyes. The creature screamed as my blade sank into its flesh. The sound was enough to rattle my brain as I twisted my sword while unleashing another sapphire blast that blew through the creature and ripped out its back.

That's when it hit me. One massive tentacle smashed into me, tearing my hands from the sword embedded into it and sending me flying. As I tumbled through the air, it turned and hurled a massive purple fireball at me. I threw my arms up, trying to both block the attack and teleport to safety, but it was too quick and too close. The attack smashed into me with enough force to shatter my armor into ethereal shards. Agony exploded through me as I careened backward through the night sky, darkness encroaching on my vision.

My Merciless Greaves of Wrath flared as I plummeted downward, magnifying the power of the attack by sevenfold before throwing it back into the ravager. A slash of crimson power struck the beast, knocking it back as it reached for Gwen. Its tentacles barely missed her as she reached the portal.

"Idiot!" Mammon hissed as she caught me. "What do you think you were doing? You could have gotten killed."

"You said she needed to reach the portal," I wheezed, barely able to catch my breath as Gwen reached out, touching the bindings holding the portal in place.

The spark inside me flared, sucking the breath from my lungs. The whole of the sky erupted in shades of purple as my mind splintered into need. The next thing I knew, Mammon's lips were locked on mine as a wave of crackling lust exploded across the horizon.

The ravager screamed, lavender fissures erupting across the whole of its body as it reached out toward Gwen with one burning claw. Only, as it reached her, Gwen spun. Except it wasn't Gwen as much as it was something else. Whoever this was looked like Gwen, but the power coming off of her was nearly indescribable. It rolled off her in lavender waves, and as her power hit us, Mammon moaned into my mouth.

"You don't get what's ours," Gwen said in a voice that was both hers and not hers. Purple sparks leapt through the air as she held out a hand toward the ravager. I half-expected flame to pour from her outstretched fingers, for hellfire to light the sky, but instead, energy ripped out of the ravager with a thunder crack. The portal overhead exploded, sending shimmering sparks raining down over the desolate tundra.

The portal above us ripped open, revealing the Darkness's lands. Whatever Gwen had done might have torn the power out of the ravager, but it had also opened the portal the magic had kept sealed. I could see what looked like millions of creatures within the breach. As they rushed toward the rift, intent on coming into our world, I felt the spot in my chest go superheated one more. The energy from my three armaments surged into the mass in my chest, causing silver, red, and emerald sparks to dance around Gwen.

The ravager howled, its teeth gnashing as its lavender wings shattered into ethereal shards. It fell, plummeting out of the sky and slamming into the ground far below. Its body exploded like a bag of black paint, causing the portal to snap shut before the creatures could rip themselves free of the void beyond.

"Gwen, what'd you do?" I asked, and as my words left my lips, she absorbed the purple ball of crackling energy she'd pulled from the ravager.

"I'm not Gwen," she said, cocking her head to look at me and there was only a flicker of recognition in her eyes. "Well, not entirely anymore. She is as much me as I am her." She smiled, and that look was enough to make me forget the woman running her hands over my body and reach out toward her, but what's more, Mammon did the same.

"Asmodai," Mammon moaned, her head snaking past me as she reached toward Gwen. "Is it really you?"

"Yes, Mammon. It is I." She licked her lips as she landed beside us. The wind whipped by her, sending her hair crashing down across her shoulders in a wave. Then she met my eyes with a gaze that made visions of her writhing naked beneath me filled my head "It is a pleasure to meet you, Builder. I'm sure we will get to know each other splendidly." As she reached out to me, her eyes flickered with purple energy and then it was just Gwen staring at me.

"Gwen?" I asked, still reaching out toward her as her legs faltered, and she collapsed.

23

"Is she going to be okay?" I asked, standing over Gwen. We had moved her near the fire Mina had made beside the tent. Both Annabeth and Mina had witnessed the battle overhead, and by the time we'd carried Gwen the short distance from where she had fallen, they had made a bed for her within the tent.

"She'll be okay," Mammon said, looking at me and putting a calming hand on my shoulder. "We just need to let her rest and regain as much power as she can from this place." She inhaled sharply. "Asmodai's energy still permeates this place, and she'll need as much of it as possible to become a proper host."

"What do you mean by a proper host?" I glared at

the Archangel of Greed and hoped she hadn't just fucked over Gwen. "If she's hurt—"

"Your friend isn't hurt," Sathanus said, looking up from her mug of dwarven tea and speaking for the first time since we'd brought Gwen into the tent. She was seated to our left, beside where Leviathan lay unconscious on a cot. The goblin hadn't woken yet, and to be honest, I was sort of worried about what would happen when she did.

"If she isn't hurt, why is her breathing shallow?" I pointed at Gwen, feeling pissed off, responsible, and betrayed all at the same time. While I wanted to believe them, the Archangels had never quite been on the up and up. "She's unconscious for fuck's sake."

"Her body is merely acclimating to Asmodai's power. Your friend is becoming the new Archangel of Lust. This will take time." Sathanus shrugged. "It's better this way. I don't know if you've met Asmodai before, but trust me, you do not want to." She shivered. "I'm sure your friend will be a much more reasonable steward to the power."

I wasn't sure if that was true or not, but either way,

that made me more concerned than ever for Gwen. What if she died or lost control?

"What if it's not okay?" I whispered, touching Gwen's hand. Her skin was feverish to the touch, and though I could feel the throb of her power in my chest, it felt different from before. Not worse, per se, but different.

"Then we will all mourn the loss of Gwen." Mammon looked at me, and I could tell she was upset, which was surprising. It was pretty much the only thing that kept me from screaming at her. "While I wasn't terribly fond of Asmodai because she once made me drop masturbate in front of a crowd of strangers, I will try my best to make it work. You should too." She exhaled sharply. "Believe me when I say I want Gwen to be okay."

"She has a good shot," Sathanus interrupted, one hand stroking her beard as she stared at the ceiling in thought. "It is her body after all, and Asmodai's essence is weak after all this time. She may have taken control, but it faded fast. I suspect that while we'll see some amalgamation of them both, it will be more Gwen than not."

"Maybe we should do something else," Annabeth

said before I could say anything. "We can't move Gwen until she's woken up, and Arthur also can't leave because they're tied together, but that doesn't mean we can't do something to take our minds off worrying." She met my eyes. "We still need more metal for Clarent, right? Perhaps you should busy yourself with that. Mammon can come get you if something changes. You won't be too far."

"Never thought I'd say that about mining this crater at dark, but count me in," Mina said, getting to her feet and coming toward me.

"I can't do that," I said, swallowing hard. "I don't want to leave her side."

Mammon put her hand on my shoulder. "It is best if you do. I will come get you." She met my eyes. "I promise."

"Besides, if she wakes up and goes on a murderous rampage, it'll be best if you're not here." She smiled at me. "That you can count on."

"What about Leviathan?" I asked, looking at the unconscious goblin. "What if she wakes up and does the same?" I looked at the tent. "They are only about ten feet apart."

"I'll watch over Levi," Sathanus said, patting the goblin's head. "If she so much as looks at one of us cross-eyed, I'll teleport her away, but I think the fresh air might do her good. She's always been sort of out of sight out of mind. Why I'd not be surprised if she forgot all about her hoard."

As I looked around the room, I realized I wasn't going to win. Every last one of the girls was giving me the "go away" look, and as much as I wanted to argue with them, I didn't see the point. They had it under control, and they didn't want me here. Part of me was angry I let Mina take my hand and lead me outside, but I did anyway.

"They're right, you know," Mina said when we were outside in the frozen tundra. "Sitting there will just make you worry more. This way, at least you can pass the time doing something else." She huffed out a breath. "Sometimes distraction is all we can hope for."

"Unless this is the last time I get to see her," I murmured, wishing I'd had more of a chance to talk to her, to tell her how I felt. This? This felt almost like when I got a call saying my parents were dead. No chance to say goodbye, nothing. If Gwen didn't wake up and Asmodai took her place, I knew

I'd never forgive myself. "It just always felt like we had more time."

"It always does," Mina said, leading me toward the spot where I'd tried to pull the Red Steel from the ground when the creature had attacked. The marker had been disturbed, but I could still see the spot thanks to the tooltip. "Now, do something else." She crossed her arms over her chest. "Or by my grandmother's silky beard, I'll whip you for being such a sissy."

"Right, sure," I said, raising my hands toward the Red Steel. As I did, I wondered what would have happened if I'd broken them like I had my ethereal armor. Would I have to remake them? Was that even possible? What about the belt and greaves? Would I have to remake them too?

I pushed the thought out of my head and concentrated while Mina pulled out her pipe and began to smoke. Getting my head in the game was hard because I kept thinking about Gwen, but I did my best. This chunk of Red Steel wasn't as deep as the others, but because of my distraction, it took me a long time to grab onto it with my magic. I tried using the method I had before for extraction, but it didn't seem to work. Instead of pushing the Red

Steel up through the earth, it seemed to be keeping it in place.

"Something is wrong." I shook my head. "Every time I try to push it up, it's like the earth just passes through it. Worse, it's like there isn't much to grab onto." I tugged on it with my power to no avail. "I can't just pull it free either."

"Interesting," Mina said, stroking her beard. "Have you tried getting it like you did with the spider ore? When you did that one, you said something similar?"

"Hmm, no. Let me try that." I took a deep breath and exhaled slowly, mentally scrolling through the techniques I'd used in the past and cycling through all of them. None seemed to work at all.

"Well?" Mina asked, pulling her pipe from her mouth and blowing a smoke ring into the air. "Is it working?"

"No." I shook my head. "They're all not working in different ways." I sighed, shutting my eyes and concentrating on the ore down below. It was a mixture of Stygian Iron and Red Steel, but as I focused on it, I felt something else. My breath caught in my throat. I knew what that something else was. Dark Blood.

Only how could that be?

I looked around quickly. "Say, did we ever get the dark blood from the dead ravager?"

"No. I looked for a bit but couldn't find it." Mina shrugged. "I just assumed it shattered in the fall."

"Or maybe that didn't happen at all," I said, thinking back to when the ravager had appeared. It had happened as I'd tried to pull this bit of Red Steel from the ground. Was it connected? And if so, why?

I reached down, trailing my fingers along the hilt of my sword. It had been imbued with the powers of dark blood, and as I did it, I knew I was right. There was dark blood power in this ore. Only that wasn't all that was there. I shut my eyes and reached out once more, trying to get a feel for its shape in my mind.

"Why can't I get a handle on its shape?" I murmured, opening my eyes, but as I did, I found time had stopped. Snowflakes hung in the air and the smoke trailing from Mina's pipe had frozen in place.

"You think you are worthy?" Asmodai asked, and as I turned toward the sound of it, I found myself staring at a woman who looked similar to Gwen. Instead of having raven locks she was a redhead, and her eyes were as blue as the ocean, but otherwise? Otherwise, they were the same. "What makes you think so?"

"How are you here?" I asked, taking a step forward and trying to keep from yelling at her. "I thought you were busy trying to take over my friend's body?"

"I'm not really here. I'm in your head." She poked my forehead, causing her finger to phase through my skull. I didn't feel her touch, so much as I felt a bit of warmth on my flesh.

"That doesn't answer my question," I said, crossing my arms over my chest.

"I am not trying to take over your friend. That isn't possible." She shook her head. "I am letting her have my power, and once that is done, I will be free of this fight and this world." She met my eyes. "You have no idea how much I am looking forward to oblivion, assuming that is what is in store for me." She touched her chin. "Where do we go when we die?" Her lips curled into a wry smile. "Maybe I'll meet my maker."

"Wait. You're just giving up?" shock, surprise, and a little bit of relief washing over me in waves. If what she said was true, maybe Gwen would be okay, maybe I'd have another chance to tell her how I felt. If that were true, I'd not waste it.

"More like passing the torch." She touched my chest with her finger. "I'll always be here." Her hand trailed down toward my crotch. "And most especially here." She tittered. "Anyway, the reason you cannot pull my ring from the ground is because I have not marked you." She smirked and placed her palm on my chest where the blaze of heat connecting me to Gwen burned.

"Wait, that is your ring?" I asked, turning my attention back to the tooltip for the ore. It had changed. No longer were there the separate boxes for the Stygian Iron and the Red Steel. Instead, there was a new one.

Uncontrollable Binding of Lust

Material Type: metal (various)

Grade: S

Depth: 3,464 meters

Difficulty: 7

Proficiency: 10/100

Overall Proficiency: 12/100

The Armament forged by the Archangel of Lust.

"It is my ring. I wore it on my finger." She extended her hand toward me, and I saw a ring sat there. It had a band of Red steel with another of Stygian Iron woven around it. In the center where a gem would normally be was a pulsing crystal of refined Dark Blood. "When I was swallowed by that horrible ravager, I used the last of my power to bind it to this place, to make it so it could not be free to roam with my power." She shook her head. "We would have remained like that, locked in our own little purgatory if you hadn't disturbed my resting place." She smiled. "I am glad you did though. Otherwise, I'd have not met you."

"You are glad to have met me?" I asked, raising an eyebrow at her. "Why is that?"

"Because you are a lover and a fighter." She

smirked. "So many are one or the other and half more are cowards." She shook her head. "I do not think you are a coward though, not after what you did to stop the ravager." She cast her gaze around the crater, and for a second she looked like she would say more. Only, before she could, she winced, and her ethereal form began to fade. "We do not have time for that though. My tenuous link to this plane is all but gone now." She touched my chest again. "I must mark you before it's too late. Then you will be able to recall my ring."

I wanted to ask her how she could do that, but all I wound up doing was nodding to the red-haired archangel. "Do it."

She nodded, biting her lip as the purple energy surrounding her form traveled up her body and into her outstretched hand. Then I felt it pulse along my flesh like warm bathwater. It wormed into me, warming me from the inside out, and as it did, Asmodai began to fade away. "Good luck, Builder." She winked at me. "Get loads of ass for me."

Then, with that, she was gone, leaving me standing there in the frozen tundra.

"Well, you going to try again?" Mina asked, and as

I turned toward her, the dwarf's eyes went wide. "Where did you get that?" She pointed, and I looked down to see a ring resting in the palm of my hand just like the one Asmodai has been wearing.

"I, um," I said, trying to figure out how to explain it when I saw Annabeth tear out of the tent and wave to me. The spark in my chest pulsed once more, and as I headed back toward the tent, I knew one thing to be true. Gwen was awake.

24

As I burst through the doors of the tent, I found Gwen looking at me. Only, I quickly realized something was wrong. The others in the room weren't moving, and by not moving, I didn't mean they were dead. No, they were frozen just like Mina had been when I'd met the spirit of Asmodai.

"Hello, Arthur," Gwen said, getting to her feet. Each movement drew my eyes along her body, highlighting each muscle as it moved. There was something sensual about it even though she'd done nothing more than rise to her feet. It was a little crazy too because as I tore my gaze from her body and settled onto her face, I realized how beautiful she was.

Now, I'd always thought Gwen was a perfect ten, and until now, the only girl who had been close to her in terms of sheer beauty had been Lucifer. Now though? Now Gwen had something else, some kind of inner spark that drew me to her in a way I couldn't explain.

"Hi," I said, swallowing hard and stepping into the tent. Only, as I did, I realized Mina hadn't followed. She was still outside, one foot raised in the air, trapped in mid-step. The snowflakes had once again frozen in place, and I realized that whatever Asmodai had done earlier hadn't been in my head. No, she'd actually stopped time somehow.

"I can feel you now," Gwen said, and as I turned back toward her, she was right in front of me. Her breasts pressed into my chest as she wrapped her arms around my neck, pulling me close to her. "Can you feel me too?"

"Yes," I whispered, my voice catching in my throat as she nipped at my ear. "How could I not?"

"I don't mean like this," she said, voice hot on my throat as she took a step backward, disengaging from me while trailing one hand down chest. "I mean inside. I can feel you. I mean, I always could before, but now I can really feel you."

The heat in my chest pulsed, and then the mark Asmodai had given me flared to life, casting the glowing image of a heart with an arrow through it against my shirt. I sucked in a breath, looking down at the spot as Gwen pressed her hand to it.

"What happened to you?" I asked, taking a step away from her. "Why is everyone frozen?"

"Because we are having a moment." She licked her lips. "And moments are not bound by time. No, they are bound to something ethereal." She dragged her teeth over her bottom lip. "A certain je ne sais quoi."

"Right, okay," I said, taking another step backward, suddenly concerned. She was looking at me hungrily, and as I studied her, I realized I didn't know what to expect if we got together. I knew it wouldn't be just sex since she was a succubus. Would she feed off me? Would that be okay?

Her face twisted in confusion. "Why are you retreating, Arthur?" Uncertainty flickered across her face. "Why do you always pull away from me?" She looked down at herself and snorted. "I am the embodiment of lust now. The master of my domain, and still you pull away from me."

"It's not that," I said, swallowing hard. The truth was, she scared me. A lot. I know I said I'd tell her how I felt, tell her I wanted her, needed her, but the truth was, I was scared. I knew it was ridiculous since I also knew she wouldn't deny me, but at the same time, whenever I was around her, I felt like the silly little boy in high school too scared to ask his crush to the dance.

"What is it?" She moved toward me again and reached out, taking my left hand in hers. "What can I offer you? What do I need to do to prove myself to you?" She curled her fingers around the Uncontrollable Binding of Lust in my hand. "Do you require power?" She pulled my gauntlet from my hand and let it fall to the ground. As it hit with a clang, she slipped the ring onto my finger. Another surge of power exploded through me as it meshed with the other three Armaments I wore. "There, now you have it." The heat in my chest burned and the light of her mark pulsed. "I give it freely to you."

"Gwen," I said, shaking my head as I stared at her. Even if I wasn't worried about the whole succubus thing, how could I possibly make her understand how special I wanted this to be? "It's not that at all."

"I know what it is, Arthur." She smiled at me as she took my hands and pulled me back a step, toward the bunk where she'd been sleeping just a few moments ago. "And I know all your fears, all your insecurities. I can smell them in the air, taste them in your words. I am saying I don't care about any of that." She met my eyes. "I just want you." She touched my chest, resting her hand on the mark.

That's when I felt her, really felt her. I saw all the events of our meeting over in my head but from her perspective. Watched as she bided her time waiting for me to come for her and not doing so. She'd wanted to be my first, but had understood when she wasn't. Then I saw her worry when I'd been trapped within the Darkness for a year. I saw her leaping to her feet at the smallest sound, hoping it was me.

I saw her after our fight when she'd resolved she wouldn't like me anymore. Then I saw her open the box of donuts and stare at it. I saw her hate die away, saw it pass from her as she stared at the donuts. I had been dumb, and she knew it, knew better than me.

No. It wasn't that at all. She didn't know better than me. She was better than me. When the archangels had come, she thought I'd choose Gabriella or Mammon. Someone with power. She had found me, but they had more claim than she could hope to have. After all, my sword had been broken.

Only, now she didn't feel inferior. Now she was an Archangel like them. Not born into power but given power because she was deserving and had earned the right. I saw Asmodai in her skull, saw their whispered conversations. I saw Gwen agree to give up herself for the cause and saw Asmodai turn her down.

Happiness overtook me, and as I stood there, thanking the Archangel of Lust for letting Gwen live, Gwen moved, snapping my attention back to her. As my eyes met hers, she shut her eyes and leaned in toward me, lips slightly parted.

The moment our lips touched, fireworks exploded in my brain. The mark on my chest blazed, but I could barely feel it as she trailed her hand down across my chest.

"Arthur," she whispered, leaning in close, so her breath was hot on my neck as she spoke. "I want you inside me." Her hands found my belt then as she pulled me toward her while backing toward the bed. "Please."

"Are you sure?" I asked as she met my mouth with her own, her other hand went down the front of my pants. As she cupped me, I moaned into her mouth.

"I've never wanted anyone as much as I want you." She kissed me again before dropping to her knees in front of me. As her tongue flicked out, tasting me, she looked up, meeting my eyes, and I realized I was about to get my favorite thing in the world. "Let me show you what I'm good at."

25

Even though it took another two days to finish mining out all the Stygian Iron from the mountaintop, I still couldn't get my night with Gwen out of my mind. Every part of me ached for her touch, for her caress in a way that was nearly physically painful. It was almost better than I'd ever imagined it could possibly be. I had to return her and Mammon back to town so they could carry on with the whole alliance thing because if I hadn't, I'd have never been able to stop touching her.

"Look, I need a break," Annabeth said as she rolled off of me and lay next to me inside the tent. "Please." She got off the bed and moved to pick up her clothes. She turned and looked at me for a long time. "And while I'm sort of enjoying all the attention, I can tell your heart isn't in it."

"That's not true," I said, shaking my head as I got up and moved toward her, wrapping my arms around her waist and pulling her against me. "I enjoy your company."

"I get that, and I'm willing to tolerate it because you've become amazing in the sack over the last few days. Like mind-blowingly amazing." She pushed me away and pulled her pants up as she turned to look at me. She stood there topless, giving me a great view of her breasts and dark nipples. Only as she looked at me, I saw them harden. She tore her gaze away. "Anyway, what I'm saying is I'm getting a bit worn out down there." She touched my chest, and as she did, she bit her lip.

"Are you sure?" I asked as desire swam through her eyes. "Because I'm still good to go." I bent down, and as I moved to lick her, she stepped back.

"Yes. While I enjoy all the attention you've been giving me, I need a break." She sighed loudly. "I'm going to start packing up, okay?" She pulled on her shirt and stepped into her shoes as she moved to the exit.

"Okay," I said, watching her go, and the only thing I could see was her naked even though I'd literally just had sex with her a second ago. Worse, I could feel myself getting ready to go again. I turned away as Annabeth exited the tent. She'd been a good sport about the whole thing, but part of me felt like I was using her, anyway.

"You need to get your head in the game," I told little me. Then I moved across the tent and pulled on my pants and underwear. It was a little difficult because little me wasn't exactly cooperating. To be fair, I had a feeling that had something to do with the mark Asmodai, Archangel of Lust, had given me. It had somehow turned me into a goddamned sexual tyrannosaurus, which was part of the problem. I could go and go and go.

I finished dressing and moved outside to find Mina had already packed everything up and had been waiting beside the fire. As I approached, she handed me a mug of dwarven tea.

"You finish getting your rocks off?" Mina asked, looking over at Annabeth who had already moved to the ledge where she'd been sculpting a dragon out of ice. It wasn't quite done, but even still, I could tell it was far better than the ice sculpture she'd created during the competition, but then again, it also wasn't melting.

"More or less," I shrugged and took a sip of tea.

"Really?" Mina asked, raising an eyebrow. "Your sculptor is practically limping. Maybe you could get off of her for just a few minutes." The dwarf smirked at me. "If you could, we'd have been out of here a day ago."

"I can't help it," I said, gesturing at my crotch before I realized what I was doing. As Mina's eyes trailed down my body to rest on my crotch, she inhaled sharply.

"I can see why she's willing to try." Mina looked at me. "Almost makes me wanna try if I didn't think I'd break ye in two." I met her eyes, and as I did, I could feel the mark on my chest begin to burn. It was a bit weird because while the dwarf was a bit on the short and stout side, she well, had a lot of cushion for the pushin' as it were. And that was aside from the fact her breasts were bigger than my head.

"I bet you'd give before me," I said, touching the spot on my chest. Already purple light was beginning to show through my shirt. "There's no question about it."

"I don't believe you even slightly," she said, eyes not leaving my crotch as I moved toward her. "Besides, it isn't like we have time to find out." She licked her lips. "We need to get all this metal back to your smith."

"I'd say we could be quick, but we won't be." I shrugged. "Not by a long shot."

"Look, Arthur," Mina said, tearing her eyes from me and focusing on my face. It was weird because it seemed like it took a lot more effort than it should have. "Please just go pack before I do something I'll regret, okay." She turned away then, visible strain on her face, and as I watched her go, I could practically see her without clothes on in my mind's eye. "And don't help me with the tent. It'll be faster for me to do it alone." She glared at me over her shoulder. "I mean it."

I shook myself trying to get back in the right frame of mind. It didn't really work, especially since I could feel the mark beneath my shirt burning with need. It was almost worse because I could feel the ring hanging on the chain around my neck. I'd originally tried to wear it, but it was too hard to wear that and my gauntlets so I'd hung it on the same chain as the sculpture Annabeth had given me. I knew part of it had nothing to do with the ring itself and more that I wasn't used to wearing stuff around my neck.

I stood there, feeling like an idiot in greaves, gauntlets, and a metal belt, but I didn't want to take off the Armaments except when I had to. I sighed and touched the ring around my neck. Then I focused on finishing my tea.

Even still, it felt like it was taking forever for Mina to break down the tent. I watched her for a few more moments before turning my attention toward Annabeth. She'd stopped working on the sculpture again and was instead, standing there looking at it. Then she glanced my way. When she saw me looking at her, she turned pointedly away and focused on her sculpture.

"Why don't you go back to town and take these with you," Mina said, startling me by pressing the sack of ore into my hand. I'd remembered it being heavy, but it didn't really feel heavy as I took it from her.

"What do you mean?" I asked, hefting the bag over my shoulder. "You still haven't really finished with the tent." I gestured around the clearing. "There's still other stuff to pack up too."

"I'd rather do it without you here." She met my eyes, and that same look Annabeth had given me in the tent flashed through her eyes. "Because every second I'm around ye, all I can think about is tearing off your clothes." She shook her head before staring at the sky. "Please just go. Come back in a couple hours, or don't and we'll just hike down. We have enough supplies to make it to the way station at the bottom."

"You want me to just leave you here?" I asked, confused.

"God, yes." Mina met my eyes. "Please just go." She fidgeted slightly, cheeks flushing. "I want almost nothing more in the world than for you to not be here."

"Wow, alright." I sighed. "Let me just say goodbye to Annabeth." I turned to move toward the sculptor.

"Arthur is going to head back to town. He'll be back in a few hours!" Mina called before I'd made it three steps.

"Okay!" Annabeth said, and I could have sworn I heard the relief in her voice. "See you soon, Arthur. Tell everyone I said hi."

As her words hit my ears, I stood there feeling a bit dumb. "Uh… guess that's it," I said, shrugging. "Later."

"Goodbye." Mina nodded to me as I teleported away.

I arrived back in the Graveyard of Statues next to the massive sculpture in the middle of town. As I stood there, I saw Maribelle's two apprentices look up from where they were working almost a hundred meters away and fix on me. As they jumped to their feet, I waved.

"Arthur!" they cried, dropping their tools and sprinting toward me. "We missed you." The crazy thing was it sounded like they really had.

"Missed you too," I said right before I felt hands around my waist.

"Welcome back, Arthur," Maribelle purred into my ears. "You seem different." She inhaled sharply. "And you smell so good." She kissed me then, pressing her body against mine before shoving me down to the ground. She climbed on top of me, pausing only long enough to pull off her shirt, eyes wild with need. "I need you right now." She swallowed hard, her hands moving down to my pants and tugging them down.

"Um… outside?" I asked as her two apprentices appeared beside us. Their nipples jutted out against their shirts as they dropped down on either side of me. The blonde one moved to help Maribelle with my greaves while the brunette kissed me, hard. As her lips ground into mine, she grabbed my hand and put it on her breast.

The mark on my chest blazed as the two girls finally got my pants off. As I tried to figure out what the hell was happening, I felt their tongues on me and realized I didn't care.

26

"Oh! Just like that!" Maribelle cried, back arching as she thrust herself down on top of me again. "Never stop fucking me!" Another wave of pleasure hit me as I reached up, grabbing her breasts. She cried out, dropping down on top of me, face pressing against my chest, and sucked in another breath.

Her two assistants were passed out on the ground next to us, and as Maribelle rolled off of me, I realized that we hadn't moved from the spot by the sculpture in the middle of the town.

"Still ready to go?" Maribelle asked, reaching down to cup me. "How is that possible?" She winced. "I'm done worn out."

"Huh, oh. Yeah." I gave her a smile as I started to get up. Her hand trailed down my leg as I did. "Come on, we should probably get cleaned up." I offered her my hand.

"I will in a minute. I don't think I can walk right now." She stared at me for a moment. "If I could, I wouldn't be helping you clean up. That's for damned sure."

One of her assistants moaned, and as I turned to look at her, something grabbed me by the back of the neck. My feet left the ground as I tried to whirl around, but pain exploded across my temple. The next thing I knew I was being suspended over a volcano. Magma boiled down below, and the smell of sulfur hit my nose, making my eyes water and my throat clench in agony.

"I gave you a very specific job, Builder," Lucifer growled, her lips dangerously close to my ear as she spoke, causing a surge of fear to ripple through me. "And since then, what have you accomplished?" She shook me over the volcano's edge.

"I've been a bit busy," I cried while reaching for my sword. Only I didn't have it because I was naked. In fact, I didn't have most of my armaments. The only one I had was the ring hanging around my neck.

"I don't want your excuses." She threw me over the edge, and I plummeted down toward the molten rock below. Fear exploded through me as I tried to think of something, anything that could save me. The heat from below burned the moisture from my body, and I knew that I'd be flash fried long before I hit the pool at the bottom. As I sucked in a breath, I gagged, my body convulsing in midair.

Lucifer caught me by the ankle. Her wings fluttered behind her all shimmering golds and silvers against a backdrop of black. She lifted me up, her arm extending heavenward until she was eye level with my crotch.

"Tell me why I shouldn't drop you into this volcano," she sneered. "Tell me why I should let you live because right now, I think I may need to teach you a lesson." She smiled evilly. "Because for the past few days you've been gallivanting around." Her other hand went to my chest and pressed on the spot where Asmodai had marked me. A surge of pain exploded from me as purple light flared and died. "You think that by gathering these marks you are strong?" She shook her head. "You are nothing but a weak man."

She flung me up into the air, and my body cartwheeled, my whole world spinning in a mishmash of color. Then her knee slammed into my stomach, driving what little breath I had from my lungs in an explosive burst. Her hand reached out, seizing me by the throat. Below, I could feel the heat of the volcano, but it was nothing compared to the pain I felt as the glow of Mammon's mark exploded into a thousand scintillating sparks.

"I promised you power." She touched my shoulder, and another surge of pain ripped through me as the light from Wrath's mark faded away. "And yet you think to compensate?" She narrowed her eyes. "You think they can give you what I can?" She grabbed my hand, and as she did, Envy's mark flared like a dying star. More pain hit me, and darkness began to encroach on my vision. "I am simply more."

She tossed me backward, and I struck the ground beside the lip of the volcano. The volcanic rock tore at my flesh, shredding my skin as I tumbled down several feet before slamming into a rocky outcropping.

Lucifer landed lightly on the lip of the volcano and came toward me, her blood-red armor gleaming against the backdrop of a stormy sky and a blazing magma pool. "You disgust me." She snorted. "You think that because Wrath, Envy, Lust, and Greed have marked you that you can do as you wish, do you?" She shook her head, causing her hair to flutter around her face. "You should know better."

I tried to get to my feet even though my body felt like a bloody wound. Only before I could do more than crawl to my hands and knees, she kicked me in the stomach. Stars flashed across my eyes as I collapsed to the ground.

"You mean to defeat the Darkness?" She looked at the sky and laughed. "You can't even face me with the combined power of four Archangels." She kicked me onto my back and stared down her nose at me. "Retrieve my hammer. Then at least someone can do something." Lucifer grabbed me by the hair and hauled me to my feet. Then she twisted, pointing back toward the volcano with her free hand. "It is down there. Why don't you swim for it?" She flung me toward the edge, but not hard enough to send me over it.

Instead, I stumbled, crashing to the ground just in

front of it. The rock was so warm, it burned my ragged flesh, but I ignored it, trying to push myself to my feet once again.

"What's that?" she asked, cupping one hand to her ear. "You're too weak? Your pathetic human body can't survive in lava?" She laughed, and the sound caused the sky above to crackle.

"I told you I'd get your hammer," I wheezed, finally able to get on my hands and knees. Only as I turned my head to look at her, I found her striding toward me.

"I told you I don't want your excuses." She knelt down next to me and patted her head. "I recognize this isn't your fault. Your kind was never meant to do more than lick my boots, and yet here we are, forced to work together." She shook her head as she sat down next to me, feet dangling over the edge. "The only question now is one of terms." She patted my head. "We can have a long-term relationship or a short-term one." She flicked her hand toward the volcano, and the lava began to rise. "Choose."

"What the hell are you talking about," I cried,

glaring at her. My hands balled into fists as I tried to reach out for my power. Only without my sword, without my armaments, I had nearly nothing to call upon. The ring around my neck even felt dead and lifeless. Like a cheap piece of jewelry. No. Whatever she'd done to my marks had cut me off from the others.

"I am talking about inevitabilities." She snapped her fingers, and the lava fell back toward the volcano's basin, splashing against the side and sending sparks flying in every direction. "You are too weak to win." She touched her chest. "I will not tie myself to a loser. I will not fail again." She got to her feet and stared down into the volcano. Then she jumped.

My mouth fell open as she arched through the air like an Olympian before crashing into the lava below. Her body cut through the pool before disappearing into its depths. I sat back on my hands, trying to understand what the hell had just happened.

Lucifer had grabbed me from town like it was nothing even though the wards there were designed specifically to protect me from her. Then she'd deactivated every single one of my marks. I was literally sitting here battered, bloody, and naked.

Thing was. If she wanted me dead, I'd be dead. That was obvious enough. That meant she wanted me for something, presumably to get the hammer, and she meant to keep me until I did what she wanted. Otherwise, she'd not have bothered to systematically cut off my connection to the archangels. After all, it wasn't like she feared my power, even with them. Or did she?

I shut my eyes, focusing on the strength of the marks, and as I did, I felt the pulse of Gwen's heat in my chest. It was barely a flicker, but it was there, and as I reached for it, I felt her reaching back. In my mind's eye, I could see her standing there, one hand extended toward me. No. That wasn't all, I could feel Mammon too. The archangel of Greed had her hand on Gwen's shoulder. My neck began to pulse, cold running over me.

"That's enough of that," Lucifer said right before she backhanded me across the face. My head snapped back, the connection shattering into a million pieces as my back hit the ground. The Devil herself loomed over me, one hand bracing a massive golden morningstar over one shoulder.

"You won't be calling for help." She smirked. "Though I'm inclined to let you do it just to show the others, and you, how powerless you all really are." She squatted down next to me and dropped the hammer to the ground beside me. It hit with a deafening thud that was like the screams of a million people all crying out in pain. "Would you like me to do that, Arthur? To let me call your friends here?" She licked her lips. "I would take pleasure in ripping them apart." She smiled. "After all, it is their fault I have been imprisoned for so very long."

"No," I squeaked, but I was too busy staring at the warhammer on the ground next to me. It was massive in a way I didn't think anyone could easily heft it and inlaid with gemstones. The head itself was blunt on one side, but the other was spiked. The crazier thing was, I could feel the power within the weapon struggling to break free of the binding placed upon it. Six glowing marks stood emblazoned on its surface in burning light, keeping the power within bound.

"Good." Lucifer pointed to the weapon. "You may notice that this weapon has been bound by my sisters. It bears their marks." She gestured at them.

"Envy, Lust, Greed, Gluttony, Sloth, and Wrath." She narrowed her eyes at me. "Break those marks for me." Her wings spread wide, casting a shadow down over me. "Or I throw you into the volcano." She smiled evilly. "As I said before, short term or long term." Her smile vanished. "Choose."

27

"I don't know how to help you," I said, looking up at the Devil as she stared down at me. "I can't break these marks. I simply don't know how." I shook my head. "And even if I did, I don't have these two." I pointed to the two marks I hadn't seen before. The ones she'd identified as Sloth and Gluttony.

"The difference is in degrees, not absolutes." Lucifer squatted down beside me and held out her hand. "I will show you how to break those you can. Once that is done two-thirds of my power will be restored." She met my eyes, and there was no hint of treachery in them. "I will then find my sisters for you. I will lay them at your feet, Builder. They will give you their marks or they will die."

"And if I refuse, you'll throw me into the volcano?" I asked, unable to break her gaze. In her eyes, I could see the swirling fires of torment, could see armies fall, but mostly? Mostly I could see power. She was strong, far stronger than she was letting on. I wasn't sure if the others could take her in a fight, but if the seals on the hammer were broken, they definitely wouldn't be able to stop her. Only… only maybe that was okay.

"I will throw you into the volcano, eyes. But first I will break your arms and legs. I will tear the skin from your body and pluck out your tongue. I will sit here and listen to you scream until you can do so no longer, and then I will cut off that sex organ you're so proud of." She gestured down at me. "I will shove it down your throat so you cannot breathe, and as your vision starts to blur, and you feel like you're about to die, I will hold you over the volcano so you can feel your body start to cook. Then, when you are so close to death as to have it be a mere formality, then and only then, will I drop you into it." She didn't smile, didn't grin. She said it coldly, and the hard truth of it was clear. She would do all of those things and more. Much more.

"Just wanted to make sure we were clear." I took a

deep breath. "Thanks for clarifying that." Inside I wanted to run, wanted to hide, but I couldn't do that. If I did, she would find me, would bring me back here, and worse, she'd be angry. It was strange because looking at her, I could see wrath. Hell, I could see all the archangels, and I knew she was better at their jobs than they were. She could visit exquisite wrath, could bring untold pleasure, but she could also want unceasingly.

"You're most welcome, Arthur." She held her hand out to me. "Should we begin destroying the bindings or should I break your knees and watch you try to crawl away?"

"Dealing with the bindings sounds good, but only on one condition." I met her eyes, and she almost seemed amused. Almost.

"There are no conditions, Builder. I have made myself perfectly clear—"

"I will need your mark." I touched my head. "You promised me the crown. Do you have it?"

"I do." She reached up, pushing her hair aside to reveal a glittering golden crown that had been hidden by her dark locks. She pulled it off and held it out to me. "You can have it after, not before. The

Devil does not lie, but man always does." She dropped it to the ground beside me.

"Fair enough." I took a deep breath, hoping I wasn't making the worst mistake of my life. Then I pulled my battered body to my feet and reached out toward the hammer. "Just tell me what I need to do."

"First, you must—"

Lucifer probably said more, but I didn't hear it because the second I wrapped my hand around the haft of the warhammer, power unlike anything I'd ever experienced surged through me. It crashed over me like a tidal wave, and as I struggled to keep myself aware of what was even happening, the marks upon my body blazed with light.

The hammer in my hand began to glow, pulsing as the energy of the bindings placed upon the weapon began to flare. That was when I realized what had happened. The archangels had each given a portion of their power to seal away this weapon, and what's more because I was connected to them, I could feel it flow into me. My body began to heal, my cells stitching themselves back together as the sky above crackled and boomed.

I felt the fury of Wrath, and as I did, her armament, Merciless Greaves of Wrath, appeared upon my body. Greed and Envy followed, their power surging through me and causing the belt and gauntlets to manifest while the ring I'd received from Asmodai began to glow.

That all happened in the split second I gripped the warhammer, but as my fingers closed around it, I felt the way the binding had worked. It wasn't so much a binding as it was a redirection. They had used a portion of their power to effectively cause the weapon's own power to feed the binding. It would be simple to break because all I'd have to do would be cut off the bindings from stealing Lucifer's own power. The thing was, I wasn't sure I wanted to do that. After all, there would be another thing that would be simple too. To modify the binding so that instead of feeding back into itself and strengthening the binding, I could open the marks on my body wide and call that power into myself

Either way, I knew one thing. Right now, I was strong. Stronger than anyone had ever intended.

I spun, swinging the warhammer in an arc toward Lucifer. The blunt end smashed into her skull with a wet crack, sending her sprawling sideways across the rocky ground like a broken mannequin. Lightning flashed, and thunder boomed as I strode toward her, warhammer raised high. I may not be the Princess of Pride, but I had her power, along with that of four Archangels coursing through me.

Wrath tinged my vision red as Lucifer started to rise. Before she could, I hit her again, slamming the warhammer into her ribs. The blow shattered her armor into flitting bits of crimson energy that died like sparks as they hit the ground. Lucifer sprawled on her back, looking up at me, eyes narrowed in anger.

"You are being a fool," she said, her words tinged with blood. "The weapon you use is mine." She kicked me in the knee, and I felt the blow crack my kneecap. I stumbled, falling as the backlash of Wrath's Armament threw the attack back at her. She screamed, her leg twisting around with a sharp crack.

The power in the hammer filled me mending my broken limb, and I knew that if it had happened for me, it was happening for her too. After all, this was her power I was using. And that was the thing though, wasn't it?

As my leg healed, I spun and sprinted for the crown she'd dropped on the ground. Lucifer rose, her wings extending as I grabbed the crown. The moment I touched the metal, she screamed. More power surged through me as the crown blazed to life in my hand. I may not have had her mark, but as long as I held this hammer, I didn't need it. The power of Pride filled me in an instant, and as it did, I realized something. I could call more than I had before from the warhammer.

While before the energy within the weapon had been siphoned into me through the marks of the other archangels, now it poured into me of its own volition.

As I placed the crown upon my head, Lucifer charged. Only, in that instant, I could see more than I ever had before. Time seemed to slow down as the ring around my neck activated, and the sight of it struck me as odd. I could see its stats.

Uncontrollable Binding of Lust

Type: Ring

Durability: 1,240

Defense: 1D3

Enchantments: Armament of Lust

Ability: Enjoy the Moment– Causes time to slow down for the user.

Only that wasn't all because I could see the stats of everything, even Lucifer.

Name: Lucifer

Experience: 435,500,796,432

Health: 173/195*

Mana: 192/192*

Strength: 97/100*

Agility: 98/100*

Charisma: 100/100*

Intelligence: 100/100*

Special: 92/100*

The hammer in my hand throbbed, drawing my gaze to it.

The Mourning Star

Type: Warhammer

Durability: 17,999,999/18,000,000

Damage: 1D50*

Enchantments: Indomitable Will, Binding of Wrath, Binding of Greed, Binding of Lust, Binding of Envy, Binding of Sloth, Binding of Gluttony

Ability: Healing Aura– The user will rapidly heal all damage taken.

Ability: Cascade– For the duration of the battle, every successful attack will cause overall damage to increase by ten percent.

While part of me wanted to open the menu for the enchantment for Indomitable Will to see exactly what it would do, I didn't want to waste the time. Besides, with the crown on my head, I could see the stats of the lightning above, of the volcano next to me. Millions of tooltips crowded my vision, and it was so overwhelming, I pushed them away in the same way I'd always done with Clarent. Instantly, the tooltips vanished back into glowing spheres of color above each and every object.

Then I turned my attention back toward Lucifer. She had been caught mid-stride, one hand reaching back as flames gathered in her palm. Her other was outstretched toward me. Her face was twisted into a snarl and blood ran down her body.

As I looked at her frozen in place, I couldn't help but think about her health. Even though I'd hit her twice, I'd barely done twenty-two points of damage to her, and that was with a weapon that supposedly had a roll of fifty damage on top of the fact she'd been hit by the backlash of Wrath's attack.

I wasn't sure if that was because she had incredible durability given by a hidden ability or if she was just healing, but I knew one thing. It'd be fucking impossible to put her down on my own. Even if I could keep hitting her, she'd eventually get the warhammer away from me, and once that happened, I'd find myself swallowed by a volcano.

Besides, I didn't want to fight her. Not really. No, at the end of the day, I wanted her to join me.

"Stop," I said, and as I spoke, the frozen moment shattered. Lucifer sped up, and she was so fast I could barely see her move even with all the power that had been granted to me. I dropped the hammer, and as it hit the ground, the crown on my head turned back into a lifeless hunk of metal, and all the stat boxes vanished.

Lucifer stopped, one fist arching toward the air to

me. It hovered only inches from my head, and I knew that if she wanted to, she could kill me.

"What are you doing?" she asked, eyes shifting to the warhammer on the ground beside me.

"Truth be told, I was hoping we could talk." I reached up and pulled the crown from my head. I offered it to her. "I can't break the bindings on your warhammer. You can have this back."

"That was not our deal," she said, anger bubbling within her. Then she stopped, going absolutely still. She shut her eyes for a moment and took several deep breaths. When she opened them, she seemed calm. It was actually sort of scary. "Why can you not break them?"

"Because they aren't meant to be broken by me." I pointed to the bindings emblazoned upon the hammer. "They are meant to strengthen me." I touched the mark of Lust blazing on my bare chest. "Each of these marks allows me to pull power from the warhammer and use it as I see fit, but it doesn't mean I can break them." I sighed. "You'd need the other archangels to do that."

"Why would they place such a binding upon my hammer?" she asked, gaze flitting from the weapon to me and back again. "You should have your own weapon. You do not need mine."

"I have a theory," I said, offering her my right hand. "It was to get you to join me."

"I do not follow," Lucifer said, glancing at my hand as confusion spread across her face.

I pointed at the hammer with the crown in my hand. "When I wore your crown and held the hammer, I felt tied to you. I'm not sure if you felt it too."

"I did." She nodded. "I felt you stealing from me."

"I think that if you were to give me your mark, you could bypass those marks. Then, instead of keeping you from your power, you would have access to it through me." I shrugged. "It's just a theory." I offered her the crown once more.

"And if you are wrong?" She took the crown from me and looked down at it.

"Then you'll have helped save the world for no reason," I said, shrugging. "Your other option is to talk to your sisters and see what they say, but something tells me that if you were going to do that, you would have."

"I cannot meet them without being in a place of strength." She handed me the crown back. "Keep this for now. I will think about what you have said, Builder." She looked me up and down. "I was not born to bow down before a man."

"I'm not asking you to bow down," I said, taking the lifeless crown from her. "I'm asking you to join the fight against the Darkness."

"It is the same thing," she said, and even before the words had finished leaving her lips, she vanished. Leaving me standing there all alone on the volcano's edge. The hammer gleamed beside me, left behind along with the crown. Lucifer was strange, but I was starting to think I understood her. At least a little.

I put the crown back on my head and lifted her warhammer. As I did, the familiar surge of power filled me, causing stat boxes to appear over everything.

28

"So, how was making out with the Devil?" Sam asked as I reappeared inside her shop. She was standing over her table, staring down at the chunks of ore I'd gathered from the volcano.

"We didn't make out," I said, approaching her. "How are you?"

"Good, but that will change if you get much closer." She turned and looked at me with hungry eyes, and I got the distinct impression she was imagining me naked.

"What do you mean?" I asked, suddenly confused. "Why would me coming closer change things?"

"If you come closer, I might not be able to resist Lust's call." She pointed at my chest, and I looked down to see the mark on my chest was blazing with purple light again. What's more Lust's binding on the hammer was glowing too. "And as much as I'd love to give in, I'm too hurt to manage that." She touched her chest where we'd torn Dred's mark from her. "You understand, right?"

"Yeah," I sighed, running my free hand through my hair. "I'm not exactly sure how to turn it off." I stared down at it and felt the pulse of heat within my chest. "My sexy knows no bounds, it'd seem."

"Sounds like you need to talk to our resident succubus, but until then, you stand over there." She pointed to the far corner. "And word of advice. Don't go anywhere crowded, okay?" She shook her head. "I don't feel like seeing you sexed to death."

"Right," I mumbled, feeling my cheeks heat up. If there was a way to control the power of lust radiating off of me, I needed to find it. As much as I enjoyed every girl I saw wanting to rip off my clothes, it was getting a bit tiresome to walk around with a constant erection.

"Anyway, we have a problem." She gestured at the

table. "I can't smelt this stuff down into ingots. It's not even close to my expertise." As she spoke, her smelting tree popped into view, and I saw she was right. While she could smelt basic metals, most of the tree was unlearned. Hell, she didn't even have more than cursory training in the main skill.

"Yeah, I can see that," I mumbled, and as I tried to increase her base skill, I found I couldn't. Lucifer's hammer and crown gave me the ability to look but not touch, it seemed. "So, what do you want to do?"

"We have a couple options, honestly." She turned and looked at me. "Option one is I can try heating up the ends of the broken blade. If I get them hot enough, I might be able to weld them together. Then I can pound it out until it becomes one piece of steel. It won't be quite as good as before, but it will be usable." She shrugged. "Probably."

"And you didn't do that before, why?" I asked, watching her. I knew part of the reason was because she'd been hurt, but if that were the only reason, she'd not have sent me to find more Stygian Iron.

"Two reasons. One, you broke the blade multiple

times. Each break is going to require a separate weld. One of those is right where the tang extends into the hilt, and the other is in the center of the blade. Those are both places prone to breakage. So, basically, you have a really good chance of breaking Clarent again. Still, I could get it done in a day or two, assuming my body holds out." She gave me a weak smile. "I'm fine by the way, but it will be months before I'm back to full strength."

"So, assuming you can even do it, the sword won't be as good as before?" I asked, watching her closely.

"Theoretically." She shrugged. "That may let you use your builder powers though. Then you could just keep it on your person and use a different sword."

That was an excellent point, and I considered it for a moment before stopping and looking at her. "What's the second way?"

"The second way is harder." Sam gestured at the ore laid out behind her. "It involves melting the sword down into a solid bar, adding more Stygian Iron to the mix, and reforging it anew." She sighed. "It was what I had planned to do, but the more I think about it, the more I'm not sure I can." She bit her lip. "It's entirely possible I'll fuck it up, and we'll wind up with a sword that looks really nice but isn't Clarent."

"That seems pretty damned horrible," I said, peering at Clarent where it lay broken on the bench to her left. Maybe she was right. Maybe the best thing to do would be to fix it and see if I could still use my Builder powers.

As I thought about it, I used the combined power of the crown and hammer to open her repair tree and looked through it, but the result made my heart sink. While she knew the repair skill, she hadn't learned any of the skills for repairing legendary weapons. Worse, she didn't even have most of the forge legendary weapon skills learned which made sense because they required the repair skills.

While she was proficient in some materials like Dark Blood, and her sword making skills were maxed, I worried she was right. She could definitely create a powerful sword, but there was no way she'd be able to reforge Clarent.

"The look on your face makes me think I can't do

it," Sam said, gesturing at me. "That's the look you have when you're looking at my stats, but you're not usually frowning so much."

"That's about the size of it," I said, right before I flipped open her Legendary Smithery skill tree. That's when my eyes widened in shock as I looked at her Legendary Armor and Legendary Skill tabs. They had both improved since I'd last looked at her stats.

Legendary Armor

Skill: 4/10.

The user can restore Clarent's Ability to summon magical armor. This armor will appear when the user uses Clarent to summon it. Once summoned, the armor will give the user increased Abilities.

Legendary Skill

Skill: 6/10.

The user can increase Clarent's Ability to spend Experience on friendly targets. Doing so will decrease the cost to learn an Ability by 25%.

Interestingly, where before the third ability in the

first line had been blanked out, there was now a new skill visible there.

Craft Legendary Armament

Skill: 5/10.

Given the proper recipe, the user can craft a Legendary Armament.

Well, that made sense. After all, Sam had crafted the Relentless Grips of Greed, so it seemed reasonable for her to gain a skill related to crafting Armaments. However, in addition to learning that skill, there was now another row of skills below it. The first was directly linked to the Craft Legendary Armament skill, and as I glanced at it, I could see why.

Legendary Armament Repair

Skill: 1/10.

The user has grown proficient in working with the Builder's Legendary Armaments, and can now repair them, should they break.

The next two skills were moved off to the left, clearly unconnected to the others and were of particular interest to me.

Legendary Enhancement

Skill: 1/10.

The user has grown proficient in working with the Builder's Legendary Artifacts, and can now enhance them.

The skill spiraled off to the left, linked to the next skill.

Legendary Breakdown

Skill: 1/10.

The user has grown proficient in working with the Builder's Legendary Artifacts, and can now extract a single legendary ability from a Legendary artifact to implant in a new Legendary Grade item. Using this skill will destroy the current artifact in its entirety.

"Well, I have an idea, but you aren't going to like it," I said, gesturing at Clarent. "You know a skill that could theoretically be used to pull my Builder ability out of Clarent and place it in a new sword. There's just one problem."

"What's the problem?" Sam asked, looking back at Clarent where it lay broken. "Because that sounds like a great idea. I can whip up a new sword, and we'll be good to go."

"The problem is you need to have a Legendary Quality Weapon to put the power into, and you don't have a way to make that." I gave her a sheepish look. "I want to say sorry, but I don't think that's the right word."

"It's not." Sam frowned. "But that's good to know. We just need to find a smith good enough to make Legendary weapons." Sam tapped her cheek. Then her face fell.

"Is this where you tell me we need the head of the Blacksmith's guild to make it, and that makes us doubly fucked because she's dead?" I asked, taking a deep breath. "Because I've gotta tell you, I've had that thought."

"No." Sam shook her head. "It's much worse than that." She took a deep breath and exhaled slowly. "There is someone I know who can craft such a weapon."

"Well, that's great, right?" I asked, nodding. "Where is she?"

"In a lake." Sam looked at the ceiling. "In a goddamned lake."

"There's a lady in a lake?" I asked, and as I said the

words, I felt stupid. "Is this one of those hyperbole things?"

"No." Sam met my eyes. "When I was up and coming, there were rumors of a woman so talented, she could create weapons so powerful they could never actually be used in battle because no one could wield such power." Sam took a deep breath. "I found her though. I thought I could learn from her, and I was wrong." She sighed. "Then when I refused to reveal her location to the Guildmistress, I was demoted."

"I'm not sure what to say to that," I replied, staring at Sam as she fidgeted. Everything about her body language told me she didn't want to talk about it, let alone take me to this woman, but at the same time, there wasn't any other way.

"You're going to ask me to take you to her, huh?" Sam looked at the floor. "You'd be right to do so."

"You don't seem to think it's a good idea," I answered, feeling like a total asshole because I really wanted to do it, to find this woman and make her forge me a new sword to replace Clarent. "Is there some other way?"

"There isn't." Sam turned and looked at the broken

pieces of Clarent. "Best I can do is try to repair this, but I don't think it will work, and with the guild mistress dead, I'm not sure there are many others capable, even if they'd be willing." Sam sighed and looked back to me. "Get your Lust Aura under control, and I'll take you."

29

"Gwen, I need your help," I said as I appeared next to her. The entire conference room turned to look at me. As I reached out for Gwen's wrist, women sprang from their chairs with so much force, their chairs clattered to the ground and came rushed me with a hungry look in their eyes.

"Arthur, what's going on?" Gwen asked, confusion filling her voice. "Can't you see…" She turned toward the room, one hand raised when she saw them all coming toward me. "Oh."

"Yeah." I took her hand, and the feeling was electric. The mark on my chest blazed, filling the room with purple light and I heard a crash as the serving girl dropped her tray to the ground, forgetting it in her haste to get to me. Already I could feel hands grabbing hold of my shirt and pants, desperate to both pull them off and pull me to their owners.

"You can explain whatever this is to me, elsewhere," Gwen said, nodding to me as I teleported. We reappeared on the edge of the volcano where Lucifer had brought me earlier. I'd chosen this spot because I was reasonably sure there'd be no one here. After all, who could get to the mouth of a volcano?

"Where are we?" Gwen asked, turning in a slow circle as she took in the surroundings.

"What the hell is going on, Gwen?" I grumbled, ignoring her question. We were next to a volcano. Duh.

"I should ask you that." She peered at me. "One minute I'm talking to the head of the farmer's guild about turnip shortages and the next you appear. Then all the women in the room turn from composed, normal people, to fucking savages." She looked me up and down. "I've seen that look before, Arthur. They wanted to fuck you to death." She put her hands on her hips. "And as someone who has actually fucked you, I know you're good, but you're not *that* good."

The Builder's Pride

"That's why we need to talk." I sighed and moved toward the edge. Below the magma boiled, but I wasn't that concerned with it. After all, as long as I could teleport, I'd be okay.

"Okay…" Gwen shook her head. "About what?"

I exhaled a breath that tasted like old socks and turned to look at her. Then I touched the spot on my chest where her mark was still glowing. "Let me break it down. This mark you gave me is making it so every female I come in contact with wants to fuck my brains out."

"And that's a bad thing?" she asked, giving me a sly smile as she came over to me. Then she grabbed my junk. "I'd say you're more than ready for the occasion."

"Stop!" I pushed her away and took a pointed step backward. "I can't do anything effectively if I can't even be around women. The entire fucking world is women."

"Think about the bright side." Gwen smirked at me. "At least it's all women." She smacked me on my ass to emphasize her point.

I felt the blood rush from my face. "That was not

something I thought about." I shook off the thought. "Anyway, every other mark I have isn't glowing." I pulled off my shirt and stood there bare-chested before her. Sure enough, the marks of Wrath, Greed, and Envy didn't glow. They just looked like tattoos emblazoned across my flesh. Only her mark glowed.

"Oh." Gwen bit her lip. "So, it's my fault." She stopped and waved her hand. "I wasn't saying that accusingly. It literally is my fault." She huffed out a breath. "So how do I fix it?" She took a step closer and poked at the mark of Lust with one slender finger, but nothing happened. It continued to glow, blazing with purple light.

"I have no fucking clue." I crossed my arms over my chest. It was weird, standing before her like this made me uncomfortable, which was crazy because we'd had sex and all, but still.

"Well, that's no help." Gwen bit her lip and walked around me in a slow circle, taking in my body. "Maybe you need to get naked?"

"Um... why?" I asked, turning to look at her as she ran her hand over the Mark of Wrath.

"I dunno. I always think better when I'm naked.

Maybe you will too…" I turned and found Gwen had discarded her clothing. She stood there naked as a jaybird. Her dark nipples stood out against her white flesh, already hard and inviting me to lick them.

"Gwen, I don't think this is going to help." I swallowed as she kissed me, one hand reaching into my pants.

"It'll definitely help," she said as she broke the kiss and nipped at my ear. "I've been so horny, Arthur. I can't even think." Her tongue flicked out, tasting my flesh. "Just fuck me, okay? Then we can figure it out." She jerked my pants down around my ankles with one quick motion, and as the chainmail hit the stone, she wrapped her hands around me.

The feeling was indescribable. A wave of pleasure unlike anything I'd ever felt hit me, cascading down the length of my body.

"Please, Arthur. Don't make me beg." She swallowed hard. "Ever since I became the archangel of Lust, the only thing I think about is sex. I need it so bad I've thought about going to the human world and just fucking a dorm full of college kids." She dropped to her knees in front of me. "I haven't though. I've stayed here trying to do right by you, trying to make the treaties work out." Her tongue flicked out again. "I just need this, okay?"

"Gwen, I'm not sure—"

She cut off my words by taking me into her mouth, and if I had thought I had experienced pleasure before, I was wrong. So very fucking wrong. She bobbed up and down on me a couple times before pulling away.

"What was that, Arthur? I couldn't hear you because my mouth was full." She looked up at me. "Did you want me to do something?"

"Um… yeah," I said, and even though I did, I suddenly couldn't think of what it was because she was kneeling before me naked and ready.

"Then tell me, Arthur." Her tongue flicked out, trailing up me. "Tell me what you want me to do."

"You know, it's rude to talk with your mouth full." I reached down, grabbing her by the hair and pushing her open mouth back onto me, and as she engulfed me once more my entire world exploded into pleasure.

30

A day later, Gwen finally rolled off of me. Yes. A whole day.

31

"Well, on the plus side, your mark has stopped glowing," Gwen said, idly running a hand up my naked chest as she lay next to me on the grassy plain at the foot of the volcano.

"I'm wondering if your horniness might have something to do with it," I said, looking down and finding she was right. The Mark of Lust had stopped glowing. "Like, you're a succubus right, so you absorb power through sex?"

"Well, yeah, but I don't see why that'd make the mark glow or make you horny." She nuzzled her head against my chest. "I should be the one making you horny."

"Oh, trust me. That is most certainly not the problem." I looked her up and down. "But that's not my point." I sighed as she ran her fingers down my chest, making it incredibly hard to concentrate.

"Then what's the problem?" She smiled in a way that let me know exactly what she was thinking, and sadly, though I was mentally prepared to go with it, I didn't think I could physically manage.

"The problem is that you are bound to me with the mark. I can feel the other archangels through the marks, especially when something really crazy happens. Like when Wrath gets mad, for instance, I can feel it." I looked at her. "You just became the Archangel of Lust since she was dead, but I think it goes without saying you weren't at her power level. I'm guessing you have to absorb a lot of power to feel sated. Like, I dunno, if we suddenly increased the size of a gas tank in a car." I gestured down at myself. "And I think maybe you were using the mark to feed through me. That's why the aura drew girls to me. So, you could feed off them through me."

"You know, you sound so sexy when you explain the world to me like it's a bunch of game mechanics." Gwen kissed me. Hard. "But I think you might be right." She moved on top of me and pressed her bare breasts against my chest. "Now, I'm not hungry though, so I'm pretty sure I just want you for your body and big ol' brain." She reached down between my legs and frowned at me. "What's the matter?"

"Are you seriously asking me 'what's the matter?' We've been having sex for almost twenty-six hours." I met her eyes as she continued to play with little me. "I need a break."

"It would seem so." She sighed before getting off of me and stretching. "Now, I need a shower and a cigarette." She looked over at me and snapped her fingers. "Come on. Back to town with you." She gave me an evil grin. "Unless you can get unbroken."

"Yeah, not gonna happen." I looked down at myself. I, unlike the succubus, did not have magical non-chaffing sex parts. While I might be able to draw on the energy of the archangels I'd bonded with to increase my strength, stamina, and general ability to not pass out, even I had my limits it seemed.

"Right, so on with the clothes." She grabbed her pants off the ground while bending over to give me a view, and the sad thing was I was so tired, I couldn't even enjoy it.

A few minutes later we were dressed and ready to go. I barely remembered coming down the volcano, but I was sort of glad we had. I was sore from having sex on grass, and I couldn't imagine what would have happened if we would have tried on top of volcanic rock.

"Well, I feel great." Gwen smiled at me before smacking my ass. "We should do that again, sometime." She took my hand in hers and squeezed my fingers. "What does your afternoon look like?"

"As awesome as that sounds, Sam—"

"She can join us, I don't mind." Gwen batted her eyes at me.

"No." I stopped, trying to get the image out of my head. "We're going to go see about getting my sword fixed."

"Ah." She looked down at my crotch. "I'm guessing not that one." She shook herself. "Geez, it's like I can't think of anything besides sex." As she spoke, the mark on my chest began to glow. Not brightly, but enough to let me know I was on borrowed time.

"You need to go talk to Mammon about the mark thing." I touched my chest. "Because as fun as spending my entire life fucking you would be, I do need to stop the Darkness because otherwise, that life will be pretty damned short."

"Right, of course." She shut her eyes for a moment and took a few deep breaths, causing the mark to fade back to normal. "I'll talk to Mammon about controlling my new powers." She licked her lips and came toward me. "Unless you want to go out with a bang." She began to laugh as she wrapped her hands around my arm. "Eh?"

"Yes, but not right now." I laughed too. Part of it was just delirium. I felt so tired I could barely think, and even though the marks of Greed, Envy, and Wrath were keeping me upright, I could tell the power I was getting from them had fallen to a trickle. I was guessing Gwen had drained them too. It was a bit of a scary thought, but at the same time, I was pretty sure once I slept for a while, I'd be okay.

"I'm gonna hold you to that," Gwen said, right before I teleported to Mammon. We reappeared in a lavish hotel room in who knows where. The entire room was lavish to the point of gaudy, with gold embroidered pillows and silver filigree on the walls.

Mammon was passed out in a chair next to a bottle of dark liquid, feet up on the table. Drool spilled from the corner of her mouth, and as I approached, the sound of her snoring was enough to let me know she was *really* asleep. Hell, she still had her boots on.

"Crazy," Gwen said, staring at the Archangel of Greed. "I didn't know she actually slept."

"I bet this is your doing." I touched the mark of Lust. "All the other marks feel really weak right now. You sucked down three archangels."

"The crazy thing is that I'm still hungry. Like I felt like I had a really nice appetizer, but I'm ready for the main course." She turned to look at me, one hand snaking down my body. "Sure you don't wanna try again? I could do that thing you like." She licked her lips. Besides, I can feel strength flowing through you now that you're holding Lucifer's hammer again. I think it'll be okay."

"Gwen, I'm almost positive that if we have sex again, I'll die." I stepped away from her, and it was hard because she kept touching me. Already the mark was starting to burn visibly beneath my chest. "Go take a cold shower or something."

"But Arthur—"

I teleported away as she started to unbutton her shirt. I knew that if I stayed until she took it off, I'd never leave, and that would have probably killed not just me, but three other archangels.

As I reappeared in Sam's shop, the blacksmith shrieked and jumped ten feet in the air. She whirled, one hand gripping her hammer, and stared at me.

"You scared the crap out of me!" she cried, grabbing her heart with one hand. "You're lucky I didn't brain you with my hammer." She sucked in a huge breath.

"Sorry, I was with Gwen, and she's trying to fuck me to death." I touched the mark, and it was still burning, but not as brightly as it had a moment ago. "She's with Mammon."

"I can still feel the draw." Sam licked her lips. "So, whatever she's doing isn't quite working." As Sam spoke, the mark of Lust on Lucifer's hammer began to flare, letting me know that Gwen was starting to draw from the Devil herself. I quickly released the hammer, and as I did, the mark on my chest faded a little.

"Sorry." I shrugged. "I'm not sure what to do about it if she can't control her power." I looked at the hammer. "And I really don't want Lucifer pissed at me if Gwen tries to suck her dry too."

"Both excellent points," Sam said, and her breathing and quickened. As I turned back to her, I saw her nipples straining against her shirt. "But I think we need to figure out something else." She swallowed hard. "Because I'm an archangel, and right now it's all I can do to keep from tearing off your clothes." She stopped and looked away, trying to focus on anything that wasn't me. "I can't go with you like this." She touched her chest. "I'm too hurt to sleep with you, and even if I wasn't, we'd make it exactly ten steps before we did just that."

"You know," I said, turning back to the hammer. "Lucifer grabbed me and beat the fuck out of me and didn't seem even remotely fazed by Lust's mark."

"Lucifer is the strongest of all archangels, and in addition to that, she has the power of every last one of us." Sam took a deep breath as her left hand went toward her breast. She stopped, visibly straining, and dropped her hands to the table behind her. Then she sat on them. "None of our powers affect her. Not well, anyway."

"Interesting," I said, grabbing the hammer once more. As I did, the mark on my chest flared like a fucking solar flare. Sam cried out, and as she leapt for me, I teleported away.

32

The surrounding scenery congealed into a purplish mass that sort of resembled grape jelly. I stood on a lone platform, the color of lavender sequins. The star-filled sky raced by like I was in the cockpit of a spaceship going near light speed, but it didn't feel like I was moving. I swallowed, trying to figure out what the hell was going on as I spun in a slow circle.

Lucifer sat cross-legged in the center of the platform, and as I turned toward her, she stood and gestured at our surroundings. There was nothing on this platform, and while it was about a hundred square feet or so in size, it was a little disconcerting because there was only the vast emptiness of space in every direction. If I fell off, I was reasonably sure I'd fall forever.

"Hello, Builder." She nodded to me. "Why have you come here?"

"Where the hell are we?" I tried to stifle my fear as the archangel stared at me. She didn't seem annoyed by my presence, more curious.

Lucifer shrugged. "A place outside of space and time. It was created as a place for angels to train and battle with no distractions. There is no real world to worry about, no magical items to use." She smirked. "No one to hear you scream."

"Why are you here?" I shook my head in confusion.

"I should ask you that." She looked me up and down. "I created this place. It is as much mine as anywhere else." She stepped on the platform, causing concentric lines of color to burst outward like ripples in a lake. "Why have you sought me, Builder?" She gestured toward the edge. "Before you reply, know that if you fall, you will keep falling until eternity ends." She smiled, and a cruel edge flashed across her face. "Which is doubly bad for someone like you because in this place you will not hunger nor thirst. There will just be an eternity of falling." She took a small step toward me. "Now, again I ask. Why have you sought me out, Builder?"

Her words sent a chill running down my spine, but I did my best to ignore them. "I have a question for you."

"Oh?" She arched an eyebrow. "And what would you ask of the Devil?"

"It's about Gwen." I touched the mark on my chest, and it was burning so brightly, I could see it through my shirt. "She can't control her powers."

"None of what you said is a question." She peered at me. "It is as though you wish for me to throw you over the edge." She gestured at my belt. "Know that if I do so, I will take away your belt so your ability to bounce around like Wrath will not save you."

"Right, okay, sorry." I sucked in a breath. "You don't seem to be affected by the Lust aura, and I want you to show me how to fix it, to keep those around me from being affected by Gwen." I touched the mark. "All of these seem to operate as a two-way street, but I feel like I'm just bending to the wills of those who marked me. That isn't acceptable. Can you help me?"

"I can." She looked at me for a long time. "Why would I choose to do this?" She held out her hand to me. "You have already received two gifts from me and have given nothing in return." She licked her lips. "That is more than most have ever gotten from me."

"Wait, you mean you planned this?" I asked, looking at the warhammer. "You knew about the way the marks worked."

"I did." She nodded to me. "You cannot walk around with such a pathetic weapon as that sword. It will not aid you in the fight against the Darkness. I have given it to you to use, knowing the bindings of my sister would aid you." She moved closer to me. "But it seems you're still too weak." She inhaled sharply.

"You're weak, Arthur. So far you've been lucky you haven't been killed outright." She shrugged. "You have no skill, no chance of beating someone who knows what they are doing. Arthur, the things you will face from here on out are stronger, faster, and better than you. If you do not up your game, you will die."

Lucifer gestured, and a glimmering rent in space appeared at her fingertips. Through it, I could see the pearly gates with huge marble statues beyond. Only, I could see the darkness encroaching upon the land, see the corruption already working at the gates. And in that darkness, I could see dead angels, their mangled bodies left to rot as an army of lizardmen, beholders, and other creatures slammed into the gates. Even watching it, I could see the stronghold would not last much longer.

"How would you defeat that army, Arthur?" Lucifer asked, and as I stood there openmouthed, she continued. "If you really want to save everyone, you'll let me train you to use your natural abilities to your advantage."

"You want to train me?" I asked incredulously.

"That is why you came here, yes? You said you wish to control the marks." She touched the mark on my chest, and the glow died. Instantly. As did the power of the ring around my neck. "You wish to know how to shut them off, to wield them to their full potential." Her hand lashed out, ripping the warhammer from me before I even realized what had happened.

The bindings upon it flared. My own marks

responded in kind, glowing to match. "I can teach you how to do it all." Lucifer sucked in a deep breath and exhaled through her teeth. "And before you give me another excuse, let me remind you of what I said earlier. We're outside of time and space right now. You can return to Hell and only a few moments will have passed, or you can go to Heaven and try to help them stop the one they call Dred." She dropped the warhammer at my feet, and the magic surrounding it died. My marks went out and the armaments I wore felt dead and lifeless. "Or you can stay." She met my eyes. "What do you say?"

"Why are you helping me?" I asked, gritting my teeth as I mulled over her words. As much as I wanted to be back out there doing something, she had a point. I mean, I'd spent a year training in Mammon's dead zone, but at the same time, looking through the portal at Heaven, I knew I was in trouble. To say I was out of my league was an understatement of gigantic proportions.

The thought gnawed at me because I could see liches like the ones Sam had faced down. Only there were hundreds of them. If I'd been stronger,

I'd have been able to kill the thing without Sam getting involved. If I didn't get better fast, I'd just wind up getting my face caved in and worse, my friends would pay for it.

I couldn't allow that. I had to get strong enough to save them all. I owed them that much.

"Isn't it obvious, Builder?" Lucifer met my eyes, and within them, I saw the millions upon millions who would die at her hands should we succeed in driving back the darkness. The thing was, if we didn't win, that wouldn't matter. "I want to win." Her hand curled into a fist. "And as incredibly pathetic as it sounds, I need you to do it." She turned her head heavenward. "The irony does not escape me."

"Can we really win?" I asked. Part of me couldn't believe I was making a deal with the Devil, but at the same time, she was right. I needed her help, and if this got me her help, well, that was fine. At the end of the day, I had to beat the Darkness, or everyone would die. If that meant I had to sell my soul to Lucifer herself, I could pay that price.

"Yes, but only if you stay. If you leave, I shall sit here alone and wait for you to fall. Then I will find the next Builder myself and hope he is not too stupid to accept my help." Lucifer pointed at the portal, and as she did, it began to flicker. "You have three seconds to make your choice. Go or stay, but know that if you stay and be obstinate in any way, I will fling you from the edge."

"I'll stay." I took a deep breath and thought about Sam, about Gwen and Annabeth. Hell, I thought about Mammon. I couldn't let them down. "If you can really make me stronger, I'll do anything."

"Excellent." As the portal vanished, Lucifer gestured at the abject darkness of the final destination. "Now, are you ready to brawl?"

I nodded in spite of myself. "Yeah, let's do this." I raised my fists and dropped into a fighting stance in front of Lucifer.

"Okay," Lucifer replied, studying me as she walked around me in a slow circle. "Your stance is all wrong." She kicked my feet out a little bit and adjusted my center of balance with her hands. "This will give you more balance and increase your natural striking speed by shortening the time you need to shift your momentum. When you swing, rotate on the balls of your feet." She demonstrated.

I complied, feeling like an idiot, but found to my astonishment she was right. My fist whistled through the air. I did it a few more times before stopping.

"Why did you stop?" Lucifer asked, narrowing her eyes at me.

"Why is it so hard to breathe?" I asked, my chest already heaving. "Normally, I have pretty good cardio."

"The air is significantly thinner than back in Hell." She bent down and picked up the warhammer. "And the gravity here is a bit stronger."

"So I'm in the training ground from hell," I grumbled, suddenly concerned I'd die from lack of oxygen. Still, I had to push through it. I threw another punch, and as I did, I could feel my muscles start to burn.

"Good." Lucifer nodded as she moved back toward the middle of the platform. "Do that about a thousand more times, then switch to your other hand and do the same thing. I'll wait, I have infinite time." Lucifer glanced at me over her shoulder, and I didn't get the feeling she was joking.

"Why so many times?" I asked, throwing another punch and nearly losing my balance in the process. I was already starting to get really tired, which was no good at all. I'd thrown what, six punches? How was I going to punch nearly two thousand more times?

"Because you want to ingrain it into your muscle memory. You need to fight without thinking. Your body needs to react without being commanded to by your mind. To accomplish this, you must drill." Lucifer gave me a 'duh' look. "Do you know so little?"

"So, it's like, you know, riding a bike?" I asked, dropping back into my stance and readying myself for another attack.

"If the bike was on fire, and you were on fire, and everything was on fire," Lucifer replied with a strange gleam in her eyes. "Actually, that gives me an idea."

The floor exploded into flame, rippling out around me in a circle so hot it sucked the moisture from my body. It steadily moved closer, inching forward as I stood there like a dumbass.

"What the hell is going on?" I screamed, not sure

how to escape the flames. Could I leap through them? Maybe, but it'd hurt a lot.

"Keep punching, Arthur. Every punch you throw will make the fire recede a few millimeters. If you stop, it will gain on you. When you get to a couple thousand punches, it will go out. Good luck." With that, the Devil sat down with her back to me and pulled out a paperback book.

I didn't see what it was about because the flames surged upward, cutting off my view of everything but the raging inferno surrounding me. It roiled, edging closer inch by inch as I stood there gasping, the air almost too hot to breathe. Sweat poured down my body and was instantly evaporated as I turned in a slow circle. As far as I could tell, there was no way out, short of throwing myself through the ring of fire.

Still, maybe the Devil wasn't lying, maybe the fire would go out if I finished the exercise. I resolved to try it mostly because I had no other choice. I dropped back into my fighting stance, and as I did so, the floor beneath my feet turned a translucent green color. I shifted my hips, throwing my momentum into the blow, and the ground turned blue, the fire edging backward a hair.

I threw another punch, but as I did so, I over-extended slightly, causing my toe to inch forward. The ground beneath my feet turned an angry red color, and the fire leapt forward, increasing in speed as I dropped back and tried punching at it again. As I did so, the floor changed back to blue.

"Oh my god," I muttered, swallowing hard. "I'm using a Dance Dance Revolution training simulator." I threw another punch. "Except it's on fire."

It almost made me want to laugh and cry simultaneously, but that'd mean I had time to stop punching, which I didn't. I kept going until my arms felt like they were going off, until everything distilled into a weird sort of emptiness in my brain. There was no thought. There was only me and the flames surrounding me. And punching. Lots and lots of punching

I wasn't sure how long I played mystical flaming DDR, but it was a while, and that wasn't the end of it, not by a long shot. Lucifer trained me for time indeterminable, and while I couldn't tell how long it actually lasted since there was no time in this place, it felt like years. Let me just say this right now, exploding hopscotch was way less fun than it sounded.

By the end of it, I had learned not only several forms of martial arts, weaponry, and everything in between, but I'd somehow managed to bulk up too. I'd also eaten something like eight-hundred pounds of fish because, for some reason, Lucifer thought it was a must for gaining muscle even though I wasn't actually required to eat while I was here. She told me this after thumbing through a human physiology textbook in search for hidden muscles to have me work out.

Either way, I was feeling pretty good as Lucifer reopened the portal, and I saw Sam standing there in her shop, still in mid-leap.

"You ready, Arthur?" Lucifer asked, slapping me on the back. The force of it surged through me, but I ignored it. "Or you want to do one more set before we go?" She gestured at a bench press in the corner of the final destination platform. The place was weird like that. Whatever type of training equipment you required magically came out of the floor. It made cleanup awesome because it disappeared just as easily.

"I'm good, thanks," I said, taking a deep breath. It felt like I'd been gone forever, and while I was sure

I'd needed the training, I was anxious to get back to work.

"You're welcome." Lucifer offered me the warhammer. "I expect this back."

"I figured." I took the weapon from her. "I really mean that, by the way, thank you for everything."

"Arthur, you did the work. I'm proud of you for that." She smirked. "If you hadn't, I'd have thrown you off the edge." She made a shooing motion. "Now go."

"Right, okay," I said, taking one last look at the Devil. It was weird because part of me wanted to stay with her longer. Truth be told, I'd spent more time with her than anyone else, which was a little weird.

"You're not leaving?" She met my eyes, and as I opened my mouth to say something, she stepped up onto her tippy toes. "Do you want to stay longer?"

Lucifer touched my face gently with her free hand, drawing me down into her while her other hand traced along my back.

She kissed me.

The kiss wasn't hungry or desperate. It was all things to all people. It was a bird's first flight from the nest, a sunrise over mountain tops. It was perfection.

As she broke our kiss and looked up at me, she shoved me backward through the portal.

33

I hit the ground hard on my back just as Sam pounced on me. As her hands reached for my pants, she stopped and shook herself. The crazed gleam in her eyes faded, and she looked down at me confused.

"What the fuck?" she asked, inhaling sharply through her nose. "You smell like *her.*" She leapt off me like I was on fire and scurried backward until her shoulders hit the leg of the table behind her. "How?"

"I went to see Lucifer about making the mark stop affecting everyone." I touched my chest, and as I did, I could feel the rising heat of Gwen's need like a raging forest fire, only it didn't affect me anymore, and what's more, it didn't affect those around me.

Figuring out how to manipulate the marks had been hard as each had worked a bit differently, but I'd had a lot of time.

"That was a bad idea." Sam swallowed her, her eyes raking over me. "I can feel her on you, feel her presence."

"What the hell are you talking about?" I asked, getting to my feet. "We barely touched the whole time. She mostly just threw fire at me, or lit the platform on fire." I shrugged. "There was a lot of fire."

"Arthur." Sam met my eyes, and I could still see the fear in her eyes. "She's marked you. Like actually marked you." She inhaled. "You've been marked by the Devil."

"I have not." I moved to cross my arms indignantly, but it was hard because I was holding the warhammer so instead I just stood there looking at it dumbly. "I think I'd know."

"Drop the warhammer then." Sam got slowly to her feet, and I saw her looking around like she was trying to find a weapon.

"Fine!" I snapped, releasing my grip on the warhammer. As it hit the ground beside me, my mouth fell open. I could still see the stats of everything. Normally, the crown Lucifer had given me didn't work when I wasn't touching the warhammer. Only it was now…

"You still see stats, huh." Sam met my eyes. "Admit it."

"Yes." I swallowed hard. When could she have marked me without me noticing? I thought back, trying to remember, and as I did, my hand went to my mouth.

"It's not your lips," Sam said, coming closer to me. Each step she took was hesitant, wary. "I could tell you kissed her, but the mark's not there." She shook her head. "Take off your clothes and let me check for marks."

"Are you sure we need to do that?" I asked, suddenly feeling uncomfortable. "I mean, if she's done it, what's it matter. I'm going to bear the mark either way."

"Fair point." Sam walked around me in a slow circle. "Do you feel evil?"

"Not particularly." I shrugged. "But I do feel like I need to get a sword." I gestured at the warhammer. "Lucifer was very clear on wanting this back."

"I'll bet." Sam took in the warhammer for a long time. "Can you try something?"

"What's that?" I asked as Sam took my hand and placed it on the spot where the mark with Dred had been.

"Tell me what you feel." Sam shut her eyes, and as she did, I felt her power reaching out to me in a way it hadn't before. It was hard to explain, but I'd not quite felt her power in the same way I had with Mammon, Sathanus, and the others. Only now… now she felt similar.

"I can feel your power. It's still recovering, but it isn't rejecting me like it once had." As I spoke, Sam opened her eyes and nodded.

"Yeah, that's what I thought." She bit her lip and stepped away. "You should check Gabriella. See if it's the same."

"Why?" I asked, confused.

"Because," Sam sighed, "Lucifer was the leader. The head archangel. The *most* high. As much as we wouldn't like to believe it, we're still bound to her in some small way. It's why defeating her proved so difficult." Sam looked me over. "Her mark is making your power feel less illegitimate." Sam sighed. "I don't know if you realize, but the reason why this wound is taking so long to heal is because my power doesn't mix well with yours." She touched the spot. "You've fused a piece of your soul here, but I was never meant to bond with the Builder." She bit her lip. "Always with the Destroyer."

"And my bond with Lucifer is changing that?" I asked, trying to follow along. If what Sam said was true, then Lucifer might be the key to reuniting the Angels and the Demons.

"A little." Sam nodded. "It's weird, like Lucifer's obviously all fucked in the head, but that doesn't matter to the ethereal powers that be." She made air quotes. "Those are beyond time, and in their eyes, right or wrong, those bonds were never truly broken." Sam gestured at me. "As her chosen, that legitimacy now resides with you." She pulled her shirt down to reveal the mark. I could see her flesh knitting together in a way that it never had before. The wound she'd suffered at the hands of Dred had always seemed more like a weird repaired hole.

Now though? Now it was healing anew, reminding me less of a patched pair of overalls and more of a quilt. Sure, it was a bit different, but it still fit the pattern in a way that seemed intentional.

"It's healing!" I exclaimed, taking a step forward, my hand reaching out to touch it, only as I did, she shied away.

"That's my point, Arthur." She looked at me. "It makes me wonder what else is possible."

"What do you mean by that?" I asked, but she waved off the question.

"I need to think about it some more, Arthur. I have an idea, but it will take time." She shook her head. "We don't have that time right now." She looked at me. "Not when we need to find the Lady of the Lake and get her to make you a new sword."

"Right, okay." I nodded my agreement. "You could still tell me though. Maybe I could help."

"If I did that, it might give you false hope. I don't want to do that." She looked at me. "Go see Gabriella, okay? When you're done, I'll be ready to go." She gave me a weak smile. "Okay?"

"Okay," I said, and turned to leave, feeling like what

she had kept to herself was important. While I got the impression I could make her tell me, I decided to let it go. She would tell me when she was ready. Besides, I wanted to chat with Gabriella, anyway.

First though? First, I had to talk to Gwen.

I clicked my heels together even though I didn't have to do it and teleported to the succubus. As soon as I appeared, she looked up from the bed. Beside her, a trio of unconscious room service girls lay naked while Mammon was still passed out on the chair. Only, I knew I couldn't have been away from her for more than a few minutes in real-world time.

"Back so soon?" Gwen asked, rising to her feet. Her naked body glistening as she threw her head back, causing her hair to crash around her pale shoulders like a dark wave. "And you smell like you're ready to go again." She licked her lips as she came toward me. "Come on, off with those clothes."

I grabbed her hands before she could jerk down my pants. "I know how to fix your problem." I touched her chest where she bore Asmodai's mark, and the light flaring from it faded away. She stopped, standing there blinking as the lust in her eyes vanished.

"What'd you do?" she asked, looking me over. "I feel…"

"Normal? Balanced?" I smiled. "Somewhere in between?"

"Yes." She nodded. "How?"

"I bound your mark shut. It's just temporary." I touched my own chest where I bore the mark. "Would you like me to show you how to control it?"

"God yes." She frowned, looking back at the bed. "I don't even like women that way, but I couldn't help myself. They just seemed so…"

"Right." I took her chin in my hand and leaned down to kiss her. As I did, the mark on my chest flared, but I ignored it. Instead, I focused on the technique Lucifer had shown me. When we'd been together, Lucifer had taught me to control each of the marks, partially by touching each mark and imparting the knowledge into me.

Now, I did the same to Gwen, pushing all the knowledge Lucifer had given me about the Archangel of Lust into Gwen's mind while using our mark as a bridge. It was easier than I expected thanks to our connection. With Lucifer, it'd always felt like trying to pound a square peg into a round hole. This wasn't like that. My peg matched her hole perfectly.

34

"Die!" Gabriella cried, whirling to attack me with her mace the moment I approached her. I sidestepped without thinking, one hand coming up to block. As her mace slammed into my gauntlet and lightning crackled across the metal, her eyes went wide with shock. "Arthur?"

Her mace fell away from me as the lighting along its length dissipated. "Oh my gosh! Are you okay?" Her nose crinkled as she looked at me, eyes raking over me in one quick motion. "What happened to you?"

"To me?" I said, taking a step back in case she decided to try to brain me again. We were standing amidst one of the fields out back. "You just attacked me!"

"I thought you were someone else." She fidgeted, looking at her feet. "It was an honest mistake. I was here all by myself trying to get the plants to grow even though I told them the land isn't right because it's too dry and we need rain. Then you came up smelling like that and feeling like that, and I didn't know what to think." She swallowed.

"Like what?" I asked, confused. "What are you talking about?" When she didn't immediately respond, I continued, "Look, Sam told me to come talk to you. She said my power is different."

"It does feel different." Gabriella crossed the distance between us and touched my chest with her hands while inhaling sharply. "I can smell all of my sisters on you." She nodded. "Sam, Lucifer, Mammon, Sathanus, Leviathan, and even Asmodai." She touched her chin. "Though Asmodai also sort of just smells like Gwen. Are they friends now?"

"Gwen bonded with Asmodai." I stopped. "Wait, what do you mean you can smell Sam?"

"Well, I can smell her mark." She gave me a weird

look, nose scrunched up in thought. "It's right, um…" She touched a spot on my lower abdomen. "Right there."

I looked down at the spot she'd touched, and as I did, I found it glowing. Only that was a bit crazy because it hadn't glowed before.

Confused, I pulled up my shirt and found Gabriella was right. There was a mark there. It was a blackened scythe with two dark wings extending from it, and it looked incredibly similar to the one I'd seen on Sam's own scythe when she'd used it against the lich.

"See, told you." Gabriella smiled at me. "You bear Samael's marks." She frowned. "That's why I was confused. You didn't smell quite like him, but for a second, I thought you were him, were Dred." She met my eyes. "You can see how I got confused."

"I don't understand how Sam was able to mark me." I touched the spot and found it hot to the touch. What's more, as I concentrated on it, I realized I could feel Sam, feel her command over death itself. The crazy thing was I could also feel how weak she was, how Hell itself had sapped much its strength, and what's more, I could feel that strength returning.

"Well, you guys basically did the whole marking thing when you saved her. You gave her a piece of your soul and stitched it into place with Mammon's power." Gabriella shrugged. "I don't know that I'm the right person to ask about this. I'm not really very smart." She sighed. "Wish I could help you more."

"I think you're plenty smart." I was still mulling over her words in my mind, but I could tell she wanted to get back to work from the way she kept furtively glancing at the field. What's more, I knew I had time to kill because I could feel Sam's haste to get ready and knew she was still far from ready to go.

"I know you do, Arthur. It's why I love you." She blushed slightly. "Anyway, this farm isn't going to water herself." She swallowed. "I need to figure out a way to get the well water all the way over here. Sam was going to make pipes later, but in the meantime we need another way."

As she spoke, I realized she was right. The ground beneath us was dry and barren, and though I could feel Gabriella's magic in the air, I could also feel that it was fighting the odds. For one, Hell's ethereal nature was breaking down her power before it got a chance to really work, and that was compounded by the fact that the ground was suboptimal. We might have been able to overcome one, but not the other. Worse, just a quick look around let me know what power she had wasn't reaching much beyond where we were. It made the fields the others had tilled and planted a waste.

"I can see what you mean," I said, reaching up and touching my crown. As I did, the farm plot popped into view.

Farm Plot

Grade: D

Size: 64 m by 64 m

Status: Seeded

I turned my gaze away from the main menu for the farm plot, focusing on the soil beneath my feet, and as I did, another tooltip opened.

Seeded Earth

Type: Rockberry

Moisture: 1/10

Nutrients: 6/10

Note: Rockberry seeds will not grow unless they receive sufficient water.

I drilled down even further, bringing up the seeds themselves.

<u>Rockberry Seed</u>

Type: Edible

Grow Time: 7-10 days.

Harvest Time: 3 days

Usage: Recurring

Requirements: Moisture: 6+, Nutrients: 4+

"Do we have other kinds of seeds?" I asked, looking up at Gabriella. She'd evidently grown bored with watching me stand there looking at the plants because she had her back to me and was kneeling on the ground trying to coax life from the seeds. This time, as I watched her, I saw the tooltip for her magic.

Angelic Growth

Skill: 8/10.

The user can reduce the Grow Time, Harvest Time, and requirements for certain types of vegetation.

"Yeah, I think so." Gabriella looked over at me. "That's Crystal's thing though. She decided what to plant." She frowned. "I told them we needed something that would tolerate the weather here a bit better, but she said we can't eat those kinds of plants, and that they planned on getting irrigation."

"That makes some sense," I said, thinking. If that was true, it'd be better to sow the fields with seeds to take advantage of the coming irrigation. Otherwise, we might have wasted land on something that wasn't as good. At the same time, none of these fields near me seemed to be growing, and what's more, Sam wasn't going to be making piping anytime soon.

"I suppose." Gabriella bit her lip. "But it wouldn't have hurt to plant some of the fields with things that actually grow here." She gestured at the plot in front of here. "I don't think I can make this work, but I'll keep trying."

"It's probably not worth it. You aren't going to make it grow without some rain," I said, looking at the sky. As I did, I felt the small of my back start to burn. The crown on my head began to glow, and as I reached up to touch it, I could practically feel Lucifer wrapping her arms around me. Her fingers entwined with mine as she pointed up into the sky where a tooltip had appeared on the clouds overhead and reading it made my eyes go wide.

Would you like to make it rain? Y/N

"Do it," Lucifer's voice whispered into my ear, and while she wasn't there, I could hear her plain as day. "Show them the might of our power. Show them that even the weather bows before us."

I stared at the message for a moment before nodding.

"Okay." I selected the Yes Icon. The crown on my head began to glow, and as it did, white-hot pain exploded from my back. I collapsed to my knees as energy washed out of me, spiraling up into the atmosphere. As the spell hit the sky above, lightning began to crackle, and the darkened clouds rumbled angrily.

As the clouds above finally let loose, spilling their contents down across the field in a torrent of water, my vision went black, and I collapsed.

35

"Arthur, are you okay?" Gabriella asked, and my eyes fluttered open to find myself laying with my head in her lap. The rain pouring down around us shimmered off a translucent barrier that kept us from getting drenched, but even still Gabriella's white dress was matted to her flesh in a way that left little to the imagination.

"I think so," I whispered, and found it hard to talk due to the migraine practically splitting my skull in two. "How about you?"

"I'm okay." She gave me a weird look. "Why wouldn't I be? It's just raining." She looked up and gestured at the shimmering shield. Besides, I made a barrier."

"Oh, I just figured you might melt because you're so sweet." I gave her a stupid grin, and she blushed so hard, her chest turned pink.

"That's a very sweet thing to say," she said, taking a deep breath before fixing her perfect blue eyes on me. "But I see what you're doing. Trying to distract me with nice words." She clucked a couple of times. "That won't work, mister. I saw you call the rain just like sister does right before you collapsed." She looked at the sky. "It was strange, almost like I could feel her here."

"I think the crown let me do it." I slowly got off her lap and sat up. It was weird because I could see the ground around us turning to mud as the greedy earth sucked in the rain, but our little spot was still dry.

"That does not surprise me." She looked at the crown on my head, her eyes studying it. "Especially knowing my sister. Her tantrums caused the downfall of Atlantis, don't you know." She nodded once. "That's neither here nor there though."

As much as I wanted to ask her about Atlantis, I was fairly certain that no man named Arthur Curie should ever go into the ocean, let alone to Atlantis.

The way things were going, that might raise a whole bunch of issues I didn't want to deal with.

"I have a question," I asked, running a hand through my hair. It'd gotten much longer in the time I'd spent with Lucifer, and though Lucifer had hacked at it with a knife to keep it from growing too long, she wasn't exactly the world's best barber.

"Oh?" Gabriella brightened. "I'd love to answer it for you if I can. Well, if that would make you happy." She frowned at the space beyond the barrier. "Otherwise, I'll have to get back to work, and while working is in my top ten favorite things, I don't like rain. It reminds me of snails and worms." Her frown deepened. "They're so icky."

"Right, okay." I nodded. "I don't like them either. When I was little the sidewalk outside the place where I lived often flooded in the rain, and there would always be worms on it. They'd eventually dry out in the sun." I stuck my tongue out. "Always made me feel bad."

"You didn't put the worms back in the ground?" She watched me carefully. "I don't like them, but I'd have helped them."

"I couldn't. It was too wet when I first saw them,

and they were dead by the time I returned." I shrugged. "To be honest, I hadn't thought about it."

"Oh." There was a lot of disappointment in that word. "What's your question, Arthur?" she asked, turning to look across the field. "I need to finish this before we can have rock berries. I'm told they make a great pie."

"Hmm, why did you attack me before?" I gestured at myself. "You said you thought I was someone else. Who did you think I was?"

"Oh." There was more emotion this time. Only now it was fear. "You reminded me of Dred." She took a deep breath. "You feel so much like him now. Not just with the power, but all around." She gestured at me. "The same drive, same determination. It flows from you and mixes with the power." She hugged herself. "Makes me glad we're on the same side."

"Wait, you think I feel like Dred?" The words made me feel ill. Dred was an agent of Darkness, but he hadn't always been. From what Sam had told me, he'd turned on her to get more power, and as it stood, I'd been pretty relentless in my pursuit of power. Could I turn out like him? Already, I could feel the archangels bonded to me, influencing me like a thousand angry cats in the night. I couldn't imagine what a lifetime of hearing those same voices would do, and they weren't the darkness. How much worse would it be to hear Cthulhu or the Empress for all that time?

I remembered Nadine. How happy she'd been when I'd killed her, how free she'd seemed. How much worse would it be for Dred?

"You do feel like Dred." Gabriella touched my arm. "But he is evil, and you are not." She gave me a soft smile. "Do not worry, Arthur. You will do the right thing when the time comes."

"I hope you're right," I said, getting to my feet. I could hear the rain pounding at the barrier surrounding me, and as I reached out toward the barrier, I realized Lucifer had shown me how to do something similar. In the end, it was the same power Sam had infused into my sword long ago.

"I think you do not give yourself enough credit." Gabriella reached out and touched my face, turning me toward her. "Just like last time." She nodded once. "You will prevail."

"What do you mean like last time?" I turned to her and found her staring at me.

"You have faced down the Darkness twice." Gabriella smiled. "Do you know how many Builders have done that?" She touched my arm lightly. "Just you, Arthur."

36

"Gabriella says you've marked me, Sam." I leaned Lucifer's warhammer against my shoulder as I stepped inside her shop. Overhead the sky was still thundering. Rain pelted the roof, reminding me of my childhood, of my life before I'd come here. The rain had been a constant, and something about hearing it outside made me miss home.

Even though I'd been a loser there, and here I was a veritable hero, I still sort of missed it, though I wasn't sure why. After all, I'd been an orphan with a sword collection who worked at Seven Eleven. I shouldn't miss it, but part of me did. Hell, part of me wondered what it'd be like to return there now. Would I still be a schlub, or would my newfound power have changed me?

"Yeah, I noticed. I don't even understand how that's possible." The blacksmith shook her head, causing her pink hair to whip around her shoulders. She turned to look at me, and I realized her shirt was open. The spot on her chest where I'd torn out Dred's mark had healed over, and the same scythe design was faintly glowing on her chest.

"Oh, um..." I took a deep breath suddenly embarrassed because I could see the edge of her nipple peeking out from beneath her shirt.

Her face scrunched up. "Are you embarrassed?" She looked down at herself. "You know we've had sex lots of times, right?"

"Yeah, but part of me can't believe you have sex with me." I gestured at her. "You're a fucking knockout."

"I am." She smirked then began buttoning her shirt up. "And evidently you've marked me." She smiled. "Guess that makes me yours."

"That wasn't my intention." I sighed. "I was just trying to save your life."

"I'm giving you a hard time, Arthur." Sam reached behind her and grabbed something off the table. "I made you something." She offered me a small box with a badly fitting lid.

"What is it?" I asked, moving closer to take the box from her. It wasn't very heavy.

"My armament." She looked down at the box. "I made it exactly as how I made Dred's armament. I figured you suck at keeping swords in good shape, so I did what I did for him. I made an earring." She touched her right ear, and I saw she was now wearing a silver stud. "I want to see if it works for you. I think it will because you bear my mark, but I don't really know. Part of me has wondered if the Armament I gave Dred even still works." She shrugged. "How wish it stopped working."

"Wait, you made me an armament?" I asked, opening the box and finding a stud similar to the one in her own ear. It sat gleaming on a small bed of cotton. Power wafted off of it, and as I took in the piece of jewelry, I felt the mark on my abdomen begin to glow.

"Yes." She nodded. "Purely for scientific purposes. You understand." She gestured at me. "Now try it on. I want to know if it works."

"If it does…" I swallowed.

"If it does, perhaps you can get Gabriella's Mark and Armament as well." Sam looked at her feet. "That would give you seven marks, which is more than Dred has, even if mine still works for him." She took a deep breath. "You might be able to beat him then."

While the idea seemed reasonable, and made me hopeful, the way she said it didn't. No. It sounded more like there was a catch, and if there was a catch, it likely wouldn't work.

"You don't sound terribly confident about it," I whispered, taking the earring from the box and holding it up into the air. Just touching it made a surge of power rush through me. Only this felt different. Wrong almost. I couldn't quite explain it, but even though I could feel the mark I shared with Sam reaching out toward the object, I instantly knew I couldn't use it.

The Cold Embrace of Death

Type: Earring

Durability: 1,300

Defense: 1D5

Enchantments: Armament of Death

Ability: Ethereal Armor– Allows the user to coat his body in Ethereal Armor that absorbs three times the user's health in battle before being destroyed.

"Dred is impossibly powerful, Arthur. He is not strong because of his Armaments alone. Ignoring that he has millennia of experience fighting archangels, he wields Excalibur, a weapon designed to lay waste to all those who oppose it. The sword that signifies his might, his strength." She gestured toward Clarent's broken blade. "Your sword lies in pieces, and as powerful as Lucifer's warhammer is, she will need that in the coming battle."

"That's why we're going to visit the Lady in the Lake." I put the earring back in the box and handed it to her. "To get a new sword to replace Clarent."

"Is there something wrong with it?" Sam asked, taking the box and looking at it.

"Don't tell me you didn't feel it when I touched it." I sighed. "I saw your face flash with pain." I gestured at her. "I can feel how weak you still are through the mark. While I might be able to use that, it would most certainly kill you."

"I'd thought maybe…" she trailed off. "Sorry…"

"It isn't your fault, Sam." I moved closer to her and brushed her hair out of her face. "It is destiny, and god, and Dred. Not you though."

"That feels like an excuse." She tightened her grip around the box. "I want to be able to help you."

"You do help me, Sam. Just by being you." I smiled at her. "Now, come on. Let's go get us a sword." I took her hand in mine. "Ready?"

"Not quite yet." She sighed and put the box on the table. Then she shuffled over to one of the cabinets and opened it. This time when she turned around, she held out another earring. "Take this instead."

"What's this?" I asked, taking the item from her.

"I was worried you wouldn't be able to actually use the armament I made." She gestured offhandedly behind her. "So, I made this as well. You know, just in case. It mimics the abilities I gave to Clarent. Basically, the earring will let you summon Ethereal Armor, as well as do your other magic without having to have the sword in your hands."

"This is amazing!" I squealed, looking at the new earring.

The Dragon-Blooded Breath of Valor

Type: Earring

Durability: 300

Defense: 1D3

Enchantments: none

Ability: Ethereal Armor– Allows the user to coat his body in Ethereal Armor that absorbs the user's Health in battle before being destroyed.

Ability: Sapphire Beam– Allows the user to blast an opponent with concentrated energy, dealing damage equal to weapon damage plus Special to an opponent.

Ability: Emerald Shield– Allows the user to create a shield that blocks three times the user's Special in damage.

Ability: Crimson Fire– Allows the user to summon a ball of flame that deals damage equal to Strength plus Agility to an opponent.

"Sam, this is really amazing," I said, looking down at it. "Just one problem."

"Your ear isn't pierced. I know, but I can fix that." She came toward me with a devilish look on her face.

"Um… aren't you supposed to numb it first?" I swallowed. I wasn't sure I wanted my ear pierced.

"I am." Sam met my eyes. "But I figure you can handle a little pain." She held her hand out to me. "But if you want to keep being reliant on your weapon, well…"

"Fine." I handed her the earring and shut my eyes.

"Are you really shutting your eyes?" Sam asked, and when I went to tell her I was, in fact doing that, she jabbed my ear.

"Fuck!" I cried, my hand going to my ear. It hurt like hell, but as my eyes fluttered open, I found Sam smirking at me.

"Well, now that we've got that out of the way, let's go convince the Lady to help us." The smirk fell off my face. "If anyone can do that, it's you." She turned and pointed to a map laid out on the table. "That's the entrance to her lands. We won't be able to get any closer than this." She pointed at a spot where an X had been drawn in marker. "The magic barriers within will blow us apart if we try to teleport closer."

"Okay," I said, staring down at the map of the

enchanted forest while rubbing my ear. It still hurt, but I knew I'd forget about it in a little while. "I always wanted to get out and see the scenery." I looked at her. "Should we bring Gabriella or Sheila with us?" I thought back to Annabeth, and while she had been helpful in the dungeon, it would have been smarter to have brought someone with more fighting ability. Only as I thought about that, I realized I had no idea where Annabeth was. I'd never gone to pick her up. Geez, I was a total asshole.

"Are you worried because of what happened with Ruby's Gleam? Annabeth told me what happened when she returned a few hours ago." Sam shrugged. "Buffy got her from the dwarven city." Sam looked at me. "Probably want to apologize for not getting her by the way."

"Yeah, I probably should do that." I looked at the ground sheepishly. "But yes, that's why I asked."

"Arthur, you have the power of five Armaments." She touched my chest. "You have Lucifer's Warhammer, and a magically enchanted sword. If you can't make it through the forest, we may as well give up on our chance to face Dred." She took my chin in her hand and forced me to look at her.

"Because I guarantee he could make it through the forest on his own."

"You don't really pull any punches, do you?" I asked, dread welling up in my gut. The way Sam talked about Dred scared me. He seemed almost superhuman, and at the end of the day, I was a Slurpee Monkey in way over his head. Still, I had to try. No. More than that, I had to win. The first step toward that would be to enter the enchanted forest and find this Lady in her stupid lake.

"It's part of my charm," Sam said, nodding to me. "Now, let's go before something else comes up."

"Right, okay. Let's get us a sword." I sucked in a deep breath, and as I exhaled, I teleported us to the coordinates on the map.

37

The blackened, snarling forest across the massive ravine spread out in front of me like a blight upon the earth. Twisted, leafless branches reached for me as red-eyed monsters peered out from the thorny brush. A narrow footpath led into its twisting confines, and as lightning crackled overhead, I couldn't do anything but stare at the small wooden sign next to the bridge leading into its depths.

"Abandon all hope ye who enter here," I said, repeating the words on the sign. "And then they drew a picture of a skull."

"I think that means it's safe to enter," Sam said, drumming one hand nervously on her thigh. "You know, opposites and all that."

"I'm pretty sure it means exactly what it says," I said, edging toward the bridge. It was rickety as fuck, and half the boards were missing, making it seem like a gap-toothed frown spread over an infinite abyss. I looked down once more, trying to ignore the fraying rope holding the bridge together. I couldn't even see the bottom.

"I could try to fly us across," Sam said hopefully, and then her face creased with concentration. Then one hand went to her back. "Or not…"

"What's wrong?" I asked, turning toward her. "Because, to be honest, flying over that," I gestured to the ravine, "seems like a great fucking idea."

"I can't call my wings." Sam frowned. "At all."

I looked at her for a moment before sighing. "Of course not…" Still, just because we couldn't fly, didn't mean we couldn't get across. "Guess there's no time like the present."

I stepped onto the bridge, the entire thing swayed. The wind began to pick up, swinging the bridge to and fro as the board beneath my foot swayed. Still, as I tested my weight, I found it could hold me. I took another step, my hand gripping the rope for support, and as I did, I found that one could support my weight as well.

"Seems okay." I looked at Sam who was watching me with both hope and fear plastered across her face. "Let me go across and wait for you." I took another step. "I don't know how much weight this can support."

"Sure." Sam nodded. "I know that between the two of us, I'd rather you fall than me. You understand, right?"

"Of course." I smiled. To be honest, I'd sort of rathered that too. I wasn't sure what was down below, but given that she couldn't fly, I could at least risk a teleport.

I moved forward, concentrating on each step, and while the boards creaked and the bridge groaned, nothing much happened. Still, the swaying was starting to get to me so that by the time I reached the center, it was all I could do to keep from throwing up. My nerves were practically shot, and worse, the bridge was swinging so hard I found myself nearly horizontal more than once.

"Arthur! Watch out!" Sam cried, and as I turned

toward her voice, a ninja swung a katana at me. Seriously. A goddamned ninja.

I leapt backward as its katana passed by me, barely missing me by an inch. The ninja's eyes blazed bright red beneath its featureless cowl, and as it changed its grip on its katana, six more jumped onto the bridge from the darkness below.

"Not cool," I whispered, unslinging my warhammer just as a trio of ninja stars came flying at me. I dropped, hitting the deck, which wound up being incredibly lucky. Well, for me anyway.

The ninja stars sank into the chest of another ninja that had been sneaking up behind me with a garrote. The ninja fell backward, blood spraying from its chest as I scrambled to my feet while bringing my warhammer to bear.

My target tried to block, but at the end of the day, I was a super-powered demigod swinging a massive warhammer designed to empower the goddamned Devil herself. My blow ripped the feeble katana from the ninja's hands right before it smashed into the underside of its chin with a wet squelch. The ninja's head exploded like an overripe melon, and it collapsed backward into its friend as I whirled around.

More ninjas had mounted the bridge, and I sprinted toward them. The bridge started to sway as I jumped through the air. This time the ninja didn't try to block, opting to sidestep instead. There was just one problem. The movement felt slow. I could see every last twitch of the ninja's muscles as my warhammer sank into the boards, blowing them out into the abyss in a spray of debris.

My left hand shot out, slamming into the ninja's chest as it finished its sidestep, driving it back over the rope railing. The ninja tumbled over the ropes as I pointed the warhammer toward the end of the bridge. There were at least six more between the end of the bridge and me. That was bad odds, but as I stepped forward, swinging the warhammer, I realized I was way, way faster than them. My blows knocked them aside when they blocked, and when they dodged, I was easily able to counter.

In no more than ten seconds, I stood alone in the center of the bridge. "Sam. Come on before more come." I stepped hard on the bridge. "Pretty sure this can support our weight." I smiled. "Just a guess though, so if it breaks and we die, I'll take responsibility for it.

"Arthur, how did you do that?" Sam stared at me wide-eyed. "I couldn't even see them move they were so quick, and you beat them like it was nothing."

"They were fast?" I asked, confused as she took a step onto the bridge.

"Really fast." She gripped the rope railing as she came closer. "I'm the Archangel of Death, and while I'm not at full power, I should have been able to follow their movements. They were a blur, and you?" She shook her head. "You moved so quickly, it was almost like you were teleporting."

"Well, I do have a lot of Armaments." I looked down at the ring around my neck. It was glowing faintly, and I wondered if I had instinctively used Lust's power to slow time without realizing it. Still, I couldn't help but wonder if maybe I'd gotten strong enough to defeat Dred. After all, when the last Builder faced him, it had been without any Armaments, and right now I had five. That put us more or less on equal ground, didn't it?

"Thing is, I didn't feel you use any of them." Sam

joined me near the middle. "I think it was just you." She touched my arm. "I think it's whatever you did with Lucifer. I mean, you were fast after the Mammon business, but this." She gestured at me. "This is a whole different level."

"Good." I nodded to her and began moving down the bridge again. "I'd hate to think I didn't earn it." I took a deep breath. "As nice as the power from the armaments is, I am just the guy who picked them up. The training? I did that."

"I can see how you feel that way, Arthur." She followed along behind me as I looked for more ninjas, but so far I didn't see any. "You always seemed like you had a chip on your shoulder, like you didn't deserve the power of Clarent."

"It's not just that really." I reached the end, and the moment I stepped onto the blackened shore of the enchanted forest, my heart did a little flip-flop of joy. Sure it was scary as fuck, but at least it was solid ground. "It's that you could replace me with anyone and it'd have been the same." I took her hand and helped her onto the steps of the forest. "I know you guys talk about how no Builder has done what I did, but at the end of the day, I just picked up good gear." I shrugged. "But the training I did is something *I* did. I worked hard and got stronger." I sighed. "It's just different."

"Sure." Sam smiled at me. "You're turning into Annabeth." Sam made a serious face. "Nothing is of value unless I work harder than everyone else for it."

"So, you're mocking me now? That's cool." I nodded at her.

"Yeah, guess you'll have to punish me later." Sam squeezed my hand. "On account of how bad of a girl I'm being."

"Looking forward to it," I said, turning back to the narrow path into the forest. All around me, I could hear the sounds of monsters, could feel their eyes upon me. We'd barely started, and though I'd beat the ninjas, I knew that was the opening act. More would be sure to come.

"Yeah. We can call it a reward." Sam extended one hand and this time her scythe appeared in her hand. Part of me didn't quite understand how she could utilize the weapon to fight since it was totally the wrong shape for practically fighting, but I wasn't going to argue. I could feel power crackling through the air as she gripped it.

"Should you be doing that?" I asked, looking her over. "You're still hurt."

"Look, if you want to walk in there with no weapon at hand, be my guest." Sam clenched her scythe tightly. "I may not be at full power, but if something tries to eat me, I aim to stab it."

"Fair enough." I gripped my warhammer and stepped forward into the forest. "Fair enough."

38

I slammed my warhammer into the mechanical ogre's skull, denting it inward like a tin can. Sparks exploded from within as black smoke filled the air. The automation wobbled, arms moving in a jerky motion as I reared back and hit it again. The blow shattered its head into bits of metal that exploded outward across the ground.

"I'm not sure what's worse," I said, chest heaving and heart hammering as I surveyed the dozen mechanical corpses strewn across the clearing. "Ogres or mechanical ogres." I gestured at the robots.

"You've not fought real ogres," Sam said, coming toward me. Her hair was mussed, but she seemed otherwise okay, probably because she'd let me do most of the heavy lifting. Truthfully, I hadn't minded. It had been fun to smash through a coterie of robotic guardians. That had been way better than the sloth-beasts and slug creatures. I shivered. Not to mention the ents.

"I kinda wanna keep it that way," I said, moving back toward the edge of the clearing now that I knew she was safe. Below a crystalline lake spread out in front of me. It was so huge it reminded me of the great lakes back home, only, you know, bigger.

"Probably for the best," Sam said, moving next to me. She gasped. "I think we're finally here!"

"Thank goodness," I whispered, wiping my head with the back of one hand. I was tired after nearly three days of nonstop fighting. "I'll be honest, I'll be glad to be done." I hefted the warhammer. "As awesome as crushing mechanical skulls is, there's something about Clarent I miss."

Sam nodded to me as we looked over the edge and into the lake about a hundred feet below. "So, uh, how do we get down there? I can't fly here, and you can't teleport."

"Uh…" I rubbed my chin as I looked around. "I

guess we jump." I smiled as I looked down at the lake. "It'll be fun."

"I am absolutely, one hundred percent not jumping—"

I cut her off by leaping over the edge. My stomach launched into my throat as gravity took hold of me, dragging me down. I put my feet together, bracing for impact as I hit the water below. Coldness sliced through me, drawing the breath from my lungs in a burst of bubbles as I surged beneath the surface.

Kicking my feet as hard as I could, I made my way to the surface just in time for Sam to smash into the water beside me. A spray of water hit me full in the face, making me sputter and gasp for breath as she bobbed to the surface.

"You're an idiot!" she scowled at me. "You could have died."

"I didn't," I said, giving her a stupid grin. "Sure, there could be a sea monster, or I could have hit a rock." I waggled my eyebrows at her. "But I really wanted to get you wet."

"You hardly had to go to all this trouble to get me

wet," Sam replied, looking me over. "And there can't be sea monsters."

"Why not?" I asked, raising an eyebrow at her.

"This is a lake. There could only be lake monsters." She shook her head. "It's like you know nothing."

"That sounds like semantics." I nodded at her as I tread water. It was a bit hard since I was holding a warhammer in one hand. "There could totally be a lake Kraken."

"If there is, I hope it eats you first," Sam said, right before she began swimming out toward the middle of the lake. "Come on."

"Where are we going exactly?" I asked, following her. I made it about a foot and a half before I slung the warhammer on my back. The weight still made it hard to swim, especially since I was wearing full armor, but I managed anyway. Still, I was pretty sure if I didn't have extra strength and stamina from the armaments and my training, I'd have already drowned.

"The lady lives in the center," Sam said, not bothering to look back at me.

"Well, how was I supposed to know that?" I asked,

shaking my head, which in retrospect was a dumb idea because I nearly swallowed a gallon of water.

"I dunno why you're being uppity about it." Sam glanced at me. "I didn't make you jump into a lake wearing full battle armor and carrying a hundred and fifty-pound warhammer."

She had a point but there was no way I was going to let her know that now. If I did, I'd never live it down.

So, I focused on swimming until we reached the center. Part of me still expected to find a lake Kraken, but when none wrapped their tentacles around my ankle and pulled me into the blimey deep, I almost relaxed. Almost.

"We're here," Sam said, and her words surprised me because I'd been so focused on what I was doing, I hadn't noticed how far we'd come.

Two pale blue hands jutted from the water in front of us, and as I stared at them, an apparition rose from the surface. Her skin was translucent, and though I couldn't see her facial features thanks to all the seaweed-like hair, a chill went down my body. She felt powerful, but more, she reminded me of the lich because she also felt dead.

"Why have you come here, Death?" the ghost said, its voice like nails raking across a chalkboard. "Why have you sought me after all this time?"

"I need your aid," Sam said, shooting me an "I'll handle it" look.

Laughter exploded from the apparition with such force the lake turned turbulent. Overhead, I felt the weather start to change, and as I did, I wondered if I could affect it with the crown. Short answer, technically, but since I wasn't sure doing so would let me remain conscious, I decided to just deal with it.

"I will never aid you, Samael." The apparition began to fade. "Not even if you were about to be eaten by the Empress herself."

"Okay, you know what, Morgan. I fucking lied. I don't give a rat's ass about you or your help." Sam's finger jutted out toward me. "The Builder requires your aid to stop Dred. Will you give it?"

"No." Morgan the ghost paused for a second, its face shifting toward me, and though I couldn't see much of its face, I could slowly see a horrific grin spread out from its mass of hair.

"Are you sure?" Sam took a deep breath. "Because I think you very much want to."

"What do you require?" Morgan said, looking at me, and as she did my world exploded into blue as a whirlpool sprang to life around me. I tried to move, tried to escape, but before I could, I slammed into the bottom of the lake. I scrambled to my feet, about to try to make a jump for it when the water above me closed with a crash, leaving me trapped in a bubble at the bottom.

Morgan stood there before me, only she wasn't a ghost anymore. Her skin was the same pale blue as the hands above the surface had been, making me think they had been hers.

She wore a simple blue dress, that while well-made, looked old and well used. Still, she definitely filled it out in a way that would have made me stop and look if I hadn't been so concerned about my wellbeing. After all, I had just been sucked to the bottom of the lake.

"Where are we?" I looked up, but I couldn't see the surface through the murk.

"In my home." Morgan gestured at the surroundings, and as she did, I realized that beyond the bubble was a chair, a bed, and various knickknacks. "Though I've created this pocket so you can breathe and to keep out nosy archangels." She snorted. "Never can trust them. All tricky bitches."

"You know, I've heard that," I said, taking a deep breath of air that tasted like a salty swamp.

"Yeah, I care." Morgan flipped her hair back, revealing her face, and I realized she was beautiful beyond words, but not in the same way all the angels and demons had been. No, Morgan was pretty in a way I couldn't quite describe because I knew intrinsically she was less pretty than the others, but I still wanted her all the same.

"You're beautiful," I said before I could stop myself. "Absolutely beautiful."

Morgan's eyes narrowed. "So, I've been told, but unless you came here to try to fuck me, let's get on with it." She made a hurry up gesture. "Samael seems to think you can defeat Dred. Why does she think this?"

"I'm the Builder—"

"There have been lots of Builders." Morgan rolled her eyes. "Each more legendary than the last, etc,

etc, etc. No one cares." She sat down in the mud, but none of it clung to her. "Gonna have to do better than that, and I swear if you pull out your dick, I will drown you." She pointed toward the water, and I saw a skeleton dressed in armor. I couldn't be sure how long he'd been dead, but it seemed like a long ass time. "Been there, done that."

"Right." I swallowed, feeling off-balance because I couldn't imagine some guy would actually whip out his dick to impress her. "See, I broke Clarent—"

"He wields Excalibur. It is not a sword you can stand against even with Lucifer's hammer." She nodded to the warhammer strapped to my back. "Clarent is old, brittle. It would not do the job. Still, neither of those facts tell me why I should help you." She smiled. "It does let me know what you seek though. A weapon to face Dred. Tell me, is that what you wish? A big sword to smite your enemies with? Perhaps one large enough to make up for whatever you're overcompensating for with all the armor?"

"These are Armaments. They grant me the strength to face Dred, assuming I had a sword that could do it." I held out my hands, displaying my gauntlets.

"Dred is not strong because he has a bunch of magic items." She spat onto the ground next to her. "He is strong because he trains harder than all those before him. He is strong because he takes what he deserves." She smiled at me. "Are you that strong? That daring." She shook her head. "I think not."

"I am strong, and I will beat him!" I growled, taking an angry step toward her and reaching for my warhammer.

"Oh?" She raised an eyebrow at me, and as she did the watery walls around us began to close in on us. "Prove it. Prove you're a big strong man." She got to her feet, and as she did, a chill ran down my spine. "Take the sword from my hand." She extended her hand toward me, and as she did, a sheathed five-foot blade filled it.

"That's it?" I asked, moving closer until I was close enough to grab it.

"That is it," she said, smiling at me. "But know that if you miss, I will require something in trade from you for another try."

"What is that?" I asked, watching her carefully.

"My dear, Builder. When you ask a question like that, it makes me think you do not think you can snatch the sword from me. After all, I'm just a tiny, frail woman. How hard could it be?" She shrugged. "Try being confident."

"I am confident," I said, taking a deep breath and focusing on the weapon in her hand.

"Then prove it, Builder." She shut her eyes. "Take the sword from my hand."

"Okay." I nodded. "Are you ready?"

"Ye—"

I backhanded her across the face, and as she stumbled backward, I snatched the sword from the air as it fell. "Thanks."

39

"Is this where you tell me I cheated?" I asked as Morgan glared at me so hard, smoke actually started to rise from my clothes. I ignored it.

"No," she growled, still glaring at me. "I just didn't expect you to hit me."

"So, what you're saying is you didn't expect the unexpected." I nodded.

"That's not what I—"

"Oh." I continued to nod. "So, I just outsmarted you." I smirked. "I could see how it'd be concerning to be outsmarted by a dumb guy like me." I shrugged.

"You're pissing me off. That is unwise." Morgan

took a step toward me, hands clenching and unclenching.

"Tell me something," I said, leaning the new sword against my shoulder. Part of me wanted to examine its stats, but I couldn't get distracted right now.

"What?" she snapped.

"Did it hurt when I hit you?" I asked, letting amusement fill my voice.

"Of course it hurt—"

"See, here's the thing. I used about one percent of my power when I hit you," I lied straight-faced. "But if you keep coming at me like you are, I might just decide I feel threatened and have to defend myself. And I won't use one percent of my power to do that. I will come at you with everything I have." I met her eyes. "Do you want me to do that?"

She stopped mid-step. "One percent?"

"One percent," I repeated.

She watched me for a long moment, and I could see thoughts flitting behind her eyes. "Go." She nodded once. "I don't like the look of you."

"Much obliged." I gave her a quick salute. "Ready when you are."

"You expect me to send you back to the surface?" she asked, incredulous. "Swim yourself."

"Are you trying to piss me off?" I took a step toward her, and she visibly tensed. "Because I feel like I've been pretty amenable." I met her eyes as I pointed the sword at her. "And you're making me feel like I shouldn't bother."

"Fine." Morgan sucked in a breath that made her breasts heave against her dress. "I will send you to—"

"To the edge of the forest," I said, interrupting her. "Sam and me both. You'll send us both to the edge."

"I can't do that," she said, but as she spoke, she looked away.

"Liar," I said, gesturing at her. "You can't even say it with a straight face." I shook my head. "My ex used to do the same thing when she lied. Just send Sam and me back, and I'll forgive the slight. No harm, no foul." I tightened my grip on the sword. "Otherwise things might not be so fun."

"Fine," she said, gesturing at me with one hand. "I didn't want to spend another second with you, anyway." As she spoke, a wave of blue energy swept out and wrapped around my body. The feel of it was like a cold breeze on a warm day, and as I looked down at myself to find myself transforming into translucent ether, I wanted to scream, to flail.

Only before I could do any of those things, I found myself standing next to the bridge where I'd fought the ninjas.

"What in the Blue hell?" Sam cried, looking around. She was still sopping wet, and as she spun in a slow circle, her boots squelched in the mud. "What just happened?"

"I got the sword," I said, gesturing at her with it. "Morgan and I had a chat, and she decided she didn't like me." I frowned. "Don't really know why. Normally, I'm fairly likable."

"Said the most annoying guy in all of Hell," Sam replied, laughter in her voice. "I don't know how you could have possibly managed to get that witch to help us, but I'm glad you did." She nodded to the sword. "Can I see it?"

"Sure," I said, offering it to her, and as she took it, I pulled up its stats.

Caliburn

Type: Longsword

Durability: 57,000/57,000

Damage: 2D20

Enchantments: Mortal Strike

Ability: none

"I wonder what that does…" I mumbled, pulling up the tooltip for Mortal Strike.

Mortal Strike: This enchantment causes the wounds delivered by Caliburn to bleed for twice as many rounds as normal. Wounds are resistant to healing and failed attempts to heal damage dealt by Caliburn results in the wound timer being reset.

"Holy fuck," I said, mouth dropping open in astonishment as Sam pulled the weapon from its sheath. Caliburn seemed to glow with the same ethereal blue light Morgan had used to transport.

"Wow," Sam whistled, looking over the blade. "This is amazing." She touched the center of the blade where it extended from the ornate golden hilt. "You can tell it has been folded many times to increase strength and blend the metals." She swallowed. "Probably sixteen or so, and the metals themselves... This isn't just Stygian Iron, Arthur." She looked at me. "This is made of Heavenly Gold too." She shook her head. "I didn't think it could be blended like this."

"Be careful with it, Sam," I said as she held it out so the light played off it. "There's an enchantment that causes the wounds to be pretty gnarly."

"Yeah, that's the product of the Heavenly Gold." Sam nodded. "Most of the weapons have effects like that. It's what makes them so devastating." As she went to sheath the weapon, I realized there was a separate tooltip for the scabbard. "Be careful too. That means if you cut yourself with it, you'll bleed just as well."

"Right," I said, taking the sword from her and opening the tooltip for the scabbard. I wasn't sure how I hadn't noticed it before.

Caliburn's Scabbard

Type: Scabbard

Durability: 7,300/7,300

Defense: 1D10

Enchantments: none

Set Bonus: Bloodless Victor

Bloodless Victor: When worn by the wielder of Caliburn, the wielder will not be affected by the Enchantment: Mortal Strike and will be able to survive mortal blows.

"That witch really thought of everything," I said, strapping the scabbard to my belt as quickly as I could.

"What do you mean?" Sam asked, watching me. "And why did you put that on? You look absolutely ridiculous with a sword on either leg."

"The scabbard makes me immune to the bleed effect granted by Caliburn, so if it cuts me, I won't die of blood loss," I said, and as I went to reveal the mortal wound thing, I stopped myself. I wasn't sure why, but something told me, I'd be better off keeping that one to myself. It was weird because while I hadn't worried about Dred having spies up till now, Morgan had seemed to know him well, and we were at the edge of her forest.

"Well, that's certainly convenient." Sam nodded. "I would have never thought of that, but it makes sense." She smirked. "You have no idea how many people have died from nicking themselves with their own weapon during a battle, or worse, had it turned on them."

"I hadn't even thought of the second one." I swallowed hard.

"Hopefully, you won't ever experience it." Sam came closer and touched my shoulder. "Now then, it seems I have some work to do." She met my eyes. "That is, if you're sure you want me to try transferring Clarent's power into that weapon."

"That's the whole point." I shrugged before looking down at the sword I'd been using. "Otherwise I may as well just continue using Seure here."

"You named it Seure?" Sam looked down at the sword. "It's not special enough to have a name."

"That's not true. Names have power, and by giving it a name, perhaps I made it a little more special." I smiled at her.

"You're an idiot," Sam said, trying to hide her grin

as she shook her head at me. "But I guess that's part of your charm."

I didn't respond as I looked down at Seure. The weapon had served me well, and yet, I was about to get rid of it. Part of me felt bad, but at the same time, a quick look at its stats let me know I was making the right choice. Mostly anyway.

Seure

Type: Longsword

Durability: 12,454/23,000

Damage: 1D20

Enchantments: none

Ability: Ethereal Armor, Sapphire Beam, Emerald Shield, Crimson Fire

"You know," I said, turning my eyes from the weapon and focusing on Sam. "You will have to add the cool hilt thing and the armor ability to Caliburn. Otherwise, I'll probably have to keep both of them." I stuck out my tongue. "They're the source of my ranged attacks after all, and while I love being a bruiser, I've played too many games where the big barbarian gets picked off by some kiting asshole."

"I don't know what any of that means, and I'll be happy to do that, though I'm not sure why. You have the new earring remember?" Sam pointed to my ear.

"You know, I'd forgotten, but I'd like you to do it, anyway." I touched my ear, feeling the earring she'd given me. "You know, just in case. One is none, and two is one and all that. Unless it's an issue."

"Not really." She looked down at Seure before moving her gaze to Caliburn. "It won't take long, probably less time than moving Clarent's ability over to Caliburn." She shrugged. "I have the stuff to do that just sitting back at my shop. All I have to do is pop out that pommel and inscribe the runic work on the blade with Dark Blood."

"Awesome. Let's get to it then." I offered her my hand, and as she took it, I teleported.

40

"Are you sure you're okay to work on this now?" I asked as Sam took Caliburn from me and laid it on her table. "You're not too weak, right?"

"Arthur, I'm fine." Sam stared at me for so long the rain pounding on the roof overhead began to drive me crazy. "Besides, I'd rather not put it off." She gestured at me. "I know you have the warhammer and Seure, but I'd rather you have a sword fit for the Builder." She took a deep breath. "It'd make me feel safer."

"Me too," I agreed because it was true. While Seure had worked well up till now, it was still a pretty normal sword, and a pretty normal sword wouldn't beat Dred. Hell, if I'd had just Seure when we'd gone into the enchanted forest, it would have been nearly impossible. Lucifer's hammer had really saved me, but as I watched Sam begin to shuffle around her shop, I knew it was time to return the weapon to its owner.

"This will probably take a few hours." She smirked at me. "Try not to get into any fights until it's done, okay?"

"Are you trying to get rid of me?" I asked.

"Yes. I was trying to be nice about it, but you don't seem to take a hint very well." Sam grinned. "Now off with you."

"Fine. I can see when I'm not wanted." I moved across the room and kissed her. "Good luck."

"Won't need it, but thanks anyway." She playfully shoved me away. "Now go. The sooner this is done, the better."

"Sure," I said, reaching back and gripping the warhammer. As I did, I focused on its owner. Once again, the small of my back began to burn, and the crown upon my head began to glow. Then I teleported.

And reappeared just beyond the edge of the town.

Lucifer sat draped in a cloak, her eyes staring off into the sky. Rain pelted her already drenched body, but if it bothered her, it didn't show. Worse, since I was outside too, I got soaked to my skin in the space of a second.

"Hello," she said, not bothering to look over at me. "How are you?"

"I'm okay. I think I'll have a new sword soon." I pulled the warhammer free of the sling and held it out to her. "So I wanted to return this."

"That is why you've come?" she asked, getting to her feet and coming toward me. Her face was strangely blank as she took the warhammer. Then she plunged the head into the earth and leaned on it.

"Yes." I nodded to her. "It really helped me out."

"Good." She paused for a second, eyes raking over me before turning them to the heavens. "Glad it helped."

"You seem distracted." I glanced toward where she stirred, but it was nothing but thunderbolts and lightning. "Should I be worried?"

"Do you ever wonder what they're doing up there."

Lucifer nodded toward the horizon. "How the fight in Heaven goes?" She turned back to me and pushed back her cowl, revealing her rain-soaked hair.

"I sometimes do, though not that often. Honestly, I've been hoping they last long enough for me to get strong enough to make a difference." I looked up at the sky for a moment.

"So you would sacrifice Heaven to save Hell?" Lucifer laughed. "Interesting."

"I didn't say that."

"You didn't have to." Lucifer met my eyes and something dark and angry swam through them. "It may not matter though. I have journeyed across this land and have found it wanting. The Darkness has encroached from all sides, and that is simply unacceptable, but do you know what is worse?"

"No?" I offered, confused by her sudden anger.

"None of mine have pushed it back." She pointed a finger at me. "Only you have done anything, and that's just pathetic."

"Hey, I'm not—"

"I do not mean to say you are pathetic, Arthur, nor your efforts. I mean to say that while I have been locked away, my people have failed to fight back effectively. We should not have needed you. We should have won on our own," Lucifer growled, and while that might have been true, I wasn't sure it was fair. After all, I'd seen Dred route Nadine's entire army in an eye blink.

"You used my name," I said, unable to hide my surprise. "You've never done that before."

"That's what you focus on." She smiled. Barely. "I am upset, and you are focused on the fact I called you by name." She shook her head. "So human."

"I wouldn't normally care, but we've spent a lot of time together, and you'd never done it before. I was always human or Builder." I shrugged. "I notice these things."

"What else have you noticed?" She took a step toward me, and as she did, the sky crackled overhead. It must have startled her because she turned her head toward it. Only that was strange because she could control the weather.

"What?" I asked, turning to look in time to see a flaming fireball explode from the sky. One that seemed remarkably similar to Gabriella's own entrance into Hell how many lifetimes ago.

"Come." Lucifer, grabbed my hand with her free hand, and before I knew what was happening, her wings unfurled, and we surged toward the crater in the distance. Overhead, the whole of the world seemed to swirl with chaotic energy. The entirety of the horizon turned crimson, and the rain that fell turned to blood.

The smell of swamp gas and death filled my nose.

"What is it?" I asked as we landed just beyond the golden flame leaping from within the crater. Even several meters back, it had been so hot, our freshly plowed fields into glass had turned to glass.

"I don't know," Lucifer growled, releasing me and gripping her warhammer with both hands. "But I aim to find out."

As she took a step forward, the ground began to shake, seizing violently enough that I fell on my ass. Lucifer sprang into the air, hovering just far enough above the dirt to keep from falling. The wind began to howl, and the sky turned to flame.

The horizon spilled open, and I could hear a thousand fading trumpet blasts. That's when I saw the army of angels overhead. There were so many, I could hardly count them, but that wasn't the problem. The problem was that there were at least a hundred darkness warriors for every last angel. And not just normal ones either. There were ravagers, liches, and everything I'd seen in my nightmares and visions and a thousand more besides.

"Heaven has fallen…" Lucifer whispered, and as I turned toward the sound of her voice, I saw a shadowy figure coming toward us through the golden flames rimming the crater.

"How right you are." A man stepped forth and flung the body of an angel to the ground in front of himself. She was missing a wing, and her body was one giant bruise. It looked like she'd once been wearing armor, but that it had been blown apart, leaving her mostly battered body naked to the open air. Her hair had been burned away, and she stared unseeing.

The sight of her laying there, so clearly defeated made a chill run down my spine. I'd have never been able to do that to an archangel. They were just too powerful.

"Michelle..." Lucifer narrowed her eyes at the white-haired man.

As his burning yellow eye settled upon Lucifer, taking her in, he ran a hand through his close-cropped white hair. Then he smiled. "Lucifer." His gravelly voice was full of amusement. "How I've longed to meet your acquaintance." He gave the angel on the ground a contentious kick.

"Destroyer." Lucifer tightened her grip on her warhammer before pointing it at him. "You will pay for what you've done."

"Do you know why I have wished to meet your acquaintance, Lucifer?" His eyes dropped to the angel. "It is because I have heard you are the *most* high." His gaze flicked back to Lucifer. "I hope that is true because this one has long ceased to be entertaining."

"You dare," Lucifer cried, and before I could blink, the archangel launched herself at him. Her warhammer lashed outward in a blur I could barely follow, and as the ground around her exploded into flames so hot, the falling rain turned to steam, the man caught the head of the warhammer in his left hand.

"Pathetic." He squeezed, and the two marks I didn't recognize on the head of the warhammer glowed like dying suns moments before the weapon shattered into a million shards of metal that flitted through the air like dying fireflies. He stepped forward then, and with almost an absent effort drove that same hand into her stomach. His fist burst through the archangel's back in a spray of crimson gobbets.

Lucifer's mouth opened and closed like a dying fish, and I could feel her power draining away through my own mark. Worse, I could feel her body struggling to heal the wound and failing as corruption seeped into her.

"Allow me to introduce myself, Lucifer. I am Dred." He withdrew his hand from her stomach, causing the Devil to fall to her knees before him. "And it would seem the rumors of you are not true. You do kneel before the right man." As she collapsed face first into the mud, he turned and knelt down beside the other downed angel. Then he gripped the necklace from around her neck and tore it free.

"No!" I cried unable to believe what had happened. He had just defeated Lucifer and stolen what looked like an Armament from Michelle. Only, how was that possible?

As he held out his left hand, causing golden light to flow out of Michelle and into him, Dred looked at me like he was seeing me for the first time. He cocked his head to the side. "You're the new one, aren't you?" A smile crept across his lips. "You know what's better than five Heavenly Armaments?" He gestured at me with the necklace in his hand before slipping it over his head. "Six." His lips twisted into a cruel smile as angels began to fall from the sky, their bloodied corpses smashing into the shores of hell like grotesque comets.

"Six?" I asked, too stunned to do anything as he sauntered casually toward me.

"Six," he repeated when he'd crossed the distance between us. "And do you know what is better than six?"

"Seven?" I asked, reaching for my sword. I wasn't sure if I could stop him, but I had to try. If I didn't, what kind of man did that make me?

"Seven is better." He took a step back and nodded to my sword. "Draw your weapon, and I will show you what is better than seven."

"And if I do not?" I asked, suddenly so scared, I could barely think. Dred had dropped Lucifer in a heartbeat, and if I was right, that was Michelle on the ground. How was I to compete with that? I didn't have a magic weapon like him, and even if I did, what would it matter? He'd destroyed Lucifer's hammer like it was a goddamned Styrofoam mallet.

"Then you are a coward unworthy of the lesson I wish to show you." He looked me up and down. "Are you a coward, Builder?"

"No. I just don't want to fight an unarmed man with a weapon. Makes me feel like a wimp." I tried to sound confident, but from the way he looked at me, I could tell he knew I was terrified. That almost made it worse.

"You are not worthy to face Excalibur." He touched the sword in the scabbard at his thigh with one hand. "But if its sweet embrace is what you seek, I shall grant it." He nodded. "Draw your weapon or don't. It will not matter to me, Builder."

I drew Seure. The blade was slick in my sweaty hands, and as I held it, I felt like a little kid again. I tried so hard to push it down, to be the hero I was supposed to be, but as Dred watched me with his stupid yellow eye, I couldn't help but feel inadequate. Still, that didn't matter. I had to stop him.

"Come on." He gestured for me to attack him. "Attack."

I took a deep breath, calling upon my power. I felt it instantly. The ground around me turned to flame, and the sky screamed in pain as the powers of the archangels filled me.

Greed. Wrath. Envy. Lust. Pride.

And one more.

Death.

They filled me, and as they did, the world seemed to slow down until it was just Dred and me.

"Wait." Dred looked me up and down as sparks of color leapt from my skin. "This won't do at all." He shut his eyes. Instantly the armor covering his chest evaporated into mist, revealing his scarred, war-torn body. His flesh rippled with so much muscle it was like his muscles had muscles. "Now hit me." He touched the place above his heart. "Here. Give it everything you have."

I wasn't sure what he was playing at, nor what his

game was, but I didn't care. If he was stupid enough to give me a free shot, well, I was sure as hell going to take it.

Grabbing hold of every last ounce of energy I could, I attacked, leaping forward and driving Seure into him. As the blade struck his skin, Seure overloaded and exploded into a billion glinting shards causing all the power I'd called to erupt outward in an explosion that threw me from my feet.

I hit the ground hard and skidded across the mud as debris rained down around me. Only, as the smoke cleared, I saw Dred standing there. His chest had been torn open to reveal the shattered bone beneath. Blood poured from the wound as he reached down at touched his chest.

"More than I could have ever hoped for," he said even though he should have been dead. "And yet not nearly enough."

He took a step toward me as his flesh began to writhe. Before my eyes, his organs reformed and the shards of his skeleton pulled themselves back together. By his second step, his muscle had covered over the whole mess. By his third step, his skin flowed outward across his body like sculptor's clay. By his fourth step, there was no trace I'd hurt him at all.

"That was your one free shot." He held his hand out to me. "Now it is time for your lesson, Builder." When I didn't move, he narrowed his eyes at me. "We can do this the easy way or the hard way. Know that insolence will cost you."

"Fuck you," I said, and even though I didn't have a weapon, I launched myself at him. My fist struck the underside of his chin, and as he stumbled, I drove my knee into his groin.

He staggered, completely caught off guard as I moved to pull his sword from his sheath. Only as I touched it, agony unlike anything I ever felt hit me. My whole world exploded into a cacophony of pain unlike anything I'd ever felt before.

"That was a mistake." Dred grabbed me by the throat as I started to fall toward the earth. His face turned to a blur as he met my eyes. "You are not worthy of wielding Excalibur." He threw me.

I sailed back across the fields and slammed into the wooden walls surrounding the Graveyard of Shadows. The wood splintered under the impact, and I felt my bones break as I burst through the reinforced earthen layer and out the other side. I hit the ground hard, toppling across it like a broken mannequin.

As I lay there in so much pain I could barely remember how to breathe, Dred walked through the hole in the wall, causing the barrier protecting the town to spark. A thunder crack exploded through the air as every last sigil burst into flames, and for a moment it was silent save for the rain.

"So, as I said before, Builder." Dred grabbed me by the scruff of my shirt, and it was then I realized my ethereal armor had shattered under the force of the blow. "This is better than seven."

He flung me through the sculpture Annabeth had carved in the center of town. As I hit the ground in a rain of debris, I saw the archangels standing there. Sam, Mammon, Sathanus, Gwen, Leviathan, and Gabriella.

"There is no feeling quite like defeating a champion before his people." He gestured at them. "Look how they tremble. How they fear me." He licked his lips. "It is delicious."

His words made me scream in rage. I was supposed

to do better, be better for them. I was supposed to stop them, and instead? Instead, I would be responsible for breaking them.

"Arthur!" Gwen cried, and as she moved to rush toward me, I put a hand out toward her.

"Stop."

Truth be told, I couldn't have told you how I did it. How I could speak let alone raise my arm. Everything in me hurt, and the craziest part of it was that thanks to my Armament of Wrath I knew Dred had taken seven times as much damage and had nothing to show for it.

"You should do as the Builder says." Dred looked over at me and nodded. "He is now wise."

"That's Michelle's necklace," Gabriella said, her voice cracking midway. She gripped her golden mace tightly, and as she raised it defensively, I could see her shaking. Fear clouded her eyes, and the sight of it made me want to die inside.

That was the fear of someone who knew she'd already lost and was going to throw her life away, anyway. Of someone who knew everything was pointless. It was different from the fear on the other's faces. They were scared of him, but not in the way they should have been.

"It is." Dred nodded to the archangel as I got to my feet before turning his eyes to Sam. "Hello, Samael." He smiled. "Did you miss me?"

"No," she said, scythe in hand. She was the only one not scared. No, in her, the fear had been replaced by unbridled fury. "Not for even a second, you son of a bitch."

"Hmm." He rubbed his chin. "That's surprising considering you always told me how much you loved my cock." His voice changed then to match hers. "Oh, Dred. I think you've ruined me for all other men."

The sound of it made something explode behind my eyes, and even though it shouldn't have been possible, I reached out to him with my power. As I did, I found what I was looking for, the ability he'd used to heal himself.

Uncanny Regeneration– User can heal from any attack that does not outright kill him.

Disregarding Wrath's teleportation ability, I pulled the skill into myself, and as I did, I felt my body knit itself together. It was a strange feeling, and I was so focused on it, I missed what happened next.

"Interesting." Dred's voice brought me back to him, and as I turned to look at him, rage unlike anything I'd ever felt surged up inside me.

The archangels all lay sprawled on the ground around him. Well, all save for one. Dred stood there, one arm crooked around Gabriella's throat as he held her struggling body against him. Already I could see the light fading from her eyes as he choked the life from her.

Crackling rage beyond anything I'd ever felt exploded through me as I leapt toward him intent to rip the bastard apart with my bare hands. I wanted to do that. I wanted to hurt him so bad he'd remember it for the rest of his short life. Hell, even that wouldn't be enough. "Let her go!"

"Make me." His eyes met mine.

Power flared off of me as I called upon the earring to gather a handful of Hellfire. I thrust it at him, and as I did, his sword whipped out from its scabbard, slashing through my attack. As the hellfire exploded into a cloud of debris, he drove Excalibur through my chest.

Crazily, the thing I remembered from that moment was the smell. Like a million iron filings. It didn't hurt near as much as it should have as he ripped the blade outward, spilling my entrails across the ground.

"Don't worry. You'll heal." He snorted as he flicked my blood onto the muddy ground. Then his blade whipped out, tearing a hole in the sky. Inside it, I saw a throne made of skulls and angel feathers, and beside it, two naked women lounged.

"Seven." He flung Gabriella through the portal before kneeling down beside me. "Unless you can stop me Builder, but unlike Nadine, I do not plan on letting you win." He raised his sword.

"No!" Gwen screamed, and the heat inside my chest swelled. Power drained from me as Dred turned toward the sound of her voice in time to catch Gabriella's golden mace with his nose. As Gwen followed through on the blow, Dred stumbled backward, falling into the portal.

He crashed to the ground inside his throne room as the succubus reached out with one hand. Again, I felt my power drain as she grabbed hold of either side of the tear.

"You can't close it yet!" I said as Dred got to his feet, his caved in face already healing. "Gabriella is still in there."

"Better her than all of us," Gwen said, right before she slammed the portal shut.

41

"Finish the sword," I snarled at Sam, jerking her to her feet. The blacksmith hung limply in my grip as rain continued to fall from the sky.

"Arthur—"

"Don't talk to me, Gwen," I said, whirling and glaring at her. "You just sacrificed Gabriella."

"I had to do it, Arthur." Gwen put her hands on her hips. "And even if you don't believe that, manhandling Sam isn't going to make it better. She didn't do anything. I did." She touched her chest. "Punish me."

"Why? That would imply I give a god damn about

you, Gwen?" I turned my attention back to Sam, and this time I reached out to her through the mark. "Wake the fuck up."

Gwen said something as Sam's eyes fluttered open. Only I didn't hear her because fuck her. "Arthur, are you okay?"

"No." I hoisted her to her feet. "I need you to complete the sword."

"I'll… I'll do my best." Sam met my eyes for a second. "What's wrong?"

"She's what's wrong." I pointed at Gwen.

"Look, I'm as upset as anyone…" Gwen trailed off as Sam looked at her.

"I'm not following." Sam took a deep breath. "Last thing I remember is Dred hitting me." She shook her head. "We're lucky to be alive."

"No. We're absolutely fucked. Get the sword." I began dragging her toward her shop. "And I won't let Gabriella pay for that. Not if I can help it."

"What are you talking about?" Sam asked, face scrunching up in confusion as she pulled herself free of her grip. "And stop dragging me, Arthur. I can walk on my own."

"Look." I released her and pointed heavenward. The rain was still falling, turning the ground around us into bloody rivers as angelic bodies kept raining from the sky like a horrific meteor shower.

"Yeah, I know about that." She took a breath. "Just slow down." She began to move toward her shop. "Tell me why we're still alive."

"He took Gabriella, Sam." I felt tears cloud my vision, and I pushed them back. "I was too fucking weak, and he came and took her. I was supposed to protect her."

"It's not your fault, Arthur. I shut the portal." Gwen moved up beside us. "Blame me."

"If he has Gabriella..." Sam started to speed up before stopping and turning to glare at Gwen. "You stupid bitch. Don't you realize that Gabriella has the last Armament? With it, He'll be unstoppable." Tears began to slide down Sam's cheeks. "We can't win."

"Sam. Stop. Get the sword." I put a hand on her

shoulder. "Forge the damned sword, and I'll save her."

"You can't." It was Lucifer who spoke, and her voice was so surprising we all turned to look at her. Blood poured through her fingers as she clutched the wound. Her other hand was clasped around Michelle's wrist, and I got the impression she'd dragged the archangel all the way here. "Not as you are, anyway." She coughed, splattering blood across the ground.

"Sally!" Gwen cried, spinning on her heel and rushing away. "Sally, come quick!"

"There has to be a way," I said, ignoring Lucifer as I met Sam's eyes. "Get me the sword, and I'll find it."

"What do you mean as he is?" Sam asked, moving toward her sister and kneeling beside her. "Tell me what you mean."

"He'll have to change." Lucifer nodded toward Michelle. "Take her mark. Take all the angel's marks." She touched her chest. "I can show you how to do it, how to harness their power, but I fear even that won't be enough."

"Then what's the goddamned point?" I asked as Lucifer began to laugh. Blood dribbled down her lips as she looked upward.

"You're still thinking small, Arthur." Lightning flashed above. "Because as it stands, the man who did this to me," as she touched her wound she met my eyes, "has somehow claimed the marks of Gluttony and Sloth. I could feel them when he destroyed my weapon. I am not sure how he has managed to do so, but we must find out."

Her words froze me, and I remembered the two women I'd seen in the throne room. I hadn't known who they were, but I had a good idea.

"I see you understand." She laughed again, and I could see the light fading from her eyes as she slumped forward onto the mud. She caught herself. Barely. "You didn't face a man with six Armaments. You faced a man with eight." The Devil picked herself back up and stumbled toward me. "If he gains control of Gabriella's, it will be nine, and even then, he will want more." She nodded toward where the rest of the archangels lay unconscious. "He will come for them."

"What of Gabriella?" I asked, taking a deep breath

as her words sunk home. Once Dred completed his heavenly Armaments, what was to stop him from coming here and taking mine?

"I think she may be fine," Gwen said, bursting past me. That's when I saw Sally. The healer knelt down beside Lucifer, her hands already glowing.

"I won't have enough power to heal this. There's too much corruption." Sally looked from me to Gwen and back.

"Use me as a battery," Gwen said, grabbing Sally's arm. "And when I'm done, get one of the others. Use us all to save her."

"To think, you'd all sacrifice yourselves for me." Lucifer shook her head. "Better to not and save Michelle."

"This isn't either or," Gwen snapped. "This time you're all listening to me." Purple fire flared out from her as she stood, wings unfurling. "Gabriella is going to be okay, Arthur. It's why I sacrificed her. Now, everyone do your goddamned jobs. Sam, make the sword. Sally, heal the Princess of Darkness."

"Okay!" Sally said, and as she spoke, Sam began moving back toward her shop.

"I'll finish the sword, though I'm not sure how much it will help, I'll be damned if I sit here and let that fucker win." As Sam marched off indignantly, I turned my eyes to Gwen.

"How do you know Gabriella will be okay?" I asked, looking at Gwen and hoping she actually had an answer.

Only, before she could answer, Lucifer began to laugh. "You don't get it do you."

"What is so goddamned funny!" I snarled, my hands clenching into fists. "Because the way I see it—"

"Gabriella loves you, Arthur." Gwen met my eyes, and I saw the truth in them. "She is the Archangel of Love and my Heavenly Counterpart." Gwen looked down at herself. "Like how Michelle is Lucifer's Heavenly counterpart."

"You mean?" I swallowed hard, thinking back over our conversations. She'd said she'd loved me, but I'd always sort of blown it off as a mindless expression.

Only I remembered how she had blushed when I complimented her. What if it was true? What did that mean? And why did I feel so conflicted about it? Gabriella had an endearing, fumbling sweetness that, well, was pure in a way I couldn't explain. I couldn't let that be sullied. Not by Dred, not by anyone.

"He gets it." Lucifer pushed Sally away and came toward me. "As long as she loves you and not Dred, he will not be able to gain control of her Armament." She pointed to Michelle. "And once you take hers, you will gain more legitimacy. It will allow you to better use Samael's Mark, perhaps her armament as well."

"But that means a woman who loves me is trapped with Dred, and who knows what he'll do to her." I turned toward the downed Archangel, and as I did, I knew Lucifer was right. I had to take this woman's power whether or not she wanted me to have it, and I had to try to find more archangels. Enough to tip the scales in my favor.

"Thing is. Gabriella was made to fall in love. If Dred is smart, he'll be nice to her, make her see his goodness, assuming he has any, and she'll fall for him too. It's what she was *made to do*." Lucifer put her hand on my shoulder. "So anything we do must be done before that happens. I fear there won't be as much time as your friend thinks." She turned and pointed upward. "Either way, that leaves us with two choices, Builder. You take Heaven's power one way or another and defeat that asshole, or you do not."

THANK YOU FOR READING!

Curious about what happens to Arthur next?
Find out in The Builder's Wrath, coming soon!

AUTHOR'S NOTE

Dear reader, if you REALLY want to read my next Builder novel- I've got a bit of bad news for you.

Unfortunately, **Amazon will not tell you when the next comes out.**

You'll probably never know about my next books, and you'll be left wondering what happened to Arthur, Gwen, and the gang. That's rather terrible.

There is good news though! There are three ways you can find out when the next book is published:

1) You join my mailing list by clicking here.

2) You follow me on my Facebook page or join my Facebook Group. I always announce my new books in both those places as well as interact with fans.

3) You follow me on Amazon. You can do this by going to the store page (or clicking this link) and clicking on the Follow button that is under the author picture on the left side.

If you follow me, Amazon will send you an email when I publish a book. You'll just have to make sure you check the emails they send.

Doing any of these, or all three for best results, will ensure you find out about my next book when it is published.

If you don't, Amazon will never tell you about my next release. Please take a few seconds to do one of these so that you'll be able to join Arthur, Gwen, and the gang on their next adventure.

Also, there are some Litrpg Facebook groups you could join if you are so inclined.

LitRPG Society

LITRPG

To learn more about LitRPG, talk to authors including myself, and just have an awesome time, please join the LitRPG Group.

Made in the USA
San Bernardino, CA
25 November 2017